"Forgive me," R_____, releasing Serine from his embrace.

"Why do you not continue?" she wanted to ask but instead let her eyes speak.

"There are two situations that stand sentry between us."

"And those are?" She knew, but she must hear him say the words. The words that would both damn and free her.

"You have a husband, and I have your son. There can be nothing but lust between us, and I want more than a fleeting moment of passion from you, Serine. I want your love, just as, I believe, you want mine, but this ill-favored love we have found for each other is indeed a bitter brew."

She turned away, unable to hold back a comment of her own. "Sometimes the more bitter the brew, the greater the benefit...."

Dear Reader,

Harlequin Historicals author Barbara Leigh has been gaining a reputation for unforgettable medieval novels, and her current title, *For Love of Rory*, is no exception. This story of a young woman who forces a wounded Celtic warrior to help her find her kidnapped son will capture the heart of any medieval fan.

Bestselling author Theresa Michaels hits her stride this month with *Once an Outlaw*, the second book in her new Western series featuring the infamous Kincaid brothers. Don't miss this delightful love story that *Affaire de Coeur* calls a "fast-paced, rip-roaring adventure..."

We are also pleased to bring you *The Welshman's Way*. Award-winning author Margaret Moore's tale of a Welsh rebel who rescues a Norman maiden from an unwanted marriage is the sequel to *A Warrior's Way*. And from Carolyn Davidson, her first book for Harlequin Historicals, *Gerrity's Bride*, a Western marriage-of-convenience story with plenty of fireworks.

Whatever your taste in reading, we hope Harlequin Historicals will keep you coming back for more. Please keep a lookout for all four titles, available wherever books are sold.

Sincerely,

Tracy Farrell

Senior Editor

Please address questions and book requests to:
Harlequin Reader Service
U.S.: 3010 Walden Ave., P.O. Box 1325, Buffalo, NY 14269
Canadian: P.O. Box 609, Fort Erie, Ont. L2A 5X3

BARBARA LEIGH

FOR LOVE OF RORY

Harlequin Books

TORONTO • NEW YORK • LONDON
AMSTERDAM • PARIS • SYDNEY • HAMBURG
STOCKHOLM • ATHENS • TOKYO • MILAN
MADRID • WARSAW • BUDAPEST • AUCKLAND

ISBN 0-373-28897-2

FOR LOVE OF RORY

Books by Barbara Leigh

Harlequin Historicals

To Touch the Sun #98
Web of Loving Lies #177
For Love Alone #254
For Love of Rory #297

BARBARA LEIGH

discovered romance at the tender age of five, when she got chills listening to Snow White sing about Prince Charming. It was then that she realized "there was life after Dick and Jane." Unable to find the kind of stories she sought, Barbara began making up her own and never stopped.

Barbara, who has five children and seven grandchildren, lives in Southern California with her husband, a large doll collection, two dogs and a cat. She writes in a loft above the family room, which is affectionately known as "fairyland."

To my husband, Richard

Chapter One

They came from the sea. A small band of wild Celts. Rough men, clad in fur and armor, with leggings made of hide and tied with wide thongs of leather. Up the rocky cliffs they climbed, merging with the falling shadows in their relentless advance toward the little village nestled against the English countryside.

They carried iron weapons along with the thick rope slung over their shoulders. And their faces held the determination of desperate men who must succeed in their quest, or face annihilation.

So stealthy was their approach that they went unnoticed until they were ready to fall upon the old men and frightened women who might challenge them. They would strike with the coming of night. Strike and be gone, taking with them the only treasure the village had to offer.

They moved like the shadows of twilight. Creeping along the edge of darkness that covered the land, intent on taking from it the most tender, most valuable crop.

So still were they that even the village dogs did not sense their presence until time had run out and the animals could do nothing but whine and die.

The last songbird joined with the denizens of darkness in a duet of evensong. A mother settled herself beside the hearth and put her child to her breast, vaguely aware that the creatures of the night had suddenly fallen silent in the prelude to darkness.

Her musings were interrupted as the dog bristled. Before the animal could move, the door burst open. One man tore the child from her arms as another covered her mouth to stifle her screams. But the babe raised an angry protest at being separated from his meal.

"Bring the woman," a voice said. "We need no mewling babe dying from hunger before we reach our destination." The mother fought to free herself. With one deft movement a man slung her over his shoulder and carried her through the village while the leader and his men surged toward the doors of the keep. The Celts ferreted out the children and herded them, serf and lord alike, into the kitchens where the rest of the household were eating their evening meal.

Bowls of meat and gruel spilled across the rough-hewn boards and clattered onto the floor as adults added their shouts of outrage to those of their young.

The sounds reached into the solar where the Lady Serine worked on her accounts. With her lord husband on crusade there was much for her to do to keep the estate intact for her little son, Hendrick. The work taxed her in both mind and body but she paid her discomfort little heed, for her whole being was centered on the welfare of her child and the security of her husband's estate.

Thinking the servants had become somewhat bawdy, Serine rose wearily from the table where she worked. Her footsteps picked up speed as she recognized the sounds of true distress in the voices below. Distress, and the deep rumbling of men's voices. A rumbling that had not been heard at Sheffield since her husband had stripped the estate of men and followed the king to the Holy Land. Had the men returned without warning? Or had her household been overtaken by uninvited guests? One glance at the scene below gave her the answer.

So intent were the invaders that they did not see the young woman slip from the solar and hurry down the worn stairs. She moved like the wind, her whole being focused on the raven-haired man as he snatched up her son. The Celt's hair had broken loose from its bonds and fell to his shoulders, framing his bearded face. His eyes blazed like coals of hell, so full of fierce determination they could strike terror into the heart of the most courageous beholder.

Swallowing her fear, Serine seized a lance from the rack at the foot of the stairs and moved toward the Celt.

"Rory! 'Ware!" a deep voice shouted as Serine delivered a blow that glanced off the leader's broad shoulders. But even the strength of her desperation did not faze the man. With his free hand he grasped her weapon and twisted it from her hands. Their eyes locked and held as challenge met defiance. Serine's eyes shifted to her child, and the Celt's resolve hardened as he delivered a swiping blow that sent her pitching backward until she fell, limp, against the stairs.

At the sight of his mother's apparent demise, the boy redoubled his efforts to escape, fighting with prowess that belied his age and size. The man gave him a little shake.

"She is not dead," he grunted as the boy's foot connected with his stomach. "Most like, she hurts less than I. Now stop your caterwauling."

But Hendrick did not stop, and the chieftain wrapped the lad in his cloak and carried him from the keep, a smile of grim satisfaction on his face.

This boy had spirit. He was a lad of whom a man could be proud. The sort of child they risked all to acquire, and to Rory and his comrades the boy was worth more than gold. He was their only hope of survival. A last chance for immortality.

Serine staggered to her feet, determination mixed with hatred in her dark eyes.

The women took up torches, clubs and knives and followed the Celts. The invaders seemed immune to their blows as they ran from the village with the children tucked beneath their arms like sacks of grain. In the confusion, several women were able to pluck their young from the invaders' arms.

"To the woods! To the woods!" Serine shouted above the melee. "Take your children to the woods."

Even the most courageous women could not hide their fear at the thought of entering the woods after nightfall, for the woods were filled with spirits that walked in darkness. They looked to one another for courage as the frightened children dug in their heels, torn between the terror of the unknown dangers of the forest and the men who threatened to steal them away.

In the end, the women made for the woods, but the moment of hesitation had cost them, and even the most fleet of foot were no match for the marauding men.

The women screamed for their children and shouted curses at the men who had taken them. Serine's voice rang out above the rest. "Steal back your children before it's too late," she urged as she rushed through the throng of fierce men and desperate women.

"Find the screaming harpy and silence her," the raven-haired leader ordered. But even as he spoke, the cooking fire in one of the huts spilled across the rushes, and the embers burst into flames that lit the darkness.

The shadows evaporated, and with them the men, who disappeared into the night. In the silence that ensued, the only sound was the cry of a bird calling mournfully, "Too late . . . too late . . . too late. . . ."

The thatched huts were but wet embers and the Celts were gone with most of the village children as the exhausted villagers congregated outside the keep, where they dropped to the ground like fallen sparrows. Young women sobbed openly while old men wept silent tears. As Lady of Sheffield it was Serine's duty to see to the health and welfare of her serfs. It was well within her ability to treat their wounds and illnesses, but there was nothing she could do to heal their aching hearts—hearts that could not be eased until that which had been lost was recovered.

"I will not allow those heathen savages to get away with this," Serine told Dame Margot. "They'll not steal my son without feeling my wrath."

Dame Margot, Dowager Lady of Sheffield, and Serine's stepmother, wrung her hands in despair. "We are but a few weak women. If only the men were here instead of off on Crusade."

"But the men aren't here." Serine's chin set in determination.

"Then there is nothing we can do. We cannot hope to overcome men who are trained to fight, even if there are no more than a score of them. They overpowered us so easily it looked like child's play." Margot shifted nervously. The Lady of Sheffield was far younger than her husband, and quite set in her ways. Dame Margot knew how it felt to be the young bride of an older lord, and indulged Serine in many ways, but she could not stand by and allow the mistress of Sheffield to endanger her life and the lives of her serfs in a hopeless cause. As dowager she must do her best to make Serine see the futility of her proposal.

Sensing that Dame Margot was making ready to try to stop her, Serine went to the top step and stood silhouetted before the door. Her russet hair caught in the wind in wild disarray and her dark eyes flashed as she called out for the attention of her serfs.

"Good people, hear me!"

Weary heads lifted and tears dried as a spark of hope crept through the crowd.

"Our children have been stolen. If we want them back we must go after them."

Hope was replaced by disbelief. Surely the young mistress had gone daft with grief.

"We cannot fight those pagans, m'lady," a voice cried out. "They'll kill us dare we challenge them again."

"I do not intend to fight," Serine told them, "but I intend to steal our children back and bring them home."

"But how can you hope to do that, Lady?" the ale-wife asked. "We have neither the strength nor the weapons."

"We do not need strength. We have skill and stealth. And what we have lost is far more precious to us than to them," Serine returned in a voice that held firm despite the quivering in her stomach. "We will steal back our children one by one if need be."

"Lady." Hildegard, the alewife, lumbered to her feet. "We were lucky in this raid. There was no killing or looting. Nor did they rape or pillage. If we follow them and put ourselves in their paths we will suffer all that we have been spared." She scrubbed a tear from her face and continued, "I want my childer back as much as anyone here, but I know when I am beaten, and I be no match for an army of thieving Celts."

Serine looked out over the women's faces. They were resigned, without hope or purpose. Their children had been stolen away while their men were off fighting a holy war. It was up to Serine to make them believe in themselves again. She must find a way to make them willing to go after their children. Their children, and Hendrick, her son.

For without Hendrick all was lost and the sacrifice of her youth to the whims of an old but powerful husband would come to naught. If there was no heir to the estate it would revert to the Crown, and Serine had sworn a blood vow that it should not be so. This was *her* land. The land for which her ancestors had fought and died. And although, as a woman, Serine could not inherit in her own right, she had given all to secure it for her son.

Drawing her courage about her like a shield of valor, she tried once more to call the villagers to her cause. "'Twas no army, but a thieving band of Celts," Serine shouted. "I doubt there were more than twenty men for all their shouting and bluster."

In truth she thought it to be nearer twice that number, but few of the women were able to count.

"And we have weapons," Serine assured them. "Nearly every woman here can shoot an arrow or set a trap."

"Oh, no! My lady," Hildegard protested, "we know nothing of such things." It boded no good that their

lady suspected they were capable of catching and killing the wildlife that lived in the forest. A serf's life was
forfeit if caught poaching on the master's land.

Serine put her hands on her hips. Her dark eyes narrowed and she scrutinized each face. She knew the
doubt and fear that plagued the minds of her people
and realized she must end those fears if her plan was to
succeed.

"I have seen you hit your mark with an arrow, or return with game from your traps. I have seen you. Many
times. The keep has windows and I am not blind. But
my land is rich and fertile. Wildlife abounds, enough
for all to share. Now I ask you to bring the skills you
have been using to stock your larders and use your
knowledge to bring about the return of our children."

The women stared, openmouthed with surprise.
What sort of lady was this who knew they took the
master's meat and did nothing? They looked at one
another in astonishment.

"Who is with me?" Serine held out her arms, calling
for support. "Who is with me? Or do I go alone?"

No one moved. They stood like statues, hardly daring to breathe. Then there was a shuffling in the crowd.

An old woman emerged, an English longbow over her
shoulder, a quiver of arrows on her back and a patch
over one eye. "I stand with you, m'lady. I can shoot as
well as any man, and will follow wherever you go. As
long as you don't go too fast."

"But how can you hope to hit your mark?" Serine
asked. "You have but one eye."

"Had two when I was born," the old woman told
her. "But I lost the one to an errant arrow. Decided then
and there I would never be satisfied until I learned to
conquer the thing that had maimed me. You'll find me

as good a shot as any man. Only one eye is needed to send an arrow to its mark."

Serine gave a sigh of relief. She saw the old woman's determination and knew her admission to her prowess with the bow gave Serine the solution she needed.

"Thank you, Old Ethyl." Serine held out her hand and the one-eyed woman came to stand beside her. "And who else?"

The fact that Old Ethyl openly carried her bow and just as openly declared that she knew how to use it gave courage to the others. Several women stepped forward, including Hildegard, the alewife, who drew a strong leather cord from her pocket.

"I cannot shoot an arrow, and that's no lie. But I can set a trap big enough to catch a small animal or a man's foot, and once my quarry is down I'll sit on him until help arrives."

Everyone laughed, for the alewife's girth was legendary.

"Go and get what you need," Serine ordered. "Bring bread and meat and a plaid to keep you warm. We know not how long we will be gone. Those who cannot keep up will stay behind. Now, be off with you. We must make all haste. We must steal back our children."

The women nodded and hurried off as Ursa, Hendrick's nurse, entered the hall.

Serine saw the misery in the woman's eyes and held out her arms.

Ursa ran to her. Tears streamed down her face. "They took my whole brood," she said, "and your Hendrick, as well. I could not stop them, but I know where they camp."

"Then they are still on English soil?" Serine exulted.

"I followed them to the place where the boats wait. Apparently ours is not the only village they raided. It looked as though they were expecting more children to be brought in before they sail." Ursa held Serine at arm's length. They had been friends since before Serine had married. To Serine, Ursa dared speak her mind. "You must go to Lord Baneford, your overlord, and ask his help. He is pledged to defend you while your husband is away."

"There is no time," Serine said. "The invaders will be gone before help could arrive."

"But surely the Celts won't sail off into the night," Ursa protested, crossing herself against the dangers of darkness.

Old Ethyl shifted the bow on her shoulders and spoke with authority. "Dark or light, they will sail with the first tide after they have achieved their purpose. When they go, your childer will go with them."

"How do you know this?" Ursa asked. "Even the elders cannot recall a raid other than through the dim memory of childhood."

"My late husband took me from the Celts and brought me here as his bride," she said quietly. "I know how they think. They strike and take what they want, then disappear into the mist. They have done it before and will again."

"Then you must have some idea from whence they came and where they will go," Dame Margot said hopefully.

"Celts are a marauding breed," Old Ethyl told them. "They have planted their seed from Cornwall to Scotland and from France to Ireland. Most have seen the advantage of blending into the land in which they chose to live, but some, like those that invaded us today, care little for convention or civilization. Our lady is right. The only hope we have is to follow them and try to ascertain their origins."

Serine cast a sharp glance at her. Old Ethyl's association with the Celts would explain many of the woman's idiosyncrasies, but before Serine could question her they were interrupted by the clanking of weapons, clumsily carried, as the women came again to the hall, dragging their ordnance behind them.

"Take nothing that you cannot lift or use," Old Ethyl told them. "You must be able to carry your own weapon and move rapidly and silently at the same time."

The women nodded and placed much of their assorted equipment on the ground as they made ready to leave.

The women crept through the darkness and came to rest on a rocky cliff. Below them a row of small boats sat waiting at the edge of the sea. Some little distance away the children huddled together, guarded by the fierce men.

"There they are." Ursa pointed. "Thank the Lord they haven't yet gone." She pressed her hands to her heart. "There is my little Dickon." She turned with a suddenness that made Serine fall back. "What is the plan?"

"The what?" Serine strained her eyes as she searched the pensive little faces for that of her own Hendrick and paid no mind to Ursa's words. Surely if Dickon was there, Hendrick must be close by.

"The plan! The plan to save the children! You promised we would save the children. You must have a plan." There was an edge of panic in Ursa's voice, for the Celts were more numerous than the fingers on both hands and they were but a few desperate women.

Serine swallowed hard. "Of course," she managed to say. "The plan." She glanced around and was heartened by Old Ethyl's steady gaze. "Old Ethyl, will you walk with me? The rest of you stay here."

"If there is any danger I'll whistle like a bird," one of the young women volunteered.

"If there is any danger, I'll shoot him with my arrow," Old Ethyl said in a flat tone that defied dispute. "What do you propose?" she asked Serine as soon as they were out of earshot.

"I have no plan," Serine confessed. "But I knew the women would refuse to come with me if I told them I had no idea what I would do, and I cannot save the children alone."

"I thought as much," Ethyl said without reproach. "Perhaps inspiration will come when we get nearer."

They watched as the guards milled around. The good English ale and the food they had stolen made them negligent as the small boats moved slowly, carrying provisions across the water toward the ship moored farther out.

"They came by water," Old Ethyl observed. "Worse luck! If they leave our shores we're like to never see them again."

Serine clutched the older woman's wrist.

"If there was a fire on the ship they would rush to put it out and we would be able to steal back our children," she whispered.

"Alas," Old Ethyl commiserated, "the ship floats on deep water." She narrowed her eye, carefully gauging the distance. "Perhaps I could get close enough to send a fire arrow to pierce the side."

"To hit the ship you would need to stand on the shore. It would mean your life if you were caught," Serine reminded her. Then, without giving the other woman time to reply, she continued. "Watch how often the little boats run back and forth. If I were to take one of them it is unlikely anyone would notice. I could secure the small boat to the ship and set them both on fire. Once they begin to burn, you and the women can loose your fire arrows, each from a different place so the Celts will think we are many. In the confusion take the children and escape."

"But how will you get back to shore if you burn your boat?" Old Ethyl's eyes shone with admiration mingled with concern for the determined young woman she had learned to admire.

"I can swim . . . some," Serine told her. "It does not look so far." She was not a strong swimmer, having done little more than paddle around a lake near her childhood home. "I can think of no other way."

Old Ethyl hitched up her skirt and shifted the bow on her shoulders. Her eye narrowed as she evaluated the situation. "Have you flint and steel in your bag?" She pointed to the bag Serine carried looped over her shoulder.

"Aye," Serine assured her. "And rags soaked in fat I thought to use in case we needed to light a fire to warm the children after we stole them back."

"Good," Old Ethyl observed. "The other women can launch the arrows. I'll go with you. I can swim well. Between us the deed shall be done."

Serine gave Old Ethyl a little hug. Tears filled her eyes as she realized how inadequate their weapons were against the might of the Celts. "Should I not return I charge you and Dame Margot with the care of my son."

"You have my word," Old Ethyl promised, knowing that it was possible neither of them would live to see another dawn.

Serine went back and conveyed the plan to the other women. Ursa and several of the youngest, swiftest women took their places behind the rocks above the camp, as Serine and Old Ethyl then made their way to the water's edge.

Rory moved among the children, offering dried meat and fire bread as well as drink. "This will soon be over," he told them in a soothing voice. "You will come to a land that is rich in beauty. You will learn skills denied you here. You will be loved and cherished. You will grow to be free men."

"You lie, Celt," a boy's voice cried out. "We will be your slaves."

"I do not lie, I assure you," the man said. He offered the boy a drinking horn filled with water, but the lad batted it away. Rory recognized him as the boy who had fought with such great spirit when taken.

"All Celts are stupid, lying dogs." The boy spat out the words. "I am already free and you will pay for what you have done."

"Do not judge us by what you have heard of the past." The man picked up the drinking horn and motioned to a nearby mercenary. "This one must be taken aboard soon lest he inspires the others to rebellion." And with that, Rory left the children and joined his brother.

"There were no men in the villages we raided," Rory observed. "And I have learned from some of the more cooperative children that their fathers have gone on crusade with their king."

"As we suspected," Guthrie said. "No Celt would leave his family to fend for itself while he traipsed off after a cause that the gods themselves do not understand. A man belongs with his wife and offspring, not following the banners to a desert land where he is abhorred."

Rory agreed. "I doubt not that if left to his own devices the boy who spoke out so bravely would grow to be like his sire, leaving his family while he fights for glory, knowing nothing but the rudiments of war."

"Poor sad, ignorant people," Guthrie said self-righteously. "It is well that we have decided to take those young ones to a better life."

"Take special note of the lad who spoke to me." Rory motioned toward the child. "The boy has courage. I want him. He will be my son."

Guthrie put his hand on his brother's shoulder. "It shall be as you wish. In all the years since the plague struck down your wife and babe I have hoped you would find someone or something to care for. Perhaps our search for children will prove to be a blessing rather than a curse."

Serine crouched behind a thick bush and swore under her breath. It was *her* son this enemy wanted for his own. It was her husband that he scorned and her home at which he scoffed. How she would love to see him burn right along with his ship. She'd show him whose way of life was inferior.

As the men walked away Old Ethyl joined her. Seeing that Old Ethyl had stripped down to her small clothes, Serine took off her dress and stuffed it beneath the bush.

"Wait!" Old Ethyl whispered as Serine started toward one of the little boats. The older woman darted forward, snatched up a horned helmet that had been left near the water's edge and jammed it onto Serine's head before they eased one of the small boats into the lapping water.

The helmet wobbled precariously as Serine huddled into a cloak she found on the bottom of the boat. Bolstered by Old Ethyl's whispered soliloquy—a mixture of prayer and encouragement—Serine adjusted her borrowed helmet and began rowing.

With undaunted determination she maneuvered the boat to the rear of the ship, careful to keep well away from the path of the dragon that graced the front of the craft. Although she was a Christian, and a devout one, a part of her still feared the dragons of the sea and the men who sent them thundering through the waves. Old Ethyl made no bones about the depth of her superstition, and as the woman's fears became more obvious Serine gave heartfelt thanks for her support.

Only when the tiny craft huddled beneath the hull of the larger one did Old Ethyl rise from her hiding place. Working together they managed to secure a watersoaked leather thong around the rudder and quickly smeared fat onto the side of the ship.

There was a flash of light in the rocks above the cove, quickly extinguished, but enough to let Serine know the women were ready to launch their fire arrows.

"It is time." Serine swallowed the words, fear boiling up from the depths of her soul.

Sensing her fear, Old Ethyl grasped Serine's arm. "I will be beside you," she said. She felt some of the tension ease in Serine's muscles. "Just as you will be beside me." And with that last reminder Old Ethyl let go her hold, but the bond between them had been sealed. Succeed or fail, they would do so together.

Sending up a prayer, Serine struck flint to steel and caught the spark on an oil-soaked wick. When the little flame flared, she put it to the fat and watched it catch and burn.

Silently they slipped into the water and moved as quickly as possible to be well away when the bag, the cloak and the boat burst into flames that licked greedily at the larger vessel.

Serine swam as quickly as she could, but it was not fast enough. Time and again Old Ethyl outpaced her and was forced to return to the younger woman's side. The flaming boat cast a glow over the water. It would be only a matter of time before she was seen and captured.

"It is your clothing that holds you back," Ethyl said. "Remove it, or we are lost."

It was an order, not a request. Seeing the wisdom of Ethyl's words, Serine held her breath, dived beneath the water and shed the remainder of her clothing. Freed from the binding restriction, she surfaced at Ethyl's side and they continued toward the shore.

Shouts of anger from the ship told them that their plan had succeeded. The men on the shore jumped into the little boats and sent them catapulting across the water, leaving the children virtually unguarded. Confusion resounded from shore to ship, and Serine managed to lift her head from the water long enough to see an empty space where the children had been held.

As the guards called for help from their comrades the women shot their fire arrows from the cliffs.

A short distance from shore Old Ethyl drew Serine to a halt. "Here I leave you and go to join the others," she said. Then, unable to hold back her emotion, she continued. "You are a fine, brave woman."

"As are you," Serine replied breathlessly as the women went their separate ways.

Serine smiled despite her exhaustion as she pulled herself toward the bush where she had left her gown.

She found her legs unable to hold her weight, and crawled from the water. Her hand groped beneath the bush as she felt blindly for her clothing. It was impossible to see, and she almost cried out when, rather than the rough material of her gown, her hand fell on the sinewy warmth of human flesh.

A hand clutched her arm and drew her from her hiding place. She found herself face-to-face with a man. In the shadowy light she could make out the bearded face and the strong, virile body.

Was he truly a man, or had one of the Celt gods come to earth to mock her success in burning the ship and freeing the children? For truly he looked like a wild heathen god as he glared down at her, vengeance written in each line of his countenance. And her heart beat madly as her cheeks flamed in anger and embarrassment, for the expression in this man-god's face was clear. And, heaven forgive her, for the briefest moment she wondered what it would be like to be loved by a pagan deity.

In the shadowy light Rory could see the naked body of a woman—slim and sleek, with thrusting breasts, a flat belly and long, shapely legs. Was this the Freya, of whom the wise man Drojan often spoke? A goddess come from the sea to taunt him for his failure to safeguard the children they had taken? Did she come to rebuke him for failing in his pledge that this would be a bloodless raid?

No, this woman was flesh and blood, with defiant eyes and a determined set to her chin. Yet the supple body formed to his so sweetly he could not help but wonder if her lips would do the same.

In truth, there was nothing to lose. His raid had failed and many of the children had escaped. The ship was crippled, and his men would be forced upon the mercy of the sea with only the dubious protection of the little boats.

What matter if he tasted the lips of this water nymph? Who was she to argue if he took the pleasures that her body so graciously offered?

It was possible that she had been a part of the plot that had so successfully sent his comrades into confusion. For that alone she deserved a Celt's wrath and a Celt's revenge.

Would those firmly set lips beg for mercy? Or would they part to welcome his kiss? What sort of woman would place her life at risk against not only the Celts but the gods of water and fire? There was but one answer...a woman with the soul of a Celt, and it was such a woman he held in his arms.

He gripped her tightly and pressed her sleek, firm body against his. Perhaps, should she please him, he would take her back with him to warm his bed. And warm it she would. If not with her love, then with her hatred. With such a woman, either emotion would prove entertaining during the long winter nights.

He bent toward her. She did not flinch or beg, and once more he felt grudging admiration. As their lips touched, sparks shot before his eyes and exploded into nothingness. Rory pitched forward, Old Ethyl's arrow buried deep in his back.

Chapter Two

"Serine! Are you hurt?" Margot asked as she rushed to Serine's side.

"Only frightened," Serine admitted, struggling to roll the Celt off her body.

Serine scrambled to her feet and looked down at the man. Blood trickled from his mouth and disappeared into his beard.

"My arrow is stuck in his lungs," Old Ethyl cackled as she hurried over to survey her handiwork. "A death blow, I vow! No need to worry about that one again."

"The children?" Serine asked, trying to forget the heat that had raced through her body as the man held her in his arms.

"The children are safe," Margot assured her. "I saw them reach the hills and came back to find you." She looked at the younger woman's state of undress and added, "And well I did."

Old Ethyl regarded Dame Margot with disdain. "We had everything under control," she said bluntly.

Serine grabbed her woolen dress from beneath the bush and threw it over her body, ignoring the scratch of the coarse material against her skin. The rough woolen garment did nothing to warm her. Her whole being felt as cold as death. As cold as the man lying at the water's edge.

"Come now, we must go," Margot urged.

"But what of...him?" Serine motioned toward the inert body.

"Leave him," Old Ethyl said, pulling her away. "Perhaps the Celts will return for him. I might stay and see if I could skewer a few more."

"There's no reason for you to put yourself in more danger," Serine assured the woman. "'Tis best we leave." She willed herself not to look back.

"It was a good job we did of making them think they'd been attacked. Look there!" she cackled as the Celts struggled to set the sails on the little boats. "The whole lot of them on the run. They must make it back to their godforsaken land as best they can in their little skiffs while their ship sinks. And good riddance!" Old Ethyl added as the women made their way through the deserted camp and hurried after the children.

Only when they reached the rocks that would block the sea from view did Serine pause. Cursing herself for her weakness, she allowed herself one last look at the man, lying like a pagan god in the moonlight. It would not have surprised her to see the figure of a Valkyrie come to take him to Valhalla, or heaven, or perhaps hell. It occurred to her that it was the Viking warriors who were said to be taken to Valhalla when they were struck down in battle. God only knew where Celts went after death. Regardless of his beliefs, or lack of them, this man had held no weapon, and Serine could not help but wonder about the fate that awaited a warrior shot in the back while he dallied with a woman.

Not that she cared! Not that she cared in any way! Only, it was too bad the Celt would not receive his just reward.

But then, perhaps he already had.

Day was breaking when Serine reached the place where the children had been hidden. The sun crested the horizon and the women called out their welcome, hailing Serine and her companions as heroes.

Exhausted from the rigors of their escape and the trauma of abduction, the children slept in the hall of an ancient monastery hidden deep in the forest.

"And there's no question in my mind," the alewife boasted, "the men could have done no more, nor done it better." She beamed at her lady and cast a loving glance at her sleeping son.

Serine studied each little face as she made her way through the area while Old Ethyl accepted the accolades of the village women.

"I vow I'd never seen anything like the way the Celts took to the water when they realized their precious ship was in danger," one of the women observed. "Forgot all about the childer, they did. It was almost too easy to steal them back, so smug were those Celts. Never thought for a minute that the smoke was anything more than night fog until it was too late."

"Only one Celt sensed they'd been tricked," Hildegard chimed in. "And he started rowing toward land as though pursued by demons, but by the time he reached the shore we were well away." She paused and glanced over her shoulder. "Think you the Celts will follow?"

"The Celts are well gone," Old Ethyl volunteered with finality. "They'll not return to our shores after the drubbing we gave them."

The women laughed and crowed in euphoric relief, rightfully proud of a job well done. After the initial burst of enthusiasm they became silent. Even the women around Margot began whispering.

As well they should, Serine told herself. After all, there was no reason to wake the youngsters, who had already gone through so much. She nodded in satisfaction as she saw two of Ursa's little girls curled up together. But her eyes were never still as she continued to search for the features of her own Hendrick.

Hendrick, the beloved child of a loveless, politically inspired marriage. Some sixteen years Serine's senior, her husband, Elreath, had no living children when he was offered Serine, as well as her family estate of Sheffield, as a boon from the king in appreciation for the old knight's faithful support in the Crusades.

Visualizing himself as the inveterate soldier, Elreath expressed his appreciation to his liege, married Serine and performed his conjugal duty with the same enthusiasm he would have shown if forced to curry his horse. He made no bones about the fact that he was beyond an age where he felt a young wife was anything other than a burden, but he was gratified by her appreciation of the treasures he had brought back with him from the Crusades, and pleased beyond measure when Serine told him she was with child.

Elreath had been on his way to the Holy Land when Hendrick was born, and did not see the child until some three years later when he returned.

The child thrived, but the father had aged and shriveled in the desert sun. For a time there was some question that he would be strong enough to join the next Crusade. There was no question as to whether Hendrick would be the only child conceived of the union, as

Elreath felt he must conserve his strength and left Serine
alone. At the end of Hendrick's fifth year Elreath had
recovered enough to pledge himself to one last Crusade. In a gracious gesture he stripped his estate of able-
bodied men and set out once more to free the Holy
Land from the infidel, leaving his estates and his son in
the able hands of his wife.

Serine had been well versed in running the estate.
With the help of the steward she had managed the
lands, the flocks and the crops, but she was not prepared for the Celt invasion, and it angered her that they
had been left alone and so ill prepared. It was only luck
that she had found a way to recover the children. And
perhaps her prayers to the Christian God were more
powerful than those of the Celts to the deities they
worshiped.

Once Hendrick was again in her arms she would take
the time to thank her maker. Hendrick, with his tou-
sled hair and laughing eyes. Hendrick, to whom she had
given life, and who now made her life worth living.
Hendrick, her son.

Lost in reverie, Serine found herself at the end of the
hall and was about to start back through the maze of
sleeping children when Dame Margot approached.

"I must speak to you," Margot said without pream-
ble.

"As soon as I find Hendrick I will be at your disposal," Serine agreed absently.

Margot took Serine's arm and guided her through the
door into what must have been a small chapel. "Hendrick isn't with the other children."

Serine refused to meet Margot's steady but sympa-
thetic gaze. "Surely they haven't taken him back to
Sheffield already. Regardless of Old Ethyl's boast, there

still may be some danger." She tried to look back into the hall over Margot's shoulder. He must be there, somewhere. Any minute he would awaken and come running to her and the night's work would not have been in vain.

"Serine, come and sit with me." Margot led her to a wooden bench. "Ursa tells me that some of the children were taken aboard the larger vessel before we were able to steal them back."

Serine nodded. "Yes, that could be true. I remember how the little boats went back and forth. Some of the children could have been taken."

But not Hendrick, her heart cried out. Not Hendrick! She knew he had been on the shore shortly before she started rowing for the ship. She had heard his voice. Heard him challenge the Celts like the lordling he was.

She could feel Margot gripping her hands. She did not want to hear the woman's next words, but they must be heard. Serine took a deep breath. "Go on," she ordered.

"Hendrick is not here."

"Perhaps he went back to look for me," Serine suggested.

Margot shook her head. "The Celts have him."

It was a statement of fact, and as such, beyond refutation. Serine turned her face toward the crumbling wall to hide the tears that sprang to her eyes.

"From all that the women have been able to glean from the children, Hendrick was taken to the ship shortly before the fire." Margot continued without releasing her grip on the younger woman's hands. "You have done a very courageous thing, Serine, and the people of your village will be forever grateful, but Hendrick is gone."

Serine gave Margot's fingers a little squeeze and pulled away. "Then I shall go after him," she said. "How many others are missing?"

"Over a dozen children," Margot admitted, "along with Gerta and her babe."

"I will go after all of them," Serine vowed. "I'll go after them and bring them back."

"I understand how desperately you want to find Hendrick and the rest of the children and bring them home, but you don't know where the Celts have taken them. It could take you months, or even years to find them." Margot tried desperately to dissuade Serine from undertaking an impossible task. "Old Ethyl believes they came from Ireland, but there are Celts in Brittany, Wales, Scotland and even France. Most have become quite civilized, but these men must be renegades. You could search the rest of your life and never find their village."

"Perhaps some of the children overheard the Celts say something that would tell us where they came from," Serine suggested. "You can question them when they awaken. I'll take Old Ethyl and go back to the area where the Celts landed and see if they left anything that would tell me from whence they came."

"Serine! You know as well as I that they left nothing behind," Margot pleaded, knowing in her heart that this brave young woman was headed for heartbreak and disappointment.

"Not so, Dame Margot." Serine drew herself to her full height, her eyes hard with determination. "There is one thing they left behind that could give us a great deal of information, and that is the wounded Celt."

"But the man was sore wounded," Margot gasped. "Like as not he is already dead."

"If he is still on English soil and there is breath in his body, I will keep him alive until he can tell me where they've taken Hendrick," Serine vowed, and without waiting to hear more of Margot's objections she hurried off to find Old Ethyl, knowing all too well that the chances of success were slim.

But even a slim chance was better than no chance at all.

"M'lady! Slow down a bit," Old Ethyl panted. "I can't keep up."

Serine glanced back over her shoulder, gauging the lengthening distance between herself and the other woman. "Don't fret yourself, Ethyl," she said. "Just keep me in sight and there'll be no problem."

"There be a problem already," Old Ethyl called after her. "No lady in her right mind would go looking for a needle in the hay. You'll find yourself sorry, you will. Mark my words, there's naught but grief left on those shores."

But Serine did not slow her steps, and the old woman somehow managed to keep but a few paces behind her, for all her grumbling.

The coast looked deserted as Serine viewed it from her vantage point among the rocks on the high cliffs.

"You see?" Old Ethyl came up behind her. "I told you there would be nothing here. The Celts have taken their fallen comrade and gone their way." She tugged at Serine's arm, her one eye scanning the coastline cautiously.

Serine caught her breath. "The ship is still here," she said as she ducked behind the rocks, pulling the old woman with her.

"It will not sail again. The Celts have left it to rot. Now come along. This is not a good place to linger."

Serine shook her off. "I'm going down there to look around. Perhaps they left something that will tell me the name of the village from which they came." As Serine spoke she spied a scrap of cloth along the shore. Her heart turned painfully in her chest and pounded against her ribs like a falcon fighting to fly free.

She jerked away from Old Ethyl's restraining hands and ran down to the beach. Only when she reached flat ground did she slow her steps and approach with some semblance of caution.

The Celt was not where they had left him. She had noted the bush carefully, for it had been her point of refuge the night before, and there was no body lying beside it. If the Celts had not come back and taken him, he might yet be alive and have moved away from the sea. Again her heart lurched at the thought of life pulsing from his body, and she found herself almost as greatly troubled by the thought of the man dying along the water's edge as she was by the loss of her son.

She bolted through a cluster of rocks and almost stepped on an outthrust arm.

It took all her control to keep from screaming as Old Ethyl slammed into her back.

The older woman peered around her lady, glaring malevolently at the man on the ground. "Guess I didn't place the arrow as well as I thought," she remarked as she nocked another shaft.

"No." Serine pushed the bow aside. "There will be no killing."

"What do you mean, no killing?" Old Ethyl challenged. "The man is a Celt! He'd just as soon rape and kill you as look at you. You can't mean to let him live!"

"I mean to *make* him live," Serine told her. "To make him live, and make him tell me where his people have taken my son." A tiny smile touched her lips. "And then I mean to make him take me there to demand the return of Hendrick in exchange for the Celt's life."

Old Ethyl shook her head, but she lowered her bow. "I don't know that Celts work that way," she said thoughtfully. "But I guess it's worth the chance. Especially since it seems to be the only chance we've got."

"I only hope he lives long enough to tell me where they've taken Hendrick." Serine dropped at the man's side, appalled at his color, or lack thereof. "That is, if he's alive even now."

"Oh, he's alive enough, I'll warrant." Old Ethyl quickly assessed the situation. "In fact, I'd wager he heard every word you said, didn't you, laddie?" She nudged his leg with her foot.

"How can you be so certain?" Serine looked up at the old woman and did not see the Celt's eyelids flicker. "A moment ago we both thought him dead."

"That was before you knelt down beside him," Old Ethyl said cryptically. "I don't think he's in any condition to harm you, but if you're determined to save him I better go and get a cart to carry him back to Sheffield."

"Thank you, Ethyl," Serine answered, but this time her whole attention was focused on the man beside her. The man who pinioned her with eyes filled with pain. The man whose hair fell in ebony ringlets across his forehead. The man who managed with all that was left of his strength to drag a breath into his punctured lungs and say, "I would have thought I had surely died and been taken to my reward, had it not been for the old hag beside you."

"Do not fear, Celt," Serine said as she placed a cool hand on his fevered forehead, "I do not intend to let you go anywhere until you tell me where I can find my son."

She fought down the jolt she knew when her flesh touched his, and tried to act as though nothing unusual had happened, nothing that could not be explained as concern for his condition, nothing that might indicate that each moment she was near him filled her with emotion she had never before known and never so much as imagined.

His voice was little more than a whisper as he fought down a quickening of his blood that was slightly less than devastating. "No man could desire eternity with you at his side on this earth." His voice faded, and he stared at her, unblinking.

"Why do you look at me so?" she demanded, unnerved by his scrutiny.

"Because I fear if I close my eyes you will disappear and the one-eyed harpy of my nightmares will return." His eyes closed against the pain, nonetheless.

"I will not disappear," Serine assured him. "At least, not until you tell me how I can find my son." But even as she spoke his head lolled back and she knew he could no longer hear her.

She turned him onto his side to ease the pressure on his wound. What was he trying to do to her? Offering compliments when he was barely conscious. It was almost obscene! A Celt offering flattery with his last breath. How dare he? If only she didn't need him so desperately. If he wasn't her only chance to discover the whereabouts of her son. If her heart didn't beat so erratically when she so much as thought about their unconscionable first meeting. If these things weren't so, she would leave him here without blinking an eye. But they were true. They were all true, and she couldn't leave him behind again.

The man did not regain consciousness as he was moved from the coast to the castle. Serine watched him closely, making certain he continued the shallow breathing that was all his wound allowed.

Secreted in her own chambers, Serine removed the arrow and bathed the wound with bedstraw tea, then applied a poultice of fresh crushed lady's mantle. But the Celt's fever did not abate and the women worried over what course to take next.

"Nettle tea would give him some nourishment and purify the blood," Margot suggested, "but before we dare try to get him to swallow we must bring down the fever."

Serine watched the man's life slipping away as the poison of the wound had its way. With him would go her only chance of finding her son. She could not allow him to die.

She knew which herbs to administer to ease the pain of childbirth, to heal a cut or draw the infection from an ulcer, but the man before her was sore wounded and she feared she did not have the knowledge to save him. Yet he must live. She must make him live . . . for Hendrick . . . and perhaps for Serine herself. Somehow she must find a way.

"I do not know if I have the skills to save him." She spoke the words aloud as the man thrashed on the bed.

"Perhaps we should send for a surgeon," Margot suggested.

"A surgeon would only bleed him. In the end he would die and all our efforts will have been for naught." Serine never looked away from the man. She was determined that he would live long enough to tell her what she wanted to know if she had to breathe life into his body herself. He must not die, she would not let him die until she learned the fate of her son.

Aware of Serine's desperation, Margot agreed to stay with the man while Serine went to gather the herbs she hoped would be of the most benefit in lowering the fever and healing the wound.

Dame Margot did not feel comfortable left alone with the Celt, even if he was unconscious. There was something about him so raw and primitive, so completely virile that it intimidated the gentlewoman.

"Does he still live?" Old Ethyl asked as she met Serine at the postern gate.

"He has a grave fever. I have little hope of keeping him alive. We can only pray that he says something in his delirium that might tell us where they've taken the children." She paused and looked back toward the keep, thinking how dismal it would be without little Hendrick there to give it life and hope for the future. "I must gather herbs to rid the wound of poisons."

"There was no poison on my arrows," Old Ethyl declared. "I depend on my skill to kill my enemies."

Serine sensed the hostility and answered patiently. "The poisons come from the arrow entering the body and breaking the tissues. The man lay in the mud for hours, which was also detrimental. No one said your arrow was poisoned."

Old Ethyl hung her head. "If I had shot true the man would have been dead."

Serine touched her arm comfortingly. "If the Celt had died there would be no chance of his telling us where they have taken the children. You said you were from the land of the Celts," she reminded her. "Can't you guess where they might be?"

"The Celts are scattered along the sea like stones in the sand." Old Ethyl narrowed her eye. "And while there's no doubt in my mind that this one came to us from Ireland, we could search for years without coming upon his village. You speak true, m'lady. We must hurry and get the herbs to heal the man. This is one Celt better left alive."

And Old Ethyl strode off down the path at a pace Serine was hard-pressed to follow.

Chapter Three

"We went back a second time," the thane told Guthrie. "Just as you said. But your brother, Rory, was nowhere to be found. Perhaps he was taken by the sea."

"Perhaps he has been captured by those who set fire to our ship," Guthrie growled.

The man shifted nervously and inched his way toward the door, anxious to be away from his liege, who was fretting over the disappearance of his brother and the loss of a ship.

"Send Drojan to me," Guthrie ordered, dismissing the man with a wave of his hand. "Perhaps the Runes will tell of my brother's fate."

Guthrie paced as he waited for the seer to appear. His anger and frustration had been unabated since he had learned of Rory's disappearance and the loss of the majority of the children. First the ship had burst into flames, then the children had been stolen from the guards and spirited off and finally Rory had disappeared without a trace. Evil spirits were to blame, of that Guthrie was certain, and Drojan would surely be able to ferret them out and force them to give up the secret of his brother's whereabouts.

"You sent for me?" The spaeman's deep voice brought Guthrie from his reverie.

"I have need of your talents," Guthrie said respectfully.

"You have only to ask," Drojan assured him. "You know that I am always at your disposal."

"I need to know the fate of my brother, Rory," Guthrie told the older man. "He did not return with us from the ill-fated raid on the villages of the English. If he lives I must go after him and bring him back. But if he has died and his body was taken by the spirits, I shall leave the English in peace."

Drojan nodded and placed his bag on the floor. After drawing a circle, he took his place within and began to lay out the Runes. He cared deeply for both Guthrie and Rory; he had known them since they were children. It saddened him to think that he might never see Rory again. He felt the loss of such a warrior was far greater than the gain of the few scrawny children the Celts had brought back with them.

But he must answer true and read the Runes with honesty and detachment, for they were the word of the gods and he had sworn to give voice to their truth.

He frowned as he put forth the Runes. Then he spoke. "Your brother is with a woman of strength and beauty. Danger and loneliness, for him, are in the past."

Guthrie wiped his hand across his face. "Then he is with Brunda, his dead wife. It cannot be read any other way, for there is always danger for a Celt on foreign soil."

Drojan continued to frown. He did not interpret the reading as did Guthrie and was about to tell him so when Guthrie continued his thoughts aloud.

"We will not seek vengeance for Rory's death. He died in the way of the Celt, and no man can ask more. We will raise the children that we have taken and teach them our way of life. But I must know that his body is given proper burial."

Drojan was torn between telling Guthrie that he saw no indication of Rory's death in the Runes, and rejoicing that there would be no more raids on English soil, which would cost lives that could ill afford to be lost. The seer glanced at the Runes once more. If Rory was indeed alive, he would surely find some way to return to his home. To wage war on the English in the hope of finding him was to invite disaster. He decided to keep his counsel as Guthrie wavered between grief and hope before coming to a decision. "I ask that you go in peace to bring back my brother's remains."

Drojan bowed his head, silently accepting the assignment, as Guthrie continued. "There was a boy. A male child with dark hair and even features—well fed and bright," Guthrie mused. "Rory expressed an interest in him. He said he wanted the boy. I will take the child into my house in memory of my brother. I will raise him and to him I will give all I would bestow upon my brother's son, and until such day as my lady wife, Damask, gives me a child of my own, this boy will be my heir."

Drojan took a deep breath. "It is good," he pronounced. "Rory will rejoice when the gods tell him how you have honored his memory."

Within minutes Guthrie had gone to search for the boy Rory had favored, but Drojan remained within his magic circle and stared at the Runes. What he saw bothered him more than he wished to admit, for the rune that he knew to be his personal symbol stood out predominantly and it was challenged by the symbol of a female crossed by the sign of Woden. Never had he seen such a lay of the Runes and it unnerved him to think that Woden might have decided to disrupt Drojan's life by sending a woman emissary.

Scooping up the Runes, he returned them to the bag and destroyed the circle. As he left the building his eyes searched the faces of the village women. Which of them might have been chosen by the war god of the North, and how would Drojan recognize her? Sometimes he wished he had not been given the powers that had catapulted him to the most respected and sought-after authority in Corvus Croft. It was a heavy burden to bear knowledge of the future, especially when the future concerned oneself.

Voices drifted through Rory's mind. Women's voices, soft and comforting, and one disturbing in its hint of sensuality. The sensual voice caused him to fight the darkness of unconsciousness and try to open his eyes and return to the world of the living. But the world of the living was a world of heat and pain. It was the pain that convinced him that he was not dead, although the features of the woman that swam before his eyes seemed lovely enough to be those of the Valkyries of which his friend Drojan spoke.

Though he clamped his lips tightly shut, Rory sometimes heard his own voice calling out against the pain and fever. Then blessed moisture touched his lips and warmth seeped down his throat. His mind returned from the passages of the past and he fought to hear and understand the words bandied above his head. English voices, speaking English words. He must hold to his consciousness long enough to discover his whereabouts and, hopefully, the fate that awaited him.

"He has said nothing that would give us the name of his village," the sensuous voice said. "He calls for a woman named Brunda, but hers is the only name he has uttered."

"We will stay with him. He may yet give us the information we need," the other voice responded.

A cool hand touched his brow. "He is burning with fever. If we cannot break it he will die, and we'll never know from whence he came."

The hand slipped down beneath his ear. The voice, no longer sensuous, cried out, "His neck is swollen. Here!"

"God save him, the poison has gone into his body. We must soak him in tepid water and bring the fever down as quickly as possible, else he will die."

Rory wanted to scream as he was dragged from the bed and lowered into a tub of water that seemed more icy than the winter streams. Too weak to fight, he remained still, suffering in silence. To his amazement, in only a matter of minutes the water did not seem so cold and his mind fought to clear itself. It was then he first realized that his life was forfeit should he, in his delirium, call out the name of his village. He must fight to keep from entering delirium again, though the effort drained his body of his last vestige of strength.

If he hoped to survive he could not give these people the information they desired. And survive he would, if only long enough to look upon the woman with the cool hands and the sensuous voice. A woman he linked to the sea nymph he had held in his arms just before he was struck down. As the lovely body floated in the eye of his memory, Rory relaxed.

"We must put compresses on the swelling in his neck," Old Ethyl said as she soaked a cloth with the liquid before handing it to Serine.

"It will be impossible to tell whether the swelling has gone down with his beard in the way," Serine fussed. "There is nothing for it but to take care of his facial hair."

Rory heard the woman's remark. He was proud of his beard. As with all Celts, his beard was the symbol of his manhood. Thick and rich and luxuriant, he wore it well and washed and combed it often. And although he trimmed it regularly, he had not been without facial hair since puberty. It boded well for him that the woman who had his care appreciated the virility indicated by his beard. He felt gentle hands brush the hair on his cheeks and he drifted into sleep as a feeling of well-being overcame him.

A well-being that Serine did not share, for she knew what she was about to ask Old Ethyl might well bring about the end of their friendship. Steeling herself against the reluctance that slipped insidiously through her body, Serine managed to form her request.

"Ethyl, shortly after you came here as a bride, you mentioned a mixture of herbs you had learned from a woman in the land of your youth. Do you remember?"

Old Ethyl closed her eyes. "Yes, I remember. I remember all too much, and all too well." She remembered the kindly woman who had spent her life concocting harmless potions that made life happier and easier for those around her, only to come upon a mixture so potent it all but brought the dead back to life, and ultimately brought down the wrath of the other healers, who coveted the recipe.

The woman did not know how to write, and made her
brew with a handful of this and a pinch of that. All
good herbs from God's own garden. Gladly she gave the
others the names of the herbs she used, but she was unable to give the exact measure and their potions were
useless, and more than useless . . . deadly.

In anger and frustration the unsuccessful healers accused the woman of witchcraft and she was burned in
her little hut along with her herbs and her secret.

"If this man came from the land of which you spoke,
perhaps that mixture might cure him more quickly than
the simple things we have available."

"It is against the law to make that brew," Ethyl said
without meeting her eyes.

"But you have done so, Ethyl." Serine turned her
steady gaze on the woman. "If you have some of the
mixture, I beg you let us use it to make this man well so
that he can lead me to Hendrick."

Ethyl walked over to the window. "I saw the bitter
brew made many times. She would take powdered
wormwood, and a pinch of myrrh and saffron. To that
she would add senna leaves and camphor. Then came
such herbs as manna, the roots of rhubarb, zedoary,
carline thistle and—" her voice faded to a whisper
"—angelica."

"But there is nothing poisonous or sinister in those
ingredients. We use them all the time for one thing or
another," Serine mused aloud. "Was it in the way she
prepared them?"

"The herbs are placed in a container half-filled with
fruit spirits and set out in the warmth of the sun. You
are right. There is nothing sinister or magical about it.
As she did with all her herbs, when she worked she recited her ingredients in a singsong voice. Some of the

other healers felt they could improve on her concoction and tried adding herbs and berries. The additives did more harm than good and people became ill rather than being cured. A woman died after taking what was said to be the exact duplication of the recipe. They went after the healer who had made the original brew. They accused her of being a witch and burned her. It was believed her recipe was lost with her, and an edict was handed down that no one was to experiment with her concoction on pain of death. That edict has never been lifted."

"But surely it was only in the land where you lived," Serine argued, sensing that her only hope of saving the Celt's life was slipping away.

"The edict was accepted by pagan and Christian alike, and the punishment ultimately the same regardless of the name of the god they worshiped."

"Ethyl, for the love of that God, please help me to save this man and find my son." There were tears in Serine's eyes. "I know how greatly this request must disturb you. Still, I must ask it."

Ethyl's hands shook. "You cannot know unless you could have heard the woman's dying screams. You cannot know the fear I have felt each time I did more than make tea from the herbs I gathered. Yet I know that herbs are capable of doing more good than harm and I could not allow the knowledge she bequeathed to me to be lost in the flames that took her life."

Serine went to her, placing her hands on Ethyl's arms. "Do not let the knowledge be lost. Let it be used to save lives, as it was meant to do. I will take full responsibility and swear that I made the potion myself."

"There is no need for you to do that, although it would be true. For the herbal remedy we make that is bitter to the tongue is the same brew that cost my mother her life.''

Serine gave a little gasp, but before she could express her horror at Ethyl's revelation, the older woman added, ''Use your skill to keep him alive, and I will return with the elixir that will, with God's help, make him well.'' Old Ethyl started toward the door. ''I will be back to help you remove him from the water. In the meantime, you can deal with his beard in your own way.''

Old Ethyl glanced at her mistress. There was something about Serine that seemed to indicate curiosity rather than concern. Was the younger woman interested in the man's appearance? Surely not! This was a Celt. An enemy! One of the men who had stolen Serine's son. Yet the features above the beard were strong and even. The man might be handsome, for all that he was a Celt.

With hope beating in her heart Serine turned back to the Celt and, to her horror, saw that he was watching her with eyes as black and deep as the depths of hell. She could not help but wonder how much he had understood and how much he would be able to remember when his fever had passed. She listened closely as his jumbled words became discernible.

''The name of the village,'' she whispered. ''What is the name of your village? Why do you want to steal children? Have you none of your own?''

''Dead!'' The Celt choked on the word. ''All dead from plague.'' His voice broke and his breath came in ragged gasps.

''Tell me the name of your village and I will go there and cure them, just as I will cure you of your fever and heal your wound,'' Serine soothed.

"We must save the village," he panted. "Without children, we will be lost. We must break the curse!"

Serine crossed herself. "Curse?"

"No children born since the plague... women barren. Must take children..." Exhaustion overcame him and he fell silent.

The sky darkened and the fire crackled against the chill of night. The pungent odor of herbs permeated the room, clearing the air of the scent of sickness, leaving the fresh smell of cleanliness with a hint of marigold ointment as Serine sat back and inspected her work.

She had not expected the Celt's skin to be so fair beneath his growth of beard. She had not expected his lips to be so full and well formed, hinting of smiling sensuousness even in his pain. She had not expected the structure of his face to be so strong, and the line of his jaw so firm. Nor had she expected the cleft set deep in his chin.

His cheeks and forehead carried a much richer color than did the area that had been concealed by his facial hair. It must have been many months since he had taken the time to shave, she mused as she pressed another herb-soaked cloth against the swelling in his neck and was rewarded by a sigh of comfort.

Twice she had added warm water as she waited for Old Ethyl to appear. And while she was alert for sounds of the woman's presence, Serine was not anxious for her return. Her tired mind focused on the man before her. What was he like? What position did he hold in his village? Had he a wife and children? If his wife were here would she snatch him from the healing waters and insist that he lie in the bed burning with fever? Or would she approve of Serine's treatment and help sponge the

heated body? Would a wife watch the rivulets of water
as they slithered down his shoulders and across his
chest? Might she take her finger to trace the watery trail
as it wended its way over the muscles of his upper body
and disappeared into the pool of bathwater that covered his lower extremities?

Without conscious reflection Serine's eyes followed
the pattern of her thoughts, relishing the taut muscles
of his diaphragm and the flat ridges of his belly. How
different he was from the jiggling bulk of the man Serine called husband. So different they might be of a
different species. She cupped the water in her hand and
allowed it to drizzle over his body, imagining the culmination of its journey within the depths of the cask.
Imagining how it might trace his manhood, urging it to
a glorious awakening. Such an act between husband and
wife would, no doubt, in happier times, culminate in an
act of love laced with passion as well as abandonment.

How different such a coming together would be
compared to her dutiful coupling with her elderly husband. How uniquely different, and how wonderful!

She sighed and squeezed the water from the cloth as
Old Ethyl entered the room. The older woman stopped
short when she saw the expression on Serine's face.

"I thought to apologize for being gone longer than
planned," she said. "But from the look on your face
perhaps I weren't gone long enough. We'd best move
him back to the bed. With the night coming on he's apt
to catch a chill."

"Yes, yes, of course," Serine agreed. "I was about
to send for someone to help me do just that." She tried
to laugh away the woman's suspicions, but the color
that rushed to her face belied her efforts of denial. It

was amazing how much that old woman could see with just one eye.

"I learned why the Celts took our children," Serine told her. "It seems their women are barren and the village faces extinction."

"That is good," Old Ethyl said as she placed a container of rich dark liquid on the table. "The children will be treated kindly until we can bring them back."

Serine shook her head. "It is bad," she argued. "They want children to populate their village. They will not easily give them up."

"Did he say where the village might be?" Old Ethyl asked.

"He said little that made sense."

Old Ethyl handed Serine a cup of horsetail tea laced with the bitter brew. "Wet his lips with the tea. Some of the liquid will slip down his throat and he will begin to heal, God willing."

Serine hesitated before administering the brew. She could only pray that Old Ethyl had been able to duplicate the recipe exactly. If the woman had inadvertently deleted one of the ingredients, or been forced to make a substitution, it could cost the man his life and Serine her only hope of finding her son.

Uttering a silent prayer, Serine dipped the cloth into the liquid and touched it to the lips of the unconscious man.

The Celt choked on the liquid and Old Ethyl stayed Serine's hand. "Gently, gently," she warned. "Drowning him in herbal juices will not heal him the faster."

Serine gently squeezed a liquid-soaked cloth, wishing that her hand did not shake so when she was forced to hold him in close proximity, just as she hoped that Old Ethyl did not notice the evidence of her weakness.

For Serine found it impossible to control herself where the Celt was concerned.

Rory's fever had diminished and he lay beneath the furs in relative comfort as Serine ministered to him.

In all truth, the Celt was probably much more comfortable than Margot and Old Ethyl, who slept on mats at the far end of the chamber.

Serine had tried to talk the women out of guarding their captive so closely, but they would have none of it.

"The man is young and strong," Margot insisted. "He will let you minister to his needs until his strength returns. Then he will do his best to escape. Of that there is no doubt."

"He is sore wounded," Serine argued. "It will be weeks before he is any threat to me. Besides, I would sound the alarm before he could rise from the bed."

"And what good is the alarm when there be only a few women strong enough to fight him?" Old Ethyl added her thoughts to the dispute. "Dame Margot and I will stay near the door and spell you should you drop from exhaustion. If the man looks to take advantage of our charity, I will see that he thinks better of it."

There was nothing for it but to let them have their way. Other than bodily evicting the two women, Serine was powerless to rid herself and her prisoner of the jailers. It was odd, but Serine felt no threat from this man. Perhaps it was due to his comatose state, but she could not bring herself to believe that he would deliberately harm her, even though his arms bulged with muscles and his chest was full and deep.

Serine remembered the touch of his body against hers, his hands—strong and firm—holding her, and his lips, those beautiful lips, touching hers. Her heart quickened imperceptibly and she brushed the hair from his forehead.

How unfair it was that Serine had been destined to wed a man so many years her senior. How sad that her girlhood dreams had ended on her wedding day, long before they ever knew the wonder of a lover's kiss.

And then the water gods had sent her this man who had come to steal her only son. Although he had succeeded in his quest, she found herself unable to hate him as he lay before her, looking for all the world as young and innocent as Hendrick himself.

She smiled, turning her face toward the wall so Margot and Old Ethyl would not notice should they happen to be watching, for it was not only the man's appearance that held her interest, there was something else about him that sent blood racing through her veins in a most unseemly manner. A virility that could not be denied even in sleep.

What might it have been like to have been given in marriage to a man such as the one resting before her? Would her heart have leapt in her bosom when her father had told her of her betrothal? Would she have waited impatiently for the day when this young, virile man would make her his own, rather than dread the stiff, dry embrace of her elderly husband?

Serine crossed herself quickly, hoping the Lord would not think her ungrateful, for her marriage had given Serine her son. She loved Hendrick above all else. It was just that sometimes, quite unexpectedly, thoughts slipped through her mind and she found herself dreaming of what life might have been had her marriage been somewhat different.

"He's something to feast the eyes upon, and that's no lie." Old Ethyl's voice crackled through the silence.

"You've all but stared a hole through him, m'lady. Why don't you lie down and rest yourself? Or better yet, go get yourself a bit of fresh air. 'Tis market day, and there be a good crowd gathered. 'Twould take your mind from your troubles.''

"Hendrick always liked market day," Serine whispered. "I cannot go. I cannot face it knowing there is no chance that I will see him."

"It would be reassuring to the villagers if you showed yourself among them. They are all proud of you and you've not showed hide nor hair since you brought the Celt to your bower."

"You know how important it is that we listen for his every word. What if he uttered the name of his village and there was no one about to hear his words?" Serine's eyes centered on the man. He seemed more alert somehow and she wondered if he could hear what was being said.

"Dame Margot and I will stay with him," Ethyl assured her. "There's no need for all of us to miss being out on a beautiful day."

"You go, Ethyl," Serine urged. "I would rather stay here."

"Stay, then, if you must." Old Ethyl shrugged. "But don't say you have not been warned if your serfs come to believe you've gone daft."

"You go on and assure them of my well-being." Serine gently nudged the woman toward the door.

"Aye," Old Ethyl grumbled, "I'll convince them you are right and well, but who is going to convince me when I see you sitting there mooning over that Celt like a lovesick hound?"

"I'm not mooning over him." Serine defended herself. "I'm hoping he will say something that will help me find Hendrick and the rest of the missing children, and at the same time I keep telling him how much Hendrick means to me and how important it is that he be returned to Sheffield. Somehow, I believe that even through the netherlands of unconsciousness he will hear me.''

"As you will, m'lady," Old Ethyl agreed sourly as she scooted out the door.

It was a sorry day when their lady sat dreaming over a fallen Celt, Old Ethyl thought. But then, all the days had been sorry since the Celts had come to disrupt their lives and take their children. Ethyl, for one, would be glad when the man recovered enough to give his information and be gone. The man had brought nothing but ill luck since he'd stepped foot on English soil. The sooner he recovered enough to leave, the better for all involved. They'd rue the day if word got back to their overlord that they were harboring a Celt in their midst!

Chapter Four

The voice was low and soft. It slipped through Rory's dreams like a song and he awoke to find his fever gone and his mind clear. Though weak, he knew instinctively that he had full control of his limbs, and that his body would obey him, albeit reluctantly. The voice continued as he checked the responses of his muscles, assuring himself that he carried only the nagging pain in his back and side. Satisfied that he was able to move on command, he relaxed, keeping his eyes closed as he turned his attention to the words the woman was saying.

"You see, Hendrick is my only child and heir to this estate. His father is no longer a young man, and it is doubtful if there will be further issue. That is why it's so important that I bring Hendrick back here. Surely you can understand my situation."

So, Rory mused behind closed lids, one of the children was the heir to the manor. The only heir. In years past that would be worth a great deal of ransom money to a Celt raider. In this case, however, it meant little or nothing. They had come for children to repopulate their village, not for wealth or jewels, or even women, for that matter. Little good women had done them over the past years. All barren no matter how sexually satisfied the Celts kept them.

"I have saved your life, and do not intend to hold you for ransom. Surely that must be worth something to you," the voice went on. "All I ask is that you take me back to your village and allow me to plead my case before your overlord, adding your voice to my appeal. That cannot be much to give for your life and freedom."

Rory suppressed a smile. He could imagine his brother Guthrie's face if he were to appear with the woman whom, by all indications, had orchestrated the destruction of their plans, and asked for the return of her son. Brother or no, they would both be lucky to escape with their lives.

"Had I left you to die you would have been cast into the bowels of hell," she continued. "Old Ethyl knows quite a bit about these things and she assures me that a Celt must be struck down with a weapon in his hand, not a woman, in order to reap the rewards of eternal life."

So this *was* the water sprite he had discovered at the water's edge and held so briefly in his arms. He remembered the wet, slick body. The proud, silent face that asked no quarter. The long, dark hair like a sodden veil, and the moonlight catching the droplets of water clinging to lashes that shielded bottomless eyes.

His eyes flickered, and of their own volition lifted to behold the woman who had been at once his defeat and his salvation.

He saw her expression turn from serenity to surprise.

"You're awake!"

"A stupendous observation," he said dryly.

"How do you feel?"

"Weak and thirsty. There is a bitter taste in my mouth. What is this place?"

She seemed to be glancing over her shoulder, and Rory tried to see past her into the shadows of the room, to no avail.

"You are in Sheffield Manor. I am the Lady Serine. What is your name?"

The woman acted somewhat flustered, and the voice he had found so sensuous and soothing in the depths of the netherworld now was edged with anxiousness.

"I am called Rory."

"From whence do you come?"

She asked the question so casually she almost caught him in her trap. He had already opened his mouth to reply when a misty memory told him that he must keep the name of his village a secret if he valued his life.

"I come from across the sea," he said non-committally.

"Does your home have no name?"

He watched her face brighten with hope, then cloud as he continued. "It is not a large estate, but I am satisfied with my lot."

"Is that where you have taken my... the children?"

He watched as her eyes shifted away from his steady gaze and knew she was wondering just how much of her little soliloquy he had heard.

"The children were taken to the village, where they will be well kept," he assured her.

"They were well kept here," she challenged, "and we want them back."

"There is little hope of that."

"We could pay..."

He lifted his hand to silence her. "It is not money we need, but the children themselves. Youth to repopulate our village. Our women are barren."

"Surely a few years without the birth of a child should not cause brave men to resort to destroying the families of others."

"It has been more than a few years. It has been almost a decade. The plague struck and took over half the village. Men, women, children, babes in arms. None were spared. Those who recovered rebuilt their lives, took in the orphaned children and remarried, but there was no issue. Within the past months the last surviving children have grown to adulthood. There was nothing left but to steal the children our women cannot bear."

"You had no right to take my child or the children of my serfs." Serine met his eyes now and challenged him openly.

"We had no choice."

"You have taken the heir to Sheffield. When my husband returns from the Crusades he will appeal to the king, and the brave men who have fought to free the Holy Land from the infidel will take up our cause and destroy your village."

"By the time they could discover where the village is located, your children will be grown men and women, and will fight to defend what they have inherited. Think you the son of a serf would not rather live as a thane's heir with plot and property to be inherited rather than come back here to serve as a serf?"

Serine had no answer for that. Her breath caught in her throat and she found herself unable to answer. If what this man said was true, the majority of the children would be far better off if they stayed with their captors.

"What you say holds merit, but my son is heir to Sheffield and does not need your charity. He is the son of a landed knight and a lord in his own right. I demand that you return him to me."

Rory raised his eyebrows. This woman had spirit, but he had expected no less. Any woman with the courage and cleverness to create a diversion that confounded dozens of Celts and sent them packing would have spirit as well as beauty.

"Will you send a message to your overlord to tell him that you live?"

Again her question seemed innocent enough, but Rory sensed the underlying threat. He could not help but admire her clever persistence as she continually rooted for the name of his village.

"When I am strong enough to travel I will give thought to your request. Until that time it behooves you to keep me well or you will never see your son again." With that he turned his face toward the wall.

The woman was quick and sharp. In his weakened condition it was only a matter of time before he made a slip and told more than was prudent. His mind raced forward to the time he would spend with this woman, who interested him as well as piqued his admiration.

He empathized with her over the loss of her son. He had lost a son to the plague. Perhaps he would add his voice to hers and petition for the boy's release. One child could not be so important to the survival of the village, and as that one child was the son of a knight, and heir to an estate, it was very possible that the English king would, indeed, come to the aid of his vassal and retaliate against the Celts.

Rory nestled down into the soft furs that encased his body. His thoughts for the woman were as soft and warm as the sense of well-being. The pain had subsided and he could feel strength and energy begin to surge through his body.

He heard a voice murmur and thought to give the Lady Serine reassurance that he would, indeed, be party to her quest. Easing himself onto his back, he opened his eyes to find himself staring into the malevolent glare of a one-eyed crone. Suppressing a gasp, Rory decided the fever must have come on him again, for the nightmares had returned.

Shutting his eyes tightly against the aberration, he determined to sleep until it disappeared.

It wasn't until Rory awakened the next morning that he first realized something was amiss. His face felt clean and he could feel the air touching his skin. Still half asleep, he ran his hands over his cheeks. The next moment he emitted a bellow that resounded throughout the building.

"My beard! You've stripped me of my beard!" he shouted as Serine ran to his side with Old Ethyl in her wake.

"I did but clean you up a bit," Serine told him. "Your beard was matted with blood and I could not tell whether or not your neck was still swollen with all that hair in my way. Besides, you look better without it."

He could not know how much better he looked, Serine thought as she allowed her eyes to feast on him. His hair, clean now, curled in a mass of midnight ringlets about his face, falling to his shoulders like an ebony cloud. Each curl an invitation to run her fingers through it and let the curls trap her hands and hold them against his head while she memorized his face.

Her reverie was broken by his continued harassing over her action.

"Be still," Old Ethyl said threateningly, "else my lady's work will have been in vain, for I'll bloody you again."

"But she cut away my hair and stripped me of my manhood!" he protested.

Old Ethyl snorted in derision. "How was she to know?" she asked. "Most men don't wear their manhood on their chin."

"That's not what I mean!" he argued. "I have worn my facial hair since the day I reached manhood."

"Then it's high time you did without it for a bit," Old Ethyl assured him. "You have no need of it here. By the time we are rid of you it will have grown back, I'll vow." She turned to Serine, ignoring the man's sputtering. "As soon as our visitor calms down, I will leave you for a while, unless you wish to go in my stead."

"You go, Ethyl," Serine said, temporizing. "I will stay with our...guest."

"As you will," Old Ethyl agreed. "I prefer good fresh English air to the fumes of an angry man." Since her lady would not go among the people to learn their mood, it was up to Old Ethyl herself to do so. With a nod of her head, Old Ethyl took her place near the door, determined that she would make certain the man posed no threat to Serine before she left for the village.

Rory paid the old woman little mind. His anger and his attention focused on Serine, who looked at him with an expression of disbelief.

"I cannot see how the loss of your beard and mustache could be of such importance," she ventured.

"It is a matter of honor," he blustered. "A man is judged by his facial hair in my country."

Serine shrugged her shoulders and moved away from his bedside before answering. "I now see the difference between your world and mine, for here a man is judged by his sons."

The instant the words left her mouth she would have recalled them, but it was too late.

Only the weakness from his wound and the infection that had so recently invaded his body kept Rory from attacking her—his infirmity, and the fact that Old Ethyl had nocked her arrow and stood ready to release it with deadly accuracy should he move toward her lady.

Realizing the depth of her mistake, Serine eased the man back against the pillows. "Please forgive me," she said. "I spoke out of turn. I did not realize that your facial hair was an indication of your virility. Feel free to grow it back, and I promise I will do nothing to rid you of it whether you are conscious or no." Her eyes sought out Old Ethyl and she indicated that she felt she had the matter well in hand, and Old Ethyl was free to go.

"It is too late," Rory lamented. "In my country a man is known for his mustache. It is as recognizable as his nose. It might be years before I could grow another that could match the one you have so blatantly destroyed."

Serine narrowed her eyes. The man was beside himself. It would almost be humorous had it not been that his anger might stop him from telling her where he had taken her son. She wanted his goodwill and would never have done anything to irritate him. At least, not until he had given her the information she sought.

"At least we have found a common ground," Serine told him. "You have taken my son and I have taken your beard. Perhaps it is time that we talked of how we

can make the recovery of both of our treasures as easy
as possible.''

The man sighed deeply and relaxed. He studied her
for a long moment. ''My hair will grow back, regardless of what you do to prevent it, but there is nothing
either of us can do to bring back your son. By now he
is far away.''

''If he is well gone there should be no problem with
your telling me where your people have taken him,'' she
challenged.

''And in doing so invoke the distinct possibility of my
own death,'' he retorted. ''Feverish I may be, but my
mind has not deserted me. You cannot make me believe that you would keep me alive for one more hour
should you learn the location of your son.''

Serine chose not to answer. His words held a good
deal of truth, but not all. At first when she had brought
him to Sheffield she had cared little as to whether he
lived or died, her only thought being to keep him alive
until he could be made to tell her of Hendrick's whereabouts, but somehow she had become accustomed to his
presence and looked forward somewhat to the sound of
his voice as it became stronger. Even if he told her where
to find Hendrick at this very moment, she would be
hard put to turn him over to her overlord, let alone give
the order that would cost him his life.

Rory took her silence as confirmation of his words
and turned his back on the slim woman who carried the
strength of Celtic iron in her backbone. She was a hard
woman who cared for naught but her son, and he ad-
mired her for it in spite of himself.

In truth, he had no one to blame but himself. Had he
not paused to dally with the water-slick nymph he had
discovered on the water's edge, he would have been well

away. And some of the children would have disappeared without a trace. Now he owed his life to Serine and he knew that when the time came for him to show his appreciation for her ministrations her one demand would be that he take her to her son.

He took a deep breath and flinched against the raw pain that still troubled him. He knew Serine and her witch-woman, Ethyl, had worked long and hard to save his life. Even more than the wound had been the onset of the fever and the poisons that had invaded his body. He doubted that the women of his village had the knowledge to save him had he been able to escape.

He owed Serine his life. It was true. And to pay that debt he would take her with him to Corvus Croft and arrange for her to speak to Guthrie. But beyond that he would promise nothing, and nothing was most likely exactly what she would get for all her trouble. For the goal of the Celts had been to bring children to their village, and thanks to the efforts and cleverness of this woman those children had been few. That her son was one of those who had been successfully taken was unfortunate, because there was little hope that the council would agree to give the boy back to his mother.

"Since you have saved my life, I am willing to consider laying your plight before Guthrie, my overlord."

"I shall go with you," she said flatly, "and bring my son back with me."

"I guarantee nothing," Rory said. "Only that you will be given a fair hearing."

"Fair! What do you call fair? You have stolen our children and raided our village and you dare speak of fairness?"

"If you can heal me and return me to my village in peace, you will be heard. My people did not steal your

children out of spite or villainy. It was due to desperation, and no one would have been harmed had you not
come after them.''

If Serine wanted to be with her son she would have to
agree to stay in Ireland.

Rory watched as she moved around the room, and
imagined her moving thusly through the streets of his
village, through the halls of Guthrie's fortress and, finally, through the rooms of Rory's own home. He
found the thoughts pleasant. Perhaps he would urge her
to stay once she realized it would be impossible to obtain the release of her son.

For all that she had cut away his beard he found
himself unable to maintain his initial anger. It seemed
almost as though there was an unspoken duel between
them, with rules yet unmade, and it challenged him to
try to guess what she would do next as she strove to regain possession of her child, unaware that fate, and a
woman's tongue, would take the matter out of their
hands.

''I tell you, our Lady Serine was brave as any man
could have been,'' Hildegard, the alewife, boasted to
the knight and two foot soldiers who had come to par-
take of her wares. ''Stole those children back and
hoodwinked the Celts in the process. They never knew
what hit them, they didn't!''

''We heard your lady's own son was stolen,'' one of
the men said as he quaffed his ale.

''That's true,'' Hildegard agreed. ''So sad for the
poor lady after risking her life and saving so many. But
there's rumors from the castle that she captured a Celt
and hopes to learn from him where they've taken her
son.''

The knight wiped his hand across his mouth. "Clever woman," he remarked. "Old Sheffield was always the lucky one. He should be coming back any time now. I vow he'll make short work of the Celt. The man will beg to tell Sheffield anything he wants to hear." A toothy smile split his face. "A man learns many things on crusade. How to torture a man until he begs to talk. How to make love to a woman." His eyes swept over Hildegard's generous figure and his hand slipped around her in an intimate embrace.

"You tell me nothing I don't already know," she said as she extricated herself. "My man's been on crusade before, and I find myself more pleased to see him each time he returns. However, should you decide to persist, Sir Knight, I'm sure he would be happy to take time from showing me his newly learned arts of love to showing you his well-earned reputation as a soldier to be reckoned with." She smiled as she said the words, but the threat was there, loud and clear for all to hear.

They all laughed together, but the spurned knight's eyes narrowed spitefully as he moved away with his companions. "Country wench," he sneered. "She'll wish she'd considered my proposition before I'm finished with her and her brave, Celt-loving lady."

He motioned to his companions. "Come, lads! We have an appointment to meet with Lord Baneford. Unless I miss my guess, he'll pay good coin to learn that there is a Celt lurking around his lands."

The men swung off through the village, almost colliding with the one-eyed crone who stood at the side of the road.

To heal, one must spend a great deal of time abed, and, although Rory healed far more quickly than he was willing to let on, he whiled away his empty hours by watching Serine as she went about her duties.

It occurred to him that she was not a great beauty, and had no outstanding feature on which to base her attractiveness. Yet there was a graceful loveliness about the woman that would not be denied. The more he watched, the more he wanted. The stronger he became, the more the demands of the flesh tortured him until he reached the place where he actually welcomed the appearance of Old Ethyl.

In truth, Rory had not responded to a woman as he did to Serine since the plague had taken his wife from him, and had not thought to again. Still, the sound of Serine's husky voice sent currents of pleasure through his body, and the touch of her hand was enough to send him into a fever.

She talked of little other than the return of her son, and he wondered how she would react if she suspected the plan he had devised to take her to his village and hold her there through her love for her child.

Surely once she became accustomed to Corvus Croft she would learn to love it. It was a beautiful place with lush green fields and sparkling blue streams. He doubted not that the children the Celts had spirited away had already fallen in love with their new home. It took very little time to change one's allegiance, for in all honesty, Rory was more than a little in love with Serine. He watched her closely. Her movements were graceful but positive. There was no room for doubt within her. And he wondered, once again, what she felt when she thought of him.

He knew that there were times her heart quickened when she caught him watching her. He could see the color that tinted her cheeks and the pulse pounding in her throat. How he longed to press his lips to that pulsing point. To feel it pound beneath his lips as he drank in her scent, her warmth, her sweetness.

As if in answer to his silent supplication, she passed his cot, reaching out to touch his forehead in her journey. When she hesitated, as though reluctant to release the gentle contact with his face, Rory reached up and removed her hand. He inhaled the scent of marigolds that was uniquely her own and brushed her hand across his cheek. Without conscious volition, he pressed his lips against her palm and buried his mouth in the softness. Then, with a groan, he swept the salty moistness with his tongue.

His fingers held her wrist and he felt her pulse jump and quicken. She did care! She responded to him just as he did to her.

He felt her other hand move into his hair, and tensed himself should he have misread her and she decided to pull him away. Her hand clenched, then lost itself in his thick locks. He pulled her to him as he gave in to his desires and sought out the pulse beat hammering in her throat. With a deep moan he closed his mouth over it and felt it drum against his tongue. He knew his time was limited. Serine had given in to the madness of the moment and he had taken her completely off guard. It was only a matter of seconds before she would realize what was taking place and put up her defenses. But one moment of heaven was worth a lifetime of darkness.

Without giving propriety another thought, Rory cradled her in his arms and gently, gently covered her lips with his as he drew out her sweetness, inhaling her, tasting her, luxuriating in the touch of her body, warm and soft against his naked chest.

Then Serine's hands drew him closer, demanding that
he give all that his kisses promised. He felt her open to
him and was lost in the depths of her mouth. He barely
restrained himself from crying out at the overwhelm-
ing passion, so long denied, that surged forth and blossomed in all its frightening glory in the arms of this
beautiful, determined woman, who could never belong
to the likes of a Celt.

The world swam as Rory's kiss demanded all that
Serine could give and promised even more. It mattered
not that this man was her avowed enemy. That he had
stolen her child and would not tell where he had been
taken. All that mattered was the touch of his lips, the
caress of his hands and the burning heat of his body
against hers. All that mattered was that she had waited
for this moment, for this kiss throughout all the watchful days and sleepless nights. Longed for this moment
throughout her life without knowing for what she
longed. And now that it had come, she had not the
strength, nor the will, to push either the man or the
moment from her embrace. His kiss was all she had
dreamed it would be and though she burned through
eternity for this moment of weakness it was beyond her
ability to care.

A soft cry escaped her lips as he buried his face in the
soft fragrance of her breasts. A surge of desire shot
through her body as swift and true as one of Old Ethyl's
arrows, and most likely as deadly. For Serine felt that
she could not live without experiencing the wonder of
Rory's love, of his beautiful, masculine body, his sensual lips and his unquenchable passion.

Incapable of denying him or herself the love they so
greatly desired, Serine was swept to the boundaries of
surrender. Unknowing, uncaring of anything other than

the man in whose arms she lay. She seemed to be spiraling upward toward the bright light of fulfillment when Rory withdrew his lips, holding her close for several minutes until their breathing assumed some semblance of normalcy before he let her go.

She moved from the haven of his arms and stood before him, slightly disheveled and very disappointed.

"Forgive me," he said, unable to keep his eyes from the pleasures he had so briefly known. "I did not mean to force myself on you."

Serine opened her mouth several times before she found her voice. "Then why did you do so?" And why did you not continue? she wanted to ask.

"I lost my head, and in the heat of the moment forgot that there are two situations that stand sentry between us."

"Those are?" She knew, but she must hear him say the words. The words that would both damn and free her.

"You have a husband, and I have your son. As long as it remains so, there can be nothing but lust between us. And I want more than a fleeting moment of passion from you, Serine. I want your love, just as, I believe, you want mine. But love should give happiness, and between us we can offer each other naught but pain. For this ill-favored love we have found for each other is indeed a bitter brew."

She turned away, unable to hold back a trite comment of her own. "Sometimes the more bitter the brew, the greater the benefit."

Chapter Five

The kisses they had shared could not be forgotten. Each time their eyes met they both reacted as though struck a blow. No matter how hard either of them tried, it was impossible to pretend nothing had happened, any more than it was possible to allow another such encounter to happen again.

Serine was a woman wed. She had never so much as thought of betraying her husband's trust by giving herself to another man. Nor had she ever met a man she would have considered interesting enough to be worth the anguish that would result in such a betrayal. Now her mind slipped a hundred times a day into thoughts of Rory's strong young arms encircling her body. His lips searching out the sensitive places in her hands and neck. The heat that had filled her whole being when he had buried his face in her breasts. There were ever so many other places of interest throughout her body that had heretofore gone unexplored. He would know where to seek them out. He would find each one and with each discovery she would find deeper pleasure and more euphoric enjoyment.

And, oh, to be allowed to do the same to him. To touch him with her lips and hands as he had touched

her. To run her tongue over his hand or taste the quickened pulse in his throat. How wonderful it would be to
know that she could make his body respond to her, as
she did to him. To give and take in the deepest passion
of love until they were both too sated to move.

Tears filled her eyes and she stumbled, sloshing water over the side of the basin she carried. To her surprise, Rory was suddenly beside her, catching her before
she could do more damage. He took the basin from her
hands and placed it on the table.

"There now, it's overworked you are," he told her.
"The crone is right. You should go into the village and
get some fresh air. You've scarce left this room since I
came here. It's myself that is supposed to be the prisoner, not you!" He had fallen into the pattern of speech
used in his homeland and laughed at his own words, but
his face held true concern.

She was alternately flushed and pale and he had no
way of knowing it was her thoughts, not her physical
condition, that caused her such distress.

Rory wanted her to leave. He could not bear the close
proximity any longer. He needed a respite from her
presence. He needed a few minutes' peace in which to
be alone with thoughts that had nothing to do with this
woman; with the scent of her, the touch of her hands,
the sound of her voice. If she did not leave him to himself for a few hours he would die of desire, of wanting
what he dared not take.

For he had already come to the realization that taking Serine once in the heat of passion would never be
enough for him. It was not just sex he wanted from this
woman. It was her love he hungered for above all else.
And though there were moments when he believed to
the very depths of his soul that her longings were the

same as his, he dared not put them into words. For if
she knew the same yearnings as did he, his heart would
break to realize it could never come to pass.

There was but one way he could prove his love and
give his soul some surcease, and that was by taking
Serine to her child.

"In a few weeks I will be well enough to travel," he
said as he walked to the window and looked out over the
countryside. "Are you prepared to go with me?"

Serine finished mopping up the last traces of water.
"I am," she told him without hesitation. "I will make
the arrangements, and we will leave as soon as you are
strong enough."

Rory was stronger than he had led Serine to believe.
It had been in his mind to escape, but he had come to
realize that he would never be free of her if he did not
take her with him. And as long as she was with him
there was a chance that the gods would smile on them
both and grant them the right to love each other.

He slammed his fist against the window casing. He
could not bear to be with her, and he could not stand to
go. He turned and saw her expression. He longed to
take her into his arms and kiss the concern from her
face. "As you will," he said without moving. "You
have brought me back from the jaws of death, and I will
take you to your son."

Serine barely contained the smile that pulled at the
corners of her lips. This was the first time he had conceded that she had actually saved his life or that he
would voluntarily take her with him. She wanted to run
to him and throw her arms around his neck and thank
him. She wanted to tell him that he would never be sorry
for his compassion, and his recognition of the fairness

of her request, just as she would never be sorry that she had saved his life.

It was the sight of his clenched fists that kept her frozen to the spot. It was the set of his jaw and the compression of his lips that made her keep her distance.

"We will surely go, and soon, but you are not yet strong. Come and lie down. Rest will restore your health."

He wanted to shout at her that he could never be restored until she was his—irrevocably, undeniably his in body and soul. But he held his silence and complied with her suggestion. It was only after he had reached his cot that he again spoke. "Then it is agreed. Once I regain my strength we will go to my village and you will lay your petition before the elders." He did not add that he gave her little hope of success. But by agreeing to her terms he paid her back for her care and insured that his life would not be forfeit before he could return to his home.

Serine's face shone with happiness, and Rory was taken aback at the depth of her joy. Perhaps some compromise was possible over the return of her son, just to see her in this light again. He was silently musing over the thought when Old Ethyl banged her way into the room, almost upsetting Dame Margot, who had taken her place near the door.

"There be trouble afoot!" Old Ethyl announced. "The village is full of it. I told you it boded no good that you would not show yourself among your people."

"What do you mean?" Serine tried to shove Old Ethyl back through the door, but the woman held her ground.

"There's men coming!" Old Ethyl said ominously.

"Lord Baneford's men have passed through before," Serine reminded her. "Passed through and gone on their way, never the wiser."

"They be wiser now," Old Ethyl insisted, "and word is out they will soon be at the gates demanding an audience."

"Perhaps he wants confirmation of our safety." Serine brushed the woman's concerns aside.

"And perhaps he wants your prisoner."

"They need not know of Rory's presence. It is nothing to them. And who is to tell them he is here?" Serine tossed her head, discounting the old woman's concern.

"I'll tell you who," Old Ethyl answered. "The whole village is agog with the story of how you thwarted the Celts and took one prisoner. Unless you cut the tongues out of your serfs, the story will be spread from here to the Holy Land. Once Lord Baneford arrives it will take him but little time to get the information he wants from the Celt."

Rory glared at the woman who thought him of an ilk that would betray his countrymen. From across the room he could catch only bits and pieces of the conversation, but heard enough to know that his presence was common knowledge, and the soldiers were coming to arrest him.

He had believed in Serine. He had even thought to aid her in her plight and add his request to hers. What a fool he had been when all the time she had only waited until he was strong enough to talk so that they could torture him into giving the location of the children. Anger bubbled in his throat as the words tumbled from his lips.

"Did I not heal quickly enough for you, m'lady? Or was it that the word of a Celt was not good enough for such as yourself? You could not wait. You could not believe in me. You could not even believe in yourself! You had to betray us both and lose any chance of seeing your son again in the bargain. Thanks to your duplicity, I will undoubtedly die, and the chance of finding your child will die with me."

"Rory, I swear I did not tell. I did not betray you."

"Hah!" he taunted. "I should have known you were up to no good, but, fool that I am, I believed in you. And now I will come to rue the day."

"It need not be so," Serine protested. "We will escape. We will go now, before the knights arrive. Old Ethyl can help and—"

"A sick man, a determined woman and a one-eyed crone. Who indeed would think such a trio strange and look at them askance?" he scoffed. "We would be caught before we could reach the harbor."

"There is talk of a strange boat in the bay. It is small, but seaworthy. Perhaps the man who owns it would sell it to us. Or perhaps we could steal it," Old Ethyl suggested wryly. "'Twould save time and trouble."

"Know you the name of the man who owns the boat?" Serine asked.

Old Ethyl cast a cautious glance at her mistress. "It is not my business to know the name of each man who puts in to our shores," she said.

"But you *do* know," Serine persisted. "What does he look like? Where can we find him, and quickly?"

"He is an older man with long silver hair and sharp black eyes. He carries the rod of learning. I do not think he means to stay long and doubt that he will readily give up his vessel."

"Then we will fight him," Serine declared. "We must have that boat."

Old Ethyl sighed. "Very well, then. I will see if I can find him. He will not have gone far. He spends much of his time talking to the travelers in the alehouse. Hildegard says he calls himself Drojan the Seer."

Rory leapt to his feet. The stool on which he had been sitting skittered across the floor. "Drojan? The gods be praised. There is hope after all."

He started toward the door, but Serine was there before him while Old Ethyl nocked an arrow.

"Do not be so hasty, Rory," Serine chided. "Remember, I am going with you, regardless of what you think of me or my motives. I shall be with you every step of the way."

"And I with you, fair lady," Rory promised. "And I with you. Now send your emissary here to find Drojan and let us be away." He jerked his thumb toward Old Ethyl.

"It is my lady who bids me come or go," the woman told him, "not a thieving Celt."

"If what you say is true and you linger here arguing, there will be no Celt, and no chance of finding Hendrick." He directed the last words at Serine, noting her reaction.

"He speaks the truth," she told Old Ethyl. "There is no time to lose. We must be away as quickly as possible. You find the man. I will apprise Dame Margot of our plans."

But Old Ethyl wasn't to be sent off so easily. Her eye narrowed and she looked from Serine to the Celt. "Perhaps this Drojan is a spy and comes to free our prisoner at the cost of our lives," she suggested.

"Drojan is no warrior, nor is he a spy," Rory contended. "Most likely he has come to see that I have a proper burial. If Guthrie thought I was other than dead he would have come himself."

"And it's dead you will be if you betray my lady again," Old Ethyl snorted. "Both you and your 'seer.'"

She did not trust the man, but then, there was no man she trusted, and her caution had held her in good stead. "Mind yourself," she warned Serine. "And do not be lax in minding him, lest he forget all his pretty promises and run like a tag-tail dog to whence he came."

As soon as the door closed behind the irate woman, Serine turned to her prisoner. "Will you run? Or have I your word that you will take me with you?"

The doubt in her eyes hurt almost as much as the doubt in his heart. "I will take you with me to my village and see that you are allowed to petition for the return of your son. On this you have my word."

Serine took a deep breath. It was the word of a Celt that she must accept—a Celt she had no reason to trust, but one she knew she would never be able to forget.

"I will tell Dame Margot. Be ready to leave as soon as Old Ethyl returns." Without giving him any chance to reply, she hurried off to make herself ready for the journey.

It took Old Ethyl but a short time to discover the whereabouts of the man. As she suspected, he was lingering around the alehouse talking with the patrons who frequented the establishment.

She stayed in the shadows listening to his conversation. Rory had spoken true. The man was definitely trying to ascertain the Celt's whereabouts, but, while it was common knowledge that the Celt had been wounded and captured, people could but speculate as to where he was being held.

The group of travelers left the table where they had been conversing with the seer and Old Ethyl moved up behind him.

"You ask many questions, Seer," she said bluntly. "I thought any spaeman worth his salt was supposed to give answers."

Drojan did not look up from his ale. He knew a Celt had been taken, but the man was said to have been sore wounded and no one would say for certain whether he still lived. His hopes had soared when first he arrived, only to be dashed to dust by the subsequent information, or lack thereof. Now he was being interrogated by a woman who cast aspersions on his abilities as a seer. His hackles rose at the impertinence of the woman who dared question him or his abilities, and he turned, ready to chastise her verbally.

The words died in his throat. It was she! There was no doubt. Before him stood a female with but one eye, who carried across her shoulders a longbow with a quiver of arrows on her back. The woman he had seen prophetized in the Runes. The woman he had been warned about. She, who carried the sign of Woden. The loss of an eye. There was no mistake.

"Who... who are you?" he managed to blurt out.

"Hah!" she scoffed. "Just as I thought. If you were what you say, you would know." She cast him a disparaging look. "I am called Old Ethyl, and if you want the answers to your questions, you will come with me."

To her surprise the man did not give any objections and simply picked up his pack and his rod and followed her from the room.

"Are you taking me to my lord Rory?" he asked as he followed her along the dusty road.

"Oh, so he's a lord now, is he?" she taunted. When the man did not answer she slowed her pace a bit. "I'm taking you to my lady Serine," she told him. "She has need of your boat."

He stopped in his tracks. "My boat is not for hire."

Her eye narrowed and she gave him a malevolent glare. "I think it will be after my lady is through with you."

Old Ethyl's words proved to be true. Drojan gladly offered the use of his boat and was more than happy to take Serine along with Rory back to the village. He even went so far as to guarantee her safe conduct and assure her that she would be free to leave any time she chose. He did not say she could take her child with her when she left the Celt stronghold, for it was not in Drojan to lie.

He balked only when Serine insisted that Old Ethyl accompany her.

"It would not be proper for a lady to travel without a companion," Serine asserted. For all her blossoming love for Rory, she found it impossible to trust him completely, or herself more than a little. Old Ethyl was her bulwark against her own emotional failings, as well as a strong ally and adviser.

"If it is a woman companion you want, why not take Dame Margot?" Rory suggested. "Surely she would be a greater asset in diplomatically presenting your demands."

Serine had given this situation deep thought and knew that Dame Margot was quite capable of acting as chatelaine to Sheffield, while Old Ethyl was equally as capable of putting a well-placed arrow into an enemy who might try to keep them from accomplishing their objective. She had little doubt that Rory realized this truth as well, but she gave him the benefit of a polite answer.

"The people of Sheffield are comfortable with Dame Margot overseeing the manor. Old Ethyl would not wish to fill such a position. My decision stands."

Rory turned away to keep Serine from seeing the laughter in his eyes as he observed Drojan's discomfort. Most people were in awe of the man's supernatural powers and treated him with respect bordering on reverence. Such was not the case with Serine, who was oblivious to Drojan's reputation, as well as Old Ethyl, who openly expressed her contempt for everything the man professed to believe.

The haste and secrecy with which they were leaving Sheffield was not lost on Drojan, but he wisely withheld his questions, silently thanking the gods who favored him with their beneficence and allowed him to spirit Rory away without further trouble. Had he been forced to return to Corvus Croft without Rory and at the same time admit that the man still lived, it would have meant the lives of most of the villagers.

"We dare not go together lest we be seen," Serine said in a worried voice. "I will go on with Rory, and Drojan can come with Ethyl."

Old Ethyl shook her head. "No! If we are to do this thing with any hope of success it is you, m'lady, who must go to the boat with Drojan. In the dusk there will be little chance of your being identified if you wear a cloak. Once it is dark, I will accompany *Lord* Rory."

"Is it that you don't trust me?" Rory hardly restrained his laughter at the woman's obvious distrust.

"Oh, I trust you completely," Old Ethyl exclaimed. "I feel certain that given the chance you would be away in the flick of an eye, and your seer with you. And my lady, who knows nothing of the likes of you, would be none the wiser until it was too late. That is why you deal with me."

Drojan all but groaned aloud. Being confined to a small boat with this woman would make the trip seem an eternity. Yet he could not deny the validity of her words, for his own thoughts of escape had paralleled exactly what she had outlined.

"It is not a large vessel," he warned them, "so take as little as possible." He looked at the younger woman askance, hoping she would prove to be a good sailor. The older crone gave him no concern. She could, no doubt, ride the waves as well as he, and probably weather a stormy sea with equal aplomb.

His quick glance told him Old Ethyl was perusing him as he was her, and with much the same assessment. For a moment he actually found himself wondering if she could read his mind. He discounted the thought, though it would serve her right to learn that he disliked her as much as she obviously disliked him. And it was as well, for he would not have her know of his grudging admiration at her reading of the situation and the outcome that would have come to pass had Ethyl not seen through his ruse.

His hand pressed against the bag of Runes. "And may the gods save me from a clever woman," he whispered.

They left as the sun dipped low in the sky. Serine went on ahead with Drojan. Within the hour they were fol-

lowed by Old Ethyl, who trudged along some three
paces behind Rory, keeping him well within her sight.

"Get into the boat." Old Ethyl nudged Rory with her
bow as they pushed the boat into the water.

"It will go aground," Rory protested.

"Then the great seer can help me to push it out,"
Ethyl said flatly. "Now into the skiff with you."

Her insistence was twofold. She did not want to take
the chance of the younger man's agility allowing him to
climb quickly into the boat while she floundered at the
side and was left behind. And Ethyl was positive that
she could move faster than Drojan, for all that she suspected he was not as elderly as his flowing white hair
would indicate. She was certain she had seen traces of
gold in the man's hair and suspected that he had been
quite fair in his youth. Fair in more ways than one.

Rory took the tiller while Drojan set the sail. In very
little time the shore was far away and the skiff pressed
its bow into the vapor of the night and slithered through
the froth-crested water.

As the sail caught the wind Old Ethyl went to the
prow of the boat and scattered an offering into the sea.

"What did you use?" Drojan asked when she turned
back into the boat.

"Bladder wrack." The word held all the elements of
a challenge. "And you?"

Drojan cast a quick look in her direction. "The
same," he admitted. He hadn't thought she had seen his
surreptitious movements. "You observe a great deal for
a woman with only one eye."

"More than many a person with two," she agreed,
"so mind yourself unless you want to be called out."

Drojan sputtered to himself as he went astern to join
Rory. Who did this fool woman think she was? It was

Drojan who was the seer. Drojan whose fame had spread throughout many lands, and this one-eyed crone acted as though he was her subordinate. He wrapped his cloak about himself and continued his grumbling long after the women had drifted off to sleep as the skiff sailed on through the night.

By the time the sun fought its way through the morning mist the wind had risen and the little vessel clipped along toward its destination. Serine kept her eyes ahead watching for the first sign of land. Rory watched Serine, knowing that no matter what the outcome of her reunion with her son and her meeting with his brother, Guthrie, Rory would ultimately be the loser. He did not want to lose Serine. Not when he had only just found her. He stared moodily at the back of her head as the little craft bobbed through the gray waters.

Old Ethyl watched both the young people in turn, knowing that she was not alone in her survey. Drojan seemed equally interested in the actions of Rory and Serine.

"Your lady should get some sleep," Drojan said noncommittally. "We won't take the opportunity to cast her over the side, if that's what you fear."

"I fear nothing from you, Spaeman," Old Ethyl returned. "My lady is too excited to sleep."

"The trip is long. She can't hope to stay awake throughout the voyage." He glanced over the sea as if to bring credence to his words.

"How long?" Old Ethyl challenged.

"I'm surprised you don't already know." Drojan baited her a bit.

The woman's eye flashed as she recognized the challenge. "I can only know that of which people speak, and your young friend would not speak the name of his home no matter how long and hard we listened to his senseless blathering.''

"A weak excuse," Drojan asserted.

"No weaker than a seer traveling all the way from God knows where to bury the corpse of a man who has never died." Again the eye flashed.

Now Drojan was taken aback. "I did not feel that my lord Rory had gone to join his ancestors, but had I told his brother, Guthrie, that he was still alive there would have been a war rather than a peaceful voyage."

The expression on Ethyl's face did not change but she lowered her eye, unwilling to let Drojan know that her ability to listen had just given her a tidbit of information she had not heretofore known.

So the Celt overlord was Rory's brother, was he? Had she known sooner she would have made Serine demand that Hendrick be brought to Sheffield in return for the prisoner. Now it was too late, but never too late to make sure the overlord was properly grateful for his brother's return.

Her silence portended to Drojan that he had made a slip of the tongue, and he hastily reviewed his statement trying to discover what he had said that caused Ethyl to mull over his words. It irked him that after several minutes of speculation the woman could barely keep from smiling. She didn't smile often, and Drojan had been surprised to see that she had all her teeth.

Since she was disinclined to speak, he studied her beneath the harsh morning light. The hood had fallen back from her head, allowing him to view her face without obstruction. It was strange that she was called Old Ethyl, he thought, for the skin on her face was smooth and unwrinkled except for little laugh lines at the corners of her eyes. Even from behind the patch she wore the lines crept forth and turned up like tiny smiles, as if even though the eye could no longer see it could still laugh at the world.

Her hands were smooth, too. And strong. He did not doubt that she could fire her arrow with the best of men, for she was not a small woman, and most likely was as strong and fit as many an archer.

She turned to him quickly, aware that he was staring at her. "Have I turned green?" she asked. "Or are you hoping that I will?"

"Neither," he admitted. "You are a fine sailor and that in itself is a relief."

"This is not the first time I've made such a journey." She reached into the bag at her feet and drew forth a loaf of crusty bread, broke it and offered him a generous chunk.

"You were not born at Sheffield, then?"

"Ask your Runes, old man. Perhaps they will tell you where I was born, for you'll never learn it from me."

She turned her back to him and her hair caught in the wind and blew against his shoulder. Without thought he brushed it aside and felt the snap, like lightning on a summer night, zing through his body. He glared at her as though she had done it purposely, but she held her pose, looking out over the water.

The good side of her profile was toward him and he took in the strong, high cheekbones, the square chin, the patrician nose. With her hair streaming out behind her, glinting like precious metals of silver and gold in the sun, she looked for good and all like a Valkyrie figure on the bow of a ship. Drojan's heart quaked within his breast as he wondered at the god who would flaw such beauty by striking out her eye so that he, Drojan, could identify her. And if this was indeed so, what great and portentous event did it foreshadow? He was an elder of his village. A man respected for his abilities as a seer throughout the many lands he had traveled. The last thing he needed in his life was a woman. Especially an argumentative one who never agreed with his premises and challenged his ability as a spaeman.

He settled back into his seat and slowly chewed his bread, unable to believe that he was fascinated by a woman the rest of the world saw as an old, one-eyed crone.

Chapter Six

The sun reached its zenith in the sky. The wind calmed. The sail fluttered and collapsed like a dying bird. The little boat rocked idly in the water. And though each occupant took their turn at the oars, there was little momentum.

"Think you Lord Baneford will take to the sea to follow us?" Serine glanced over her shoulder as though expecting to see an armada advancing upon them.

"The same wind that blows for us fills his sails," Rory reminded her. "If he has sent out a ship it, too, is dead in the water."

"I had not thought of that." Serine smiled into Rory's eyes. She wanted to believe him. She wanted to believe *in* him. She wanted it more than all else in the world. All else, save Hendrick.

"Baneford's emissary would not have known anything was amiss until he arrived for his audience this morning," Rory said. "It is doubtful he would have the authority to follow, much less have the vessels immediately at hand." His words were assuring and she relaxed, changing the subject to more mundane conversation.

"Why would Baneford's men want to follow?" Drojan directed his question to Old Ethyl. "Once their message is delivered to Sheffield, their duty is done. They care little by whom it is received. I'm sure Dame Margot will be able to do all that needs to be done."

"They will be angered when they learn that the Celt is gone," Old Ethyl said quietly.

A glance in Ethyl's direction told Drojan that her concern was genuine. But he had met one of the men during his travels. They had shared bread and ale together while Drojan had ferreted out news of the man's mission. For the life of him, he could not see the reason for such anxiety.

"Perhaps we are speaking of different messengers. The men of whom I speak arrived at the gates seeking an audience with Lady Serine shortly before noon two days ago. They were told the lady was indisposed and unable to see them. They were in no great hurry, for the Lord of Sheffield was not expected to arrive for some weeks."

Had the women been so addled that they neglected to accept a message from their overlord? Had it truly been fear for Rory's life that kept the messenger cooling his heels? Or did Serine know that her lord and husband had made his last Crusade?

The one-eyed witch would know, and Drojan intended to draw her out without volunteering his own information. "Surely your lady received the messenger before her departure."

"Had the messenger been received, there would have *been* no departure," Ethyl said flatly. "Baneford will not take lightly the loss of a prisoner. Nor will he take lightly the loss of the heir to the estate."

"The loss of a child will be of little importance to the overlord, I'll wager. It is Sheffield's grown sons who will inherit."

"Hah!" Old Ethyl all but growled. "I was right! You are a faker and a liar, else you would know how ridiculous you sound."

"Ridiculous or not, it is the way of the world. Men die and their grown sons inherit."

"Sheffield has no grown sons," Ethyl informed him. "It is Hendrick who will inherit, and if you are less a fool than you seem you will say nothing until you are certain of your facts."

Her words did, indeed, silence him, for the abduction of the heir of an English estate was worth a man's life, but the abduction of the lord himself was *war*.

Drojan did not doubt but that he had come upon information that could change all that would happen over the next days. Somehow he must find the opportunity to speak privately to Rory. But that would have to wait until they reached Corvus Croft, for the small boat afforded little privacy and even when the eyes of the women were closed, their ears were open.

"You may return to your home once Rory is safe in his own land," he told her.

"We will not go back until Serine has custody of her child, the heir of Sheffield. Even a one-eyed woman can see that, Drojan the Seer." She sneered out his name, and he bristled at the implication that he had not known the child was also the heir.

How could he have known? Drojan asked himself. Men the age of the Lord of Sheffield always had grown sons. Until this instance, it seemed.

Much of his knowledge was gleaned from listening, and many of his predictions were but the culmination of his ability to sort out the facts and form the most likely conclusion to a particular situation. Only when he laid the Runes did he see things that no one else could know. Things like the unwarranted appearance of a woman with one eye who needed to be taken down a peg. And take her down he would.

"I, too, am surprised," he said smoothly. "As well informed as you pretend to be regarding Sheffield and its people, I would have thought you would have taken it upon yourself to determine the portent of the message from Baneford, rather than relying on hysterical gossip. If, in fact, you didn't start the gossip and the hysteria yourself."

Ethyl's hand closed over her bow, only to find that Drojan held it firm against the side of the boat with his foot. "I gave my lady the best report I had." She all but snarled the words as she tugged at her bow.

"As did I." He released the bow as he spoke and she came to her feet quickly, the bow, as well as a nocked arrow, in her hands.

The little boat swerved, causing Ethyl to lose her balance. Drojan caught her before she pitched over the side and they dropped into the bottom of the boat, the arrow skittering harmlessly away.

Ethyl did not move. Her breath came in shallow gasps, though her heart beat wildly. She swallowed, trying to pull together her thoughts, for she was at a loss as to how to assess the emotions that surged through her body.

She would not thank Drojan for his rescue, though she realized her impulsive action could have had dire consequences. Instead, she tried to hold steady her voice and still her leaping heart as she said, "Perhaps we should each rethink our opinions of each other's abilities."

As Drojan released her, his blood quickened as it had not done in a decade, for the body that had fallen against his was strong and firm and resilient. So filled with life that he had been unable to stay his response, not as a seer but as a man.

Before he could form a reply, the sail fluttered and Drojan scrambled for the tiller to turn the boat into the breeze.

A somber crowd lined the shore as the skiff approached the village. Serine strained her eyes in the hope of catching sight of Hendrick running across the green lawns with the other children. And though she recognized several youngsters, Hendrick was not among them.

"Is this your village?" Serine clutched Rory's arm. "Are you certain this is the right place?"

As though in answer to her words, the villagers caught sight of Rory in the bow of the boat. A cheer went up and Rory got to his feet and waved to the throng.

Now not only were the children running, but several men raced toward the castle, while women hiked up their skirts and scrambled after them, cries of joy coming from their throats.

The boat was brought to shore by the willing hands of the villagers who waded out into the water. Rory was all but lifted from the vessel and passed from one exuberant hug to another as he made his way to the shore, where he was almost snatched from the ground by a man of near size and build.

The resemblance told Serine this man must be the brother of whom Rory had spoken. She watched him closely and was pleased that his pleasure at finding Rory alive was all she could have hoped.

"And who have you brought with you?" the man asked amid a second series of back poundings that would have felled a lesser man.

"Serine saved my life."

Any other words Rory might have spoken were lost in the cheer that rose from the crowd. A husky lad easily swung Serine up into his arms and carried her the few feet between skiff and shore, leaving Drojan and Ethyl in the boat alone.

As soon as Serine was placed on dry ground the group began moving toward the castle.

Ethyl turned to Drojan and then measured the depth of the water with her eye. "Well, Seer, it looks as though we are left to fend for ourselves in getting to shore. A shame your countrymen think so little of you that they do not care if you drown."

Drojan understood that with the unexpected return of Rory the villagers were catapulted into celebration. Had Ethyl not spoken of their defection he would have thought little of it, but with her obvious disapproval it took on serious proportions.

"I fear we will both get wet," he admitted. "In their haste to join the merriment they have forgotten their most elemental hospitality."

He swung over the side of the boat and sank to his waist in the water.

"I do not intend to present myself to your village looking like a drowned rat," Old Ethyl told him. "You will have to carry me."

Drojan blanched. "I have not the strength of the young," he asserted.

"Then get someone from the village." She prodded his shoulder. "If you leave me here in the boat I will sail back to Sheffield and be damned to you, for when I return I won't be alone."

Drojan did not think she could find her way back to England alone and return, but even with his powers of perception he could not be certain. And he believed that if the woman was not carried to the shore she would, indeed, set sail and there would be the very devil to pay. "Very well." He sighed. "I will take you to the shore."

He dug his staff deep into the murky water to hold his balance as she perched on the side of the skiff. And so it was that Drojan reached the shores with Old Ethyl on his back, and somehow, from what he knew of the woman, he felt this act might well portend the demeanor of their future.

As they paraded through the village Serine took in the neat houses before passing into the area where the craftsmen sold their wares.

Rory had not lied, it seemed, for the people that called out their greetings and paused in their work carried the sound of free men.

Not that Serine had thought Rory would lie to her. Still, it seemed strange that these people would seem so bound together in joy and sorrow when they had but to leave to find a new life filled with all they lacked in Corvus Croft.

Time and again Rory pulled himself from his brother's grasp to stop and ruffle the hair of an apprentice or greet a craftsman and his wife.

Perhaps she had been wrong about Rory, Serine mused. Perhaps he was not a lord of Corvus Croft and worth a ransom or a great boon. Yet the regard of the people for this man was impressive, and the affection between Rory and his brother not to be denied.

"Well met!" the tailor called from the door of his shop. "'Tis a fine apprentice ye have acquired for me. He learns quickly and makes me a proud and happy father." The man beamed at a towheaded boy that Serine recognized as one of the Sheffield children.

Her face lit with joy. The children had indeed been brought here. She smiled, ready to call out a greeting, but the boy looked uncomfortable and turned away, unwilling to meet her eyes.

She scanned the crowd, ferreting out the familiar little faces that peered from doorways and windows and from behind the skirts of some of the village matrons. She longed to hold out her arms and take them all to her breast, but dared not. There was but one child she could take into her arms. One face that would bring the ultimate joy to her aching heart, and that face she did not see.

What had they done with her Hendrick? He must be about somewhere? Surely nothing had happened to him? She positioned herself more closely to Rory and his brother as they entered the bailey, trying to catch the gist of their conversation and find the opportunity to ask the all-important question. But, in the end, she did not need to ask. For as they came to a halt in the great hall of the castle, Guthrie shouted for food, drink and his wife.

"And the lad!" he ordered as the varlet sped away with his orders. "I kept the boy you favored the night of the raid. The one you sent early to the ship and who was rescued from its flames. I vowed to keep him as my own and give to him all that would have been yours had he been your own son."

Rory's eyes met those of Serine. They did not need to speak to know that the Celt headman spoke of Serine's child. "And how has he adjusted to his new home?" Rory asked without giving inference that the lad was the cause of great conflict between himself and the woman who had saved his life.

"He is a wild one, he is," Guthrie boasted. "Outspoken and set in his ways for one so young. You'll find him a challenge, I vow, but well worth it."

"As my son and heir, I am given a free hand with him, am I not?" Rory asked, knowing that Serine hung on his every word.

"You may do anything with the boy except break his spirit or take him back to his place of birth. Beyond that, you are welcome to teach him anything you like. Even my wife has taken a liking to the boy, so should you decide he is too much trouble I would be more than happy to keep him in my household. I will miss him sorely when he is gone, but not as much as I thought to miss you when I believed I would never see you again." And Guthrie's arm came down around his brother's shoulder once more.

As the men spoke, Serine had come to stand at Rory's side. And, although the moment was informal, it was then Rory decided to reveal her true identity to his brother.

"This is the Lady Serine." Rory drew her forward. "It is through her skill and many hours of selfless attendance that I am alive." Although there were times when he wondered if she hadn't wished him dead. "She has come to ask a boon in return for my life."

In her colorless clothing Serine lacked the obvious symbols of status that would have proclaimed her a lady of rank far above a Celt overlord in a little village half a league from nowhere. She drew herself up to her full height, wishing Rory had given her time to prepare herself to more advantage. But of course, perhaps it was his plan to make her look as insignificant as possible so that her plea would be discounted before it was given.

"I fear we have but little here in the way of riches," Guthrie said thoughtfully, "but I will gladly pay what ransom I can for the return of my brother."

"I want no ransom," Serine said with quiet dignity. "I want my son returned to me."

"Your son is here?" Guthrie looked to Rory for confirmation.

"He was one of the children stolen in the raid," Rory told him.

In his euphoria at having his beloved brother returned to him Guthrie was prone to promise Serine any boon her heart desired, but at the end of the great hall he spied the dour countenance of Drojan. The man was water soaked, and his face resembled a prune. There was a warning in his expression, and even from the length of the room, Guthrie was inspired to hold his tongue and contain his gratitude.

"Tell me his name and I will do all that I can to see that you are reunited," Guthrie promised with diplomacy that surprised even himself.

"My son is Hendrick, the heir to Sheffield." Serine looked the man square in the eye and did not flinch when realization touched him.

"I will send for my wife, Damask. Perhaps the child is with her."

Serine nodded her head. There was nothing more she could do that would save her honor and identify her through her aplomb as a woman of good blood. In her heart she wanted to drop to her knees and beg. In her mind she wanted to snatch up her son and flee aboard the little skiff that bobbed in the harbor. But she knew this could not be. She would stand like a puppet, waiting for her son, her beloved child, to enter the hall, and then she would wait again to see if he would acknowledge her, or turn away, as the children from her own village had done when she'd tried to meet their eyes.

A gossamer woman lighted the shadows of the hall. Guthrie held out his hand and the sylph skimmed forward across the rushes, stirring the scent of cinnamon and cloves as she ran.

Barely touching her husband's hand, she curtsied low before turning toward her brother-in-law and throwing herself into his arms.

"Oh, Rory, Rory, we thought you lost. Guthrie was beside himself. I doubt he ever allows you to fight again."

Rory lifted the shining being in his arms and whirled her around the floor as the castle folk cheered their merrymaking.

Breathless, she regained her feet and tottered to the arm of her husband. "Fie on your brother, my lord. He is bad for me. He causes me to lose my breath and behave like a hoyden. I am shamed before the children." Her gaze crept toward the hallway to the kitchens, and she held out her hand. "Bid my little lord to come to me," she called.

There was a pause and the sound of scuffling somewhere deep in the recesses of the scullery. A few moments later a well-dressed boy appeared. A hand urged

him forward, but he moved willingly when he saw
Guthrie and his wife. He wiped the cinnamon and
honey from his chin, brushed off his sleeve and smiled.

He had reached the middle of the floor when he took
the time to survey the scene. His eyes fell first on Rory,
and they narrowed in direct challenge. He had admiration for Guthrie and abject worship for Damask. He
discounted the seer, who had taken his place with his
superiors on the dais, but his mouth dropped open
when he recognized the unique countenance of Old
Ethyl. He took another step, wondering if he dared ask
about the welfare of his mother, whom he hadn't seen
since she had fallen against the stairs of the keep at
Sheffield that last, desperate night.

Old Ethyl spoke not, but her eye, like the arrows she
aimed, centered on a woman who stood but a few feet
away. Her dress was of a drab wool, green in color, and
her hair fell to her waist in a mahogany veil, but when
he raised his eyes to her face there was no question that
his mother had come to save him and return him to his
true estate. Without thought to anyone else in the hall,
he brushed past them all and flew into his mother's
arms.

"I thought you dead!" His words were wrung from
his heart, and the men who overheard them were moved
to shame at his open admission.

"And I thought you lost forever," Serine said as she
clutched him to her breast. "Do not fear. We will return to our home. They dare not deny me, for they
know that they owe me more than they can ever re-
pay."

Her eyes flashed across the others on the dais, and she
openly dared them to deny her words. With her son at
her side, Serine challenged the Celts—the ones she de-

spised for their raid on her property, and the one she loved for his raid on her heart. She turned and faced Guthrie, the headman.

"Hendrick is my son and heir to the Sheffield estates. Rory is your brother and, as I understand Celtic law, heir to all you possess until your lady wife delivers you a son. I have delivered your heir to you, hale and hearty, though I was forced to bring him from the jaws of death to do so. In the name of justice, I ask that you give me my son in return."

Guthrie looked from one pair of defiant eyes to the other. The boy learned quickly and there were many things that he had absorbed during his short tenure on their shores. He also knew that Hendrick was superior to most of the children they had taken in their raid. Superior both in looks and intelligence. The child's quickness of wit had made him a favorite with thane and thrall alike.

From what the children had been able to tell of their life in England, this was the woman who had birthed Hendrick and raised and molded him into what he was today. She would be a force to reckon with, but more than that, she was a woman worthy of his brother, Rory. Somehow Guthrie must give Rory the chance to win her, or for Serine to win Rory. The child was but a pawn when it came to the ultimate choice between the fate of the heir of a small estate in England and the survival of a dynasty in Ireland.

Guthrie lowered his eyes so that she could not read the intent therein. "It shall be as you wish, my lady," he agreed easily. "The child shall be returned to you as you request, and so shall remain for as long as you reside in Corvus Croft. My brother will see to your comfort, and that of your woman. I am sure he wishes to have his house in order as quickly as possible.''

Without looking back, he took his wife's arm and moved from the hall, leaving his brother and his seer to deal with the outraged woman.

''Is the man daft?'' Serine ranted as Rory hauled her bodily from the hall. ''Surely he realizes that I did not come here as your leman. He must know that I wish to take my child and return to England.''

''You asked that your son be returned to you, and returned to you he is,'' Old Ethyl said as she kept pace with the hurrying men and the infuriated woman.

Serine turned her anger on Rory. ''You gave me no chance to explain my position or present my plea. I demand you make your brother hear my case. He has no right to keep either myself or my son in his godforsaken country.''

Rory managed to move Serine from the great hall of the castle to a suite of rooms a short distance away.

''Is this where you live?'' Serine gave a disdainful look at the furnishings. ''Have you no estate of your own? How is it that you seem so determined to have a son when you have nothing to give?''

Rory sighed. He was weary and his lung did not allow him to take a deep breath. The trip had taken its toll, not to mention the exuberant welcome he had received. Rory had not told his brother of the seriousness of his wound, nor had he said that he had left Sheffield under duress and long before he would normally have deigned to travel. Now he was faced with an enraged woman who ranted with all the self-righteous indignation of a harpy.

Allowing himself a breath that reminded him once again of the discomfort of his wound, Rory stemmed the venom that flowed from her lips. "Silence!" His voice echoed through the room, leaving both Serine and her son staring at him in wide-eyed wonder. "You will have the chance to plead your case before my brother," he promised. "Right now you are reunited with your son. You have seen that the boy has not been mis-treated, nor have the other children taken from your village. You yourself will be our honored guest until such time as you return to your home. Now cease your clacking. I need to rest, for there will be feasting in our honor before the week is done."

He turned away and Serine saw the lines of fatigue on his face. Despite her initial anger, she realized that her fate and that of her son still depended on Rory's wel-fare. It would do her little good to have nursed him back to life if he fell dead from exhaustion upon his return.

She swallowed her angry words and amended her thoughts. "Where do you want me to stay?"

For days and nights she had been constantly at his side. It would seem strange to awaken and not hear the sound of his breathing, yet she could not ask, and knew that now that he was again in his own element, she would not offer to stay near him.

"There are several rooms here. The boy will take the small one there." He gestured toward a narrow door. "You may choose from any of the other rooms, but you will not share a room with your son. I will not take the chance of having you steal him away during the night." Rory all but staggered from the room with Drojan at his side.

"He said nothing about my sleeping quarters," Old Ethyl observed. "I will stay with the boy. The room is small, but snug. We will be comfortable together there."

Serine realized the wisdom of the woman's words. Should they be forced to escape, it was well that Ethyl would be with Hendrick and able to whisk him away at a moment's notice.

Left to her own devices, Serine opened the door closest to the one through which her son had disappeared. The room was sparsely furnished, but comfortable. The bed looked inviting and she wandered toward it thinking to ask Rory's permission to make it her own, but the bed beckoned and she climbed onto the soft fur covering. She had hardly lain back when her eyes closed and she drifted into a sound, dreamless sleep.

It was but a few minutes later when Rory himself came through a door on the far side of the room. He rolled onto the bed in exhaustion. It hardly registered in his mind that Serine had claimed this room as her own. It had belonged to Rory from the time he was a lad and had remained in Rory's possession when Guthrie assumed the responsibilities of Corvus Croft after their parents had died of the plague. Rory seldom slept elsewhere when in residence and did not intend to do so now. He closed his eyes, unaware of the woman lying beside him. But sometime during their slumbers the two bodies came together, seeking the forbidden comfort of the other's arms.

Serine slept deeply, unconsciously lulled by the deep breathing and strong, steady heartbeat of the man beside her. Over the weeks she had cared for Rory she had become attuned to his comfort. Only when she was certain he was sleeping peacefully had she been able to find rest herself. And now, without conscious thought, she snuggled against his warmth and fell into dreamless slumber.

Chapter Seven

It was long past daybreak when Guthrie burst through his brother's door. "Come, lie-a-bed! We must make ready to celebrate your safe return. Awake and meet the...day!" The last word died on his lips as he saw two figures spring apart upon his unannounced entry.

There was no mistaking the woman, and Guthrie smiled to himself as he mumbled his apologies and backed quickly out of the room. So Damask had been correct in her assumption that there was something going on between Rory and the woman whose child he had taken.

Since the plague had demolished the village Rory had been a changed man. Those who knew him knew that he had not been able to bury his grief and had, until very recently, still sorrowed over the loss of his wife and child. And even though many of Rory's friends had counseled him to put his memories behind him, until now Guthrie had seen no sign that his brother had heeded their advice.

Perhaps all would work for the best, for the woman did not seem to have been an unwilling occupant of the shared bed.

Guthrie rubbed his hands together in satisfaction as he hurried back to his own quarters to tell his wife what he had discovered.

The headman's mood would have been altered had he been aware of the scene taking place on the other side of the heavy door.

Serine leapt to her feet and stood, hands on hips, in the middle of the floor. "How dare you?" She shot the words at Rory, ignoring the confusion on his face.

"This is my room. What are you doing here?" he countered.

Guthrie had undoubtedly seen them together and would, just as undoubtedly, come to the wrong conclusion. It would be doubly difficult to convince Guthrie to let Serine and her son leave when the man thought there was the possibility of a marriage in the future. His brother had been very outspoken about the future, about wanting Rory to remarry. For, according to Celtic law, Rory was heir to the leadership of the village until there was issue of Guthrie and Damask. Only if Rory died without issue would the leadership pass on to any child Guthrie might adopt as his own.

The law was as old as time and the cause of many a fratricide. Rory wished he could forget all about the situation, and hoped that Guthrie would do the same.

However, at the moment, Rory's problem was the outraged woman before him.

"You did not say this room was yours," she sputtered.

"Well, it *is* mine, and I did not know you were in here." He remembered the sweet, scented, warm body that had snuggled so gently against him in his dreams— dreams he now knew were reality. For even in the chill of the morning, he could feel the warmth of her beauty next to him. And he knew he would never be happy until he experienced that feeling again and again. "Who did you tell of your choice? I will have them punished for not apprising me of your whereabouts."

Serine frowned. "I told no one," she managed to say. "I thought to lie down but a moment, and awakened only when the door burst open and I found you wrapped about me."

"I thought it was the other way around." He laughed as he climbed from the bed and drew his cloak about him. "There was no harm done, Serine. I will tell my brother and we will all have a good laugh."

He walked toward her, the last remnants of sleep still on his face, causing him to look even more boyish and innocent of indiscretion. Indeed, how could Serine chastise him properly when in truth she had relished the warmth and security she had known in his arms. In her dreams she had felt the texture of his skin. The masculine scent had permeated her senses and she had been lulled more deeply into slumber by the steady beat of his heart and the reassuring sound of his breathing.

She could rail at him all she wanted, but she could not hide the truth from herself. She had crept into his arms because, more than anything in life, that was where she had wanted to be.

"I will choose another room," she said with all the dignity she could muster.

"There is no need," Rory assured her. "This room is close to that of your son. I will sleep elsewhere."

He might have said more, and she would have questioned him as to his meaning, but again the door opened and this time Hendrick peered into the room.

"Oh, there you are, Mother." He beamed at her, and cast a cautious glance at the man standing nearby. "I wanted you to come to breakfast. They have a gruel called porridge. I want you to try some. Perhaps we could have it at Sheffield. It is very good."

Hendrick sensed the tension, but, child that he was, found himself unable to analyze it correctly. He only knew he wanted to leave the room and take his mother with him. He tugged at her hand, and with one last look in Rory's direction Serine followed Hendrick from the room.

Hendrick talked nonstop as his mother completed her toilette in the little room he shared with Old Ethyl.

"I knew you would find a way to come after me," Hendrick was saying. "They said you'd never find their village, but I knew you would. I *was* surprised when I saw Old Ethyl with you rather than Dame Margot. I thought Dame Margot would want to come with you."

"I'm afraid Dame Margot has her hands full, as Lord Baneford's men are searching for Rory and it was all we could manage to escape."

"Margot is a wise one," Ethyl interjected from her place near the door. "I'll vow she's kept them wondering." As Ethyl herself was wondering about the conversation she had had with Drojan the day before. She sensed the man was keeping something from her, but could not put her finger on what it might be. She pulled her mind from problems that she could not solve and turned the conversation back to Dame Margot. "Margot will not let Lord Baneford's men get the better of her. She'll lead them a merry chase."

Serine nodded in agreement, never guessing the gist
of the chase or the seriousness of the circumstances that
Margot found herself facing.

The circumstances were so grave that Margot had
been forced to go into the village, where she sought out
Hildegard, the alewife.

The woman bobbed what had to be taken as a curtsy
as the dowager entered her little shop. "An honor it is
to have you here, m'lady." Hildegard rushed over to
sweep away the crumbs on the least-wobbly bench.

"It is not to honor you that I come," Margot said
somewhat stiffly. "It is to glean some gossip."

"Aye!" Hildegard chortled. "If it's gossip you want,
you've come to the right place."

"You are aware that Lord Baneford's men have come
with news of the death of the Lord of Sheffield?"

The woman shrugged her shoulders. "As is every
other creature in the vicinity." Why was Dame Margot
asking such a silly question? Anyone with an ear in their
head had heard the bell toll for the better part of the
day, knelling out the number of years of their lord's life
before pausing and beginning again.

"The heir must lay claim to his property. Somehow
we must get word to Serine to bring Hendrick back in
all haste, else they will lose all."

Hildegard wrinkled her brow. "M'lady, I doubt that
the Celts will willingly part with the lad, for all that they
owe the mother a debt of gratitude for saving the
worthless life of one of their own. For all her diplomacy, and Ethyl's skill with the bow, it may be a while
before we see our little lordling again."

"You may well be correct," Margot agreed, "but Serine and Ethyl will find some way to return if they are aware of the urgency of the situation."

Dare she trust the alewife? The woman was a known gossip and openly admitted her inability to keep a secret longer than it took to hear it and find someone who had not.

"Had we known where to find the Celt's village our lady would never have had the need to keep the Celt alive," Hildegard reminded her mistress. "I doubt that we'll know the Celt's lair until Lady Serine returns."

Margot drew a deep breath. "By then it will be too late. We should have kept that seer, Drojan, as hostage. That would have brought someone back quickly enough."

"Aye," Hildegard agreed, "but it probably would have been an army to wipe out the village." She mopped the bar, and then her forehead and neck with the same cloth, and looked questioningly at Margot. "What can be so important that it cannot wait?"

"If Hendrick does not return to claim his estate, Sheffield may be claimed by one of Baneford's knights."

The face of the man who had come to the alehouse some weeks ago flashed through Hildegard's mind. Yes, a man like that would undoubtedly go to any lengths to obtain a lush, ripe estate like Sheffield. Eager and greedy he was. And the alewife was certain he would stop at nothing to gain his desires. And Hildegard herself had been one of his desires, if she recalled correctly. Of course, as lord of the manor he would undoubtedly set his sights higher than the village alewife, but that did not mean he would not use his position to have his way with her, and Hildegard's husband,

who had recently returned from the Crusade along with
the body of his lord, would not like that at all.

Hildegard took a deep breath. "It is just possible I
may be able to help you," she whispered. "There was a
man came in here the other night who claimed to know
the seer, Drojan. Perhaps he can tell us where the man
resides."

"He will become suspicious and demand money for
his information," Margot fussed.

"I will tell him you wish to know your future and
trust no one else to tell it."

"Perhaps it will work. If the man knows where Drojan lives we will be able to send a message to Serine."

"I'll send word as soon as I learn something," the
alewife promised, and she bobbed once more as Dame
Margot left the shop.

It took two days and a keg of ale, but in the end
Hildegard had the information she wanted, as well as
the pledge that the man would take a messenger to
Drojan's village. Her only sorrow was that the messenger was to be her own husband, and in truth, that sorrow was blended with relief, for if there was to be
trouble with a new lord of the manor, Hildegard did not
relish the thought of having her beloved husband executed should he believe she had been insulted.

Both Hildegard and Margot breathed a sigh of relief
as they watched the men set forth. They had done all
that could be done, and their fate was in the hands of
the gods.

The day of celebration for the return of Rory McLir
lasted the better part of a week. During the day the men
participated in games of skill and daring, the wine

flowed and the food filled the tables in delightful abundance.

To the relief of both Rory and Serine, nothing was mentioned regarding Guthrie's discovery, although Serine was certain she had seen sly glances pass between Guthrie and his wife when Rory was solicitous, or even mildly polite.

The games in which the men partook were rough-and-tumble to the point that Serine actually placed her hand on Rory's arm to caution him against participating. She was rewarded by his smile as he pressed her hand with his and sank back onto the bench from which they observed the activities. Serine also noted the look that passed between Damask and Guthrie and wanted to shout out that it was only the fear that Rory would reopen his wound and undo all her hours of nursing that prompted her warning. But even as she opened her lips to speak the words, she knew them to be only partially true.

She cared deeply about Rory. She awoke a hundred times a night listening for his breathing, as she had listened during those long days and nights in Sheffield. A hundred times again, she told herself that he was fine and she was foolish. She willed herself to sleep, only to wake again longing for the sound of his breathing and the warmth of his body near hers.

She prayed that these improper thoughts would cease to haunt her. She prayed that she might remember her position at Sheffield and not think or behave like a fallen woman, but her mind gave her no peace. The moment she was taken by slumber she saw Rory's strong, beautiful body. She relived the touch of his lips inducing new and wondrous sensations throughout her body, and his hands... And again she would come awake, trembling with desire and quaking with fear that he would somehow sense her most secret longings and fulfill them, leaving her lost between his world, where she could not stay, and her land, where he would not go.

She closed her eyes against the assailing memories and reveled in the gentle pressure of his hand, still warm over hers. When she opened her eyes Drojan was staring in her direction. Was the seer reading her mind? It was said seers could do such things. Could he possibly know of the turmoil in her soul?

She glared back at him, challenging his deep stare with one of her own. He did not move, nor did he flinch under her gaze. In truth, he seemed not to be aware of her presence, though he was but a short distance away. She looked more closely and realized that his concentrated stare was not for her, but for the woman who sat at her shoulder. It was Old Ethyl on whom the man directed his attention, and a surreptitious glance told Serine that Ethyl returned it in kind.

For a moment Serine wondered if they might be giving each other the evil eye, so great was their concentration, for it was beyond even Serine's imagination to recognize the fact that Drojan and Old Ethyl found themselves in the first throes of love.

A shout from the field brought Serine back from her musings and Hendrick jumped to his feet in front of her as he cheered on his particular hero.

He turned to Rory, open appeal on his face. "Why will you not allow me to join in the games?"

"You have not lived in Corvus Croft long enough to learn the tricks of the Celt's fighting games. You would be beaten soundly." He placed his hand on the boy's arm. "When the next games come around you will be allowed to participate."

"How will I learn the wondrous secrets of your games?" Hendrick persisted.

"I shall teach you myself," Rory said magnanimously.

"I think you will find that the boy knows more than you suspect, brother," Guthrie interjected. "I have shown him how to use the staff and sparred with him several times."

Hope flared in Hendrick's eyes. Perhaps Guthrie would be able to convince his brother to let him compete.

"You?" Rory clapped his hand to his head in mock horror. "Then I will have to make him unlearn everything he knows."

Guthrie was on his feet. "Are you saying you can best me with the staff?" It was an old challenge, and for the most part a harmless one. Both men longed to participate in the competition but neither truly dared, for Guthrie was headman and by Celtic law did not compete unless there was a serious challenge, and Rory was in a weakened condition.

"Even with the stiffness from my wound I can best you," Rory boasted.

"The challenge is taken." Guthrie could hardly suppress a smile as he stood and, with a bow to the ladies, started toward the field.

Even Serine's restraining hand and soft plea did nothing to deflect Rory from following his brother. She turned troubled eyes to Damask, who answered her with a smile.

"Do not concern yourself for Rory," the young woman said. "Guthrie will not harm him. They will put on a good exhibition, nothing more. It is good sport for all."

Damask settled back in her seat, secure in her assessment of the situation. But Serine did not feel comfortable in having Rory participate in a fight of any kind. The concern on her face was plainly visible, and even Guthrie remarked on Serine's demeanor.

"It looks as though your erstwhile nurse will surely pin your ears back if I do not manage to do so."

"Serine cares only for her son. Her feelings for me are secondary." Rory shrugged off his brother's words.

"Nonetheless, the woman who cares so little for you looks as though she is about to cry."

Rory glanced over his shoulder and saw that his brother's words were true. "She probably believes that if I die of overexertion she will lose any chance of returning to Sheffield with her son."

"Do you want her to take the boy and go?" Guthrie asked bluntly.

"Yes! No! Hellfire! I don't know what I want." He shook his head as though to shake off the thought. But he did know. Rory wanted Serine. He wanted her sleek, luscious body. He wanted her quick, inquiring mind. He wanted her love. Wanted to be first and foremost in her mind and in her heart.

How he missed the touch of her hand. The sweet, clean scent of her as she bent over him during his illness. He reached for her a thousand times a night, searching in vain for the comfort of her small, capable hand, reliving over and over again the moments when their lips had touched and when his body had known the nearness of hers. Even the pain had been worthwhile in having her close, in reaching out and feeling her silken hair against the bedclothes. He wanted to become entangled in the limbs of her body as his fingers had tangled in her hair. He wanted to draw her to him and see the awakening of love, as he had seen her awaken from her slumbers.

He wanted ... he wanted ... he wanted ...

He grasped the staff and strode onto the field, leaving his brother to follow in his wake. At the center of the field he turned, his staff already coming about to meet Guthrie's, and the match was met.

It was only when Guthrie's blow forced him to his knees that Rory realized how his pain could be eased, at least for a short, blissful moment, and to the horror of the crowd and the amazement of the headman, Rory allowed the next blow to fall unchallenged as he dropped unceremoniously to the ground.

Rory was carried to his room. Not the room he had taken after Serine had claimed the one he usually used, but the room in which Serine had spent the previous night. Ensconced in the bed with the scent of the woman he loved permeating his senses, Rory savored his success. A success that was climaxed when Serine herself rushed into the room.

"You fool! How could you endanger yourself in such manner? You're nothing more than a headstrong child and should be treated as such." She whipped back the blanket and ran her hands over his chest. "Now, where does it hurt the most?"

It didn't hurt. It felt wonderful! Rory could do nothing more than moan with pleasure closely akin to pain.

Serine went to her bag and took out an ointment, which she carefully rubbed into his skin. And while the medication took the last vestige of strain from his heretofore unused muscles, the touch of her hand brought on a certain amount of discomfort to a different portion of his person. He squirmed as he tried to change positions to keep her ignorant of his arousal.

She had but to look at him to cause his blood to surge. The touch of her hands was more than he could abide without physical response, yet he knew she would neither understand nor approve. No more than would the one-eyed harpy who had appeared at the door with Drojan moving behind her like a shadow of doom.

"I will take care of Lord Rory," Drojan announced pompously. "You may return to the games."

In his attempt to put as much distance as possible between himself and Ethyl, Drojan did not see the look in Rory's eyes.

"There is no need," Serine said quietly. "I have no wish to watch any more of your sport. I will stay here with Rory. You may take Ethyl and return."

But Drojan was not about to take orders from a woman, and a foreign woman at that.

"I will stay!" he insisted, all but pushing Serine aside.

"The Lady Serine will take care of me." Rory almost growled the words as he saw the old man's stubborn determination about to ruin his plans. "You may go and take Ethyl with you. I'm sure she wants to see the rest of the competition. In fact, she may even want to compete."

His comment sent Ethyl's head up. Her eye pierced him and he felt as though she could see right through his ruse. He also knew that she didn't give a damn. From the moment he had said she might be eligible for competition, Ethyl's interest centered on his suggestion.

"How could *I* compete?" she ventured. "I would hardly want to handle the sticks after what has befallen you at the hand of your own brother."

"You possess a different skill," Rory reminded her. "Surely you're aware that the women in my country are allowed to compete equally with the men."

Old Ethyl nodded her head. "That is true."

"Then Drojan must take you back to the field of games and see that you are allowed to participate. I am not bad hurt and Serine can see to my needs."

Ethyl looked at Serine, who nodded in agreement. "Go ahead," she affirmed. "The wound has not opened and I will have some of the house wenches bring up water for bathing. We will soak the pain away."

A knowing look passed between them, for each woman had taken it upon herself to ignore the potential danger and secretly smuggle a vial of the brew out of England, on the off chance that due to the unexpected exertion Rory might take a turn for the worse. Though no words were spoken, both women understood that Serine would be using the brew and the less said about its existence, the better.

"That is a wise course," Ethyl agreed. "Drojan will escort me to the field and I will show him what an archer is capable of doing." Without further ado she took Drojan's arm and steered him from the room, oblivious to his protests.

Through the milling crowds they went until they reached the archery field. Ethyl was delighted to see other women armed with bows, nocking their arrows.

"Tell them I would shoot," she urged Drojan.

"You are not a woman of the Celt. You will be shamed, and myself with you for allowing such folly." He grumbled out the words and held back.

"Your worries are groundless, old man. I shall not shame myself."

It pleased her to think how surprised he would be when he realized just how great was her skill with the bow.

Giving the reluctant Drojan a nudge, she allowed him to introduce her to the Marshal of the Field and took her place among the rest.

A ripple of pure joy surged through her as she lifted the bow and nocked the arrow. Here she could excel. Here she could show Drojan that she was not just an ugly old woman. She let the arrows fly and they sailed unerringly to the target.

She had qualified for the first round.

One round after the other Ethyl took with her skill while Drojan stood in open-mouthed wonder.

"Did not your Runes tell you of my skill?" Ethyl chided. "Did they not tell you I was a woman to be reckoned with?"

"I do not cast the Runes for information about the skill or failings of a woman," the man grumbled.

Again she took her place, and again came out the winner. Now she was competing against the best women in the village.

"You have been lucky, woman." Drojan grasped her arm and jerked her toward him. "But now you will face Luccea, and she is the best on the isle. Withdraw with your laurels intact."

Ethyl looked into the man's face. There was concern in his eyes. True concern for her feelings and her welfare.

"Do not trouble yourself about my laurels, Drojan. Look into your soul and you will see that I can beat any woman, or man, for that matter, that you put against me."

Drojan's hand slid up the smooth, sinewy flesh of her arm. It vibrated against his palm, and his body awakened and vibrated with it. "You do not realize the potential outcome of this match, Ethyl. For the love of Woden, come away... now.''

But Ethyl's blood was singing with success and throbbing with excitement over the attention given her by Drojan. She did not leave her position, and her arrows continued to fly true.

''I swear by the Druids, Ethyl outshot every woman in the vicinity and then took on the men. It was uncanny. The last man cast down his bow and walked away when he hit the bull's-eye and she split his arrow. None other would come forth to meet her challenge. Guthrie was irritated, but Damask applauded Ethyl's success.'' Drojan had burst into the room and begun his accounting of the day's events not even bothering to notice whether Serine and Rory were in any condition to appreciate or even care about Ethyl's skill.

''I could have told you that the old woman was an excellent shot. I'm living proof of her prowess,'' Rory remarked.

And although Drojan pressed for more information, Rory held his silence. It would do little good to admit he had been felled by the arrow of a woman, although it somehow seemed to soothe him to know that she was now the acclaimed champion of his own village. At least his pain had not been from the errant arrow of someone who relied on little more than luck.

This time it was Serine who took the matter to hand. ''Lord Rory needs to rest,'' she said firmly. ''I think it best that you return to the celebration and make certain Old Ethyl doesn't get into her cups and decide to use her skill on some of your men.''

Drojan was taken aback at her words until he saw the tiny smile she could not suppress. ''Very well, if you have no need of me, I shall return to the festivities and hope you have recovered enough to rejoin us on the morrow, Rory.''

The seer had almost reached the door when Rory's voice stopped him. ''Have you told our new champion what will be expected of her through her newly acquired honor?'' he asked.

Drojan shook his head. ''I tried to talk to her while she still challenged the women, but there was no making her listen. She had the bit in her teeth and would have nothing less than complete victory. She was stubborn.... She was headstrong.... She was...'' Drojan paused and bowed his head, but when he looked up, his eyes were shining. ''She was magnificent!''

And with that he strode out of the room without looking back.

''How odd that he would leave without so much as a word of farewell,'' Serine mused. ''What do you make of it?''

Rory stared at the closed door and then raised his eyebrow. ''I would say that perhaps your Old Ethyl isn't as old as you think her to be. And I would also say that Drojan has come to that same conclusion.''

''Oh, but that simply cannot be,'' Serine began. ''Why, Old Ethyl has been in the village since I was a child. I cannot remember when I did not see her here and there. She's probably almost twice my age. She must be... two score.''

''And Drojan is most likely older than that. Apparently it matters little, for I have not heard of an age limit on loving.''

''But surely, I mean, they couldn't... That is, they wouldn't want to...'' She stopped in confusion as she realized what she had been about to say.

"Do you mean that they couldn't want to make love to each other the way I want to make love to you?" He reached out and traced the planes of her soft cheek. "They couldn't relish the other's touch, or long to feel their lips part, one against the other's. They could not desire the completion of the joining of their bodies, hot and throbbing with love that is sometimes lost in the quick, scalding lust of the young. Oh, no, Serine, I think they can feel all those things. And I believe Drojan has just awakened to the fact that he wants Ethyl just as I want you."

"Rory... Don't speak of things that cannot be. I am a woman wed. To betray my lord would be the basest of sins."

"And what is betrayal? How far must one go to betray?"

"Why, to make love. The joining of a man and woman."

"But up to that point there is no major sin, is that correct?"

"I did not say..."

"If I kiss you, and your lips part under mine and I know the honey of your mouth, there is no joining. There is no sin." And his lips found hers, and she opened to him as he searched her mouth, relishing the sweetness of his quest. "And if I bend to your neck and take pleasure in the way you squirm against me, again there is no joining... no sin."

He did not give her time to reply, for his mouth was sliding down her throat and across her shoulder as his hands deftly pulled aside her gown. But gowns are curious garments, made either to be worn a certain way or not at all. His hungry mouth was already seeking the delights of her body, and as he buried his face between her soft breasts his voice, muffled with passion, came to her.

"If I were to discover pink blossoms amid the pale fields of pleasure would it be a sin to taste each one, or would the sin be to ignore such a delight?"

Serine thought she would die if he did not fulfill his promise. Her mouth was dry. Her body was so filled with heat that she shivered against his touch. "Taste it, my lord, my love, my Rory, for I swear before God, it is no sin."

He moaned with delight at her admission. Taking her blushing orbs into his hands, pressing his lips against them, he let his hot breath encircle them before his tongue followed.

It wasn't until her shift fell to her hips and his mouth slid down her body that she thought to object.

"My love, we tread very close to the sins of which we were speaking," she warned, reminding him that it wasn't to be just as he wanted.

"You have seen me unclothed, and looked long."

"I thought you asleep and almost unto death."

"How could a man sleep with your eyes touching his body, caressing him as surely as if you did so with your hands... or your lips... or your pink, moist mouth?" He almost choked on the words, so greatly did he wish his thought to become reality.

"And would you allow me that?" Her mouth barely moved as the words formed and slipped from her lips.

Rory thought his ears had betrayed him, but he read the question again in her eyes and his answer came without more thought. "With all my heart," he managed to say as she slipped from the cocoon of her clothing and brushed aside the robe that had partially covered his body.

All the weeks she had watched and yearned. All the new awakenings that had troubled her dreams and her soul were absorbed in the rush of pleasurable passion that flooded her desire-starved body and wiped away all thought save that for this time, for this special moment, this man was hers to love as she had dreamed of loving.... Loving him ... only him.

And it took but a few minutes for Rory to discover that Serine had meant exactly what she had said. For, in her mind, only the act of coupling itself was forbidden, and, saints forgive him, Rory would not have faulted her theory for all the world.

Chapter Eight

"Everyone is asking about Rory," Hendrick told his mother as he watched her fuss about her room. "Lord Guthrie was quite concerned when neither of you appeared at the evening meal. Even Drojan the seer seemed concerned, though it was hard to tell, for he was with Old Ethyl and had little time for anyone else."

The lad noticed the bright color in his mother's cheeks, unaware it was from the memory of the previous night when Serine had satiated herself in the loving exploration of Rory's delectable body.

"I'm sure Rory will be able to join his brother today. He seems greatly recovered. There is no need for you to stay with me." Serine smiled as she noted the tiny frown of concern on her son's face. "Why don't you go down and watch the jugglers? Perchance there will even be a dancing bear. You'd like that, wouldn't you?"

Hendrick cared little for the antics of dancing bears. They were usually mangy, smelly creatures with little enthusiasm who must have their feet and legs prodded in order for them to perform. Far better to watch the men. Perhaps, without Rory and his mother to keep watch over him, Hendrick might be able to convince

Guthrie that he should be allowed to try his hand at some of the simpler games.

He had almost reached the door when he remembered the rest of his reason for coming to his mother's room. "There was a man who asked for you," Hendrick told her. "He said he traveled with a friend from Sheffield and wanted to be assured of your safety."

Serine's heart sank. "What man? What did he look like?"

Hendrick shrugged. "He said he'd been in Sheffield when Drojan was there and brought a message for the seer from Dame Margot."

"Dame Margot?" Serine repeated like a simpleton. "What would Margot want with the seer?"

"Something about reading the Runes. Anyway, the man is called Short Will and he will be at the games should you wish to speak to him."

"I *do* wish to speak to him," Serine said forcefully.

"Then I will tell him when I see him." Hendrick did not give his mother time to object as he fled the room and ran toward the sound of the day's activities.

Even Rory's love-warm kisses and promises of more erotic delights could not entice Serine back into his bed. He finally gave up and agreed to meet her at the gaming. It seemed odd to him that she would be so anxious to join the others, but he had never been one to understand the ways of women and cast the thought aside as he readied himself for the day.

A quick glance from the window told him that Serine was with Old Ethyl in the bailey below. Rory reminded himself that he must find a way to apprise Old Ethyl of her duties should it be that Drojan had not yet done. He also ought to congratulate her, as Serine must surely be doing.

Serine did congratulate Ethyl during their first moments together. That done, their conversation became intense.

"Hendrick says there is a man here who wishes to see me," Serine said in a hushed voice, a false smile on her face.

"The man who wishes to see you is Ellis, the alewife's husband."

"He was on crusade," Serine exclaimed. "What is he doing here?"

"I just told you!" Ethyl did not try to hide the impatience in her voice. "The man has a message for you."

"Hendrick did not recognize him. He said the message was for Drojan and had something to do with the casting of the Runes."

"If you believe every story you hear you are a bigger fool than you seem." Ethyl whipped the words at her mistress.

"I am no fool." Serine glared at the older woman.

"Then try to keep from acting like one," Ethyl told her. "Taking a supposedly wounded man to your apartments and staying with him throughout the day and night does nothing to enhance your reputation. Now, you go toward the games and I will go toward the vending tents. Perhaps we will see Ellis or the man who accompanied him here and learn what it is they truly want."

Serine nodded her head. "You are right, Ethyl. Perhaps we will."

The women went their separate ways, but it was Serine who went sailing around the corner of one of the viewing pavilions and smacked into Ellis, the alewife's husband.

"Lady Serine!" he gasped. "I thought never to find you in this maze of people."

"Ellis? Is it really you? Where is Hildegard, and how did you find this place?"

"Dame Margot sent me with Short Will to find you." Short Will popped out from behind the huge soldier and pulled his forelock in deference to the lady. "Short Will had run across the seer, Drojan, in his travels and knew where to find him. I came with him, bringing a message of great import to you, m'lady."

"And what is this message?" Serine asked carefully.

"I have the paper here." Ellis fumbled through his clothing and came out with a small oilcloth pouch. "I do not know what is in the packet, m'lady, and that's the truth, but your lord husband perished in the Crusades. His body has been brought to Sheffield and Dame Margot has given him right and proper burial. M'lady, you must return to Sheffield as quick as possible. It takes a strong hand to rule a manor. And your voice is the only one the serfs will hear."

"I will make my formal petition to Lord Guthrie," Serine promised. "Stay out of sight. Blend in with the crowds and I will get word to you as quickly as possible."

Her heart was pounding loudly as she hurried down the path toward the viewing pavilion, the packet containing the note tucked away in her sleeve. For a few precious hours she had thought perhaps she would find a way to stay with Rory and raise Hendrick in Corvus Croft for a while before returning to Sheffield. No matter how she loved her land, she loved Rory more. The thought of leaving him tore at her heart. It was

loyalty, not love, that caused the tumult in her breast.
Loyalty to her land, to her heritage and the heritage of
her son. Loyalty fighting the love for the man who had
stolen both her son and her heart.

But leave him she must. It was for Hendrick's freedom that she had followed Rory to Corvus Croft, and
she knew she must return her son to his rightful estate
despite her aching heart.

The thought of leaving was almost more than she
could bear. But bear it she must, for she knew that it
was mandatory she lay her plea before Guthrie without
wavering in her premise. She could not risk allowing
anyone to know that she did not want to go. She had
just discovered what it was to know the glory of loving
and being loved, and there was every reason in the
world for her to stay—for Rory was every reason in her
world. She dared not think of leaving him for the pain.

She looked around and saw Rory talking to his
brother. Steeling herself, Serine started toward them.

"You look well, brother," Guthrie observed. "It
seems your lady knows the way to a man's recovery, and
perchance to a man's heart, as well."

Rory was reluctant to admit the extent to which his
brother was correct, but he could not hide the fact that
Guthrie's words rang true.

"To me, Serine is all that is good," Rory admitted.
"I hope you were not too concerned when you bested
me yesterday."

Guthrie laughed and clapped his brother's shoulder.
"I was worried at first, then it occurred to me that I had
not dealt you a blow strong enough to warrant such a
fall. When I saw Serine leap from the stands and run

toward you, I decided to leave you to your own devices. I take it I made the right choice."

"Absolutely," Rory concurred.

Before he could say more, Serine was at his side. He welcomed her with a smile. The smile faded when she spoke.

"My lord Guthrie, I have waited these long days for the opportunity to have my request formally heard. I feel I have been overly patient. Could you not grant me a hearing this afternoon?"

Guthrie stared at the woman in disbelief. From his brother's demeanor he had assumed that she was willing to forget her quest and remain in Corvus Croft without further protest. A glance in Rory's direction told him that the younger man had thought the same. The sudden sadness on the face of the brother who had endured so much tragedy in his life made Guthrie realize that Serine's request must be considered and a ruling given.

"Very well, then, I will call the council together and we will consider your request, Lady Serine. Be ready to present your case this afternoon." He then turned to his brother. "If you have anything either for or against the lady's plea I will hear it at that time." He turned his back on the couple and his attention to the games that had again started, but his mind mulled over what could have gone so suddenly wrong between Rory and the woman he so obviously loved.

The evening shadows fell across the peaceful countryside. The birds sang out their final farewell to the day, but Serine did not hear them. She stared blindly into the setting sun.

She had been eloquent in her plea. She could not have been more persuasive in her own behalf, and, in truth, Rory had not hindered her cause. Nor had he encouraged the council in her behalf. He had answered their questions tersely and without elaboration, saying only that Serine had nursed him tirelessly and most surely saved his life after he was wounded during the raid.

To give him credit, he had not said that Old Ethyl had shot the arrow, though he knew it to be true. And Old Ethyl had not volunteered the information, which in itself was amazing.

In the end it had made no difference. The council had ruled that Serine would not be allowed to take her son from Corvus Croft. It had been then she had made her fatal mistake.

"You cannot keep Hendrick here." The words burst from her lips without hesitation or thought. "He is the Lord of Sheffield and if he is not returned to his estate at once it will mean war. You can hold him for ransom, but you cannot hold him as your captive. My son is a lord of England."

"Your son is but *heir* to Sheffield, Lady, and—" Guthrie tried to argue before Serine cut him off.

"My husband is dead. It is Hendrick who is lord of Sheffield Manor and all the rest of his father's holdings. I demand that he be returned to his rightful estate."

Rory had grabbed her then. "Serine, think what you say. It will do you no good to lie about your situation. Guthrie is well aware that you have a husband, living and on crusade."

She had stared defiantly into his eyes. "My husband is dead and my son is Lord of Sheffield."

Guthrie came to stand between them. "It matters little. You would never have found Hendrick had it not been that Drojan brought you to our village. By the time your son's whereabouts are discovered, he will be a man grown, and it will be for him to decide whether or not he wishes to claim his estate in England or remain here in Corvus Croft." He returned to his seat and conferred with the council again before once more addressing Serine.

"You are welcome to remain here with your son," the headman said. "But you will not be allowed to leave Corvus Croft with Hendrick, on pain of death."

Serine shook herself back to the present. Night had all but fallen and twilight crept across the land. She felt betrayed by both Rory and the council. When Rory found her, her mood was as dark as the advancing shadows.

He came to a stop at her side and waited for her to speak.

"Your people care more for their partying than they do for you," she said bitterly. "They would as soon you had died, and perhaps they would have found a reason to celebrate that, too."

"Serine, there was no reason to lie about Hendrick's estate. Surely you knew I had told Guthrie all that I knew about you."

"Sheffield is mine. It is of my blood and of my family, not Elreath's. And while all Elreath's holdings now belong to Hendrick, it is Sheffield that is most important to me."

"You denied me last night because of your husband and today you tell me the man is dead. Have you had a vision? Or are you keeping something from me?"

He tried to look into her eyes, but Serine evaded his gaze and clutched the slit in her sleeve where the missive was concealed. She hated concealing anything from Rory, but when he had not proclaimed himself her ally during the meeting of the council, he had aligned himself with her enemies.

"I did what I felt I had to do to obtain the release of my son," she said without meeting his eyes. "I would do it again. I will do whatever is necessary to gain my son's freedom and protect his estate."

"Even if it means staying here with him until he reaches his majority?" Rory challenged.

"It won't come to that," Serine said flatly as she brushed past him and returned to her rooms.

The thought, a brief glimmer of hope, had come to her that the existence of a living husband no longer kept her from Rory's bed. She was free to know the full measure of his love. Now it was anger and distrust that formed a barrier between them, more devastating even than her marriage vows had been.

For Rory was not satisfied with her answers and her sudden change in demeanor. He would have sworn that she spoke truth the night before when she had bared her soul as well as her lovely body to him. And if this was so, something had happened after she had left.

Serine awoke to hear someone banging on the door. Before she could move, Hendrick ran forward to the door of the apartment they shared, while Ethyl watched from the doorway of her room.

"We have come for the archer," the men declared as they filled the doorway.

Serine placed herself between the excited men and her liege woman. "Why do you seek Ethyl?" she demanded.

"We have discovered a stranger in our midst. It is for the archer to prove whether the man is innocent or guilty of being a spy."

Serine looked from the men to Ethyl. She had told Ethyl of her meeting with Ellis, how she had blurted out the truth of the situation in Sheffield when the council denied her request. And how Rory had looked at her with distrust, as if he knew she wasn't telling him the truth. But how could she tell him what was true and endanger one of her serfs?

Now, however, it seemed a moot point. From what the men said, Ellis had been discovered, and most likely his cohort with him. For some reason Serine had yet to understand, the people of Corvus Croft had come to fetch Ethyl.

Ethyl disappeared into her room, only to emerge a few minutes later totally transformed.

She had split the heavy material of her skirt down the middle and bound it about her legs with leather thongs. Her smock had been discarded and her arms were bare. They looked strong and sturdy. Not the aged flesh of an old woman at all, Serine thought as she watched Ethyl take up her bow and arrows and join the men as they made their way to the village.

Serine followed behind the group, Hendrick close beside her. When they reached the place where the stranger was being held, she saw that Rory was already present, as was Drojan.

She recognized Ellis immediately. He did not acknowledge her presence, but his eyes rolled with fear, as he knew not what fate awaited him.

Ellis stood near a wall of tightly packed straw and daub. The man looked as though he would bolt and run, but listened when Guthrie spoke.

"This man has been found within our village. He is a stranger and will not tell from whence he has come. The council has ruled that he must face the arrows of truth and summoned the village archer for that purpose." He stepped back and turned to Ethyl. "Do you understand what you must do?" he asked quietly.

"I understand," Ethyl replied firmly.

"Very well." Guthrie nodded. "Whenever you are ready."

"She's not going to kill him, is she?" Hendrick's voice piped up over the mumblings of the crowd.

Serine tried to silence her son, but it was Rory who explained to them both.

"The archer will shoot six arrows outlining the accused man. If he is innocent of any crime he will come away unscathed, for the archer is our champion and we are assured of her skill. The man must stand perfectly still. If he flinches he must take the consequences, if he flees he will be killed."

"Oh," Hendrick and his mother said in unison.

"Why does he wear a cloak?" Serine asked. "Doesn't that make him a more difficult target?"

"The cloak is symbolic," Drojan answered. "It indicates that his intentions are hidden by a cloak of secrecy and the archer must pierce through that secrecy and strike as close as possible, pinning the bulky cloak to the wall without seriously injuring the accused."

"It sounds barbaric," Serine gasped.

"It *is* barbaric," Drojan conceded. "It is also effective and has saved many a brave man's life. Here in Corvus Croft we live in constant danger from those who would conquer us from both land and sea. We have only our instinct to guide us. The village archer is one of the most valuable weapons in ferreting out those who seek our demise."

"I only hope Ethyl will be able to come up to your expectations," Serine said.

"I would stake my life on her ability," Drojan returned, unaware that before the sun set he would be asked to do just that.

Ellis glared at the target wall. He understood that he must stand still and that the village archer would place arrows as close as possible without causing undue harm. Ellis was a brave man, having soldiered through two Crusades and many local skirmishes, minor wars and disputes in Sheffield. He did not look forward to standing as target, but knew it was the only way to prove his innocence. He vowed to stand his ground.

Guards had placed a voluminous hooded cloak about his shoulders and shoved him flat against the wall. The hood covered the better part of his face. He welcomed the shelter, for it blocked his vision; he felt it best that he not be able to see too clearly, but could not help but peer through the narrow opening at the archer who was taking up the bow.

His mouth dropped open. This was no ordinary archer. This one-eyed creature was more than vaguely familiar. He lifted his head and brushed back the hood, his mouth still agape, his heart pounding in his throat and banging loudly into his head. He uttered a prayer, closed his eyes and looked again, but there was no mistake. No two alike were on the face of the earth. The archer who would hold his life in her hands was Old Ethyl, the cranky crone from Sheffield.

Brave he may have been, but Ellis knew when he was beaten. A red mist closed about him and without warning he pitched forward in a dead faint.

Drojan had had the man carried to his own house, with the better part of the village following. While Drojan examined the man, Rory questioned Serine.

"I wonder why our prisoner reacted as he did," Rory mused as he paced the floor. "It is difficult to believe that Old Ethyl's appearance is so fierce as to send a grown man into unconsciousness." His eyes never left Serine, for he knew her to be nervous and ill at ease. "Unless, of course, he knew her. Do you suppose that might be the case?"

"What will they do to the man if he is unable to stand before the archer?"

"It is an inadvertent admission of guilt. Unless, of course, there are circumstances of which we in Corvus Croft do not know. Are there such circumstances, Serine?"

"What makes you ask such a question?" she returned.

"Because I cannot think that a blooded soldier would faint at the sight of a one-eyed female archer, unless he had known her for a very long time and had no idea of her abilities. Such a man as might have found his way here from Sheffield, perhaps?"

Serine stared at her hands for a very long time before she answered. She knew she was putting her own life as well as Hendrick's—as well as Ellis's—in Rory's hands, and she felt he had failed her in not convincing his brother that her child should be returned to Sheffield, but she had no other choice.

"There is trouble in Sheffield," she replied. "Baneford will take back the land if I cannot take Hendrick back to claim what is rightfully his." She handed him the missive Dame Margot had written, and waited as he read. "Ellis is the alewife's husband. He was on crusade and only recently returned. He brought me word of Elreath's death and Margot's plea to return in haste with Hendrick or lose all we possess."

"Why did you not tell me?"

"How could I say I had received a message, without exposing the messenger? Ellis had no idea he wasn't to know where to find me. A traveler had recognized Drojan and knew where the seer could be found. It is thus they have found their way to Corvus Croft."

"Was this Ellis planning on helping you escape?" Rory demanded.

"He delivered the message, that was all. I doubt he had but the smallest idea what it said, as he can do little more than write his name."

Rory ran a strong hand through his thick mane of hair. "If I tell this to Guthrie the man is as good as dead. And if I do not tell my brother they will, most likely, tell Ethyl to execute him." His head snapped up. "Does she know who he is?"

"Of course," Serine said. "She could not help but recognize him. Ellis is well-known in Sheffield."

"If she refuses to kill him they will execute her, too," he said despondently. "It is the law."

"Your laws be damned," Serine exploded. "The man is my serf and you have no right to touch him without my permission."

"By your own admission the man is a spy—"

"Ellis is a messenger and not subject to your barbaric decree."

They were standing but a foot apart and screaming into each other's face when Drojan reentered the room.

"Thank the gods my walls are thick, or you would shout them down and inform the whole of Corvus Croft of your business."

"Is Ellis all right?" Serine asked.

"He will live, until the council orders him killed, if that's what you mean." Drojan nodded. "It looks as though he may have burst a blood vessel in his head. I doubt he will be able to stand for the test today."

Serine squared her shoulders. "I will stand in his place."

"It's no good, Serine. The archer is not allowed to perform the test on someone she knows, for there is no certainty that personal feelings rather than the will of the gods would guide her arrows." Rory tried to calm her, but even he could think of no good way to solve the dilemma.

"But in the cloak she could not know it was me," Serine insisted.

"You are too short," Drojan observed. "And the risk is too great for Rory to try. There is no doubt in my mind that she would be hard tried not to send an arrow straight into his heart should she discover he played her willing target. But there is a way to resolve our problem." He started toward the room where Ellis rested. "Go and tell Guthrie that Ellis will be able to stand for judgment in a very few minutes."

The door shut and Rory and Serine stared at one another for a long moment before doing as they were bade.

Chapter Nine

Swathed in the cumbersome cloak, the man again took his place before the target. He stood completely still, pausing only to flex his legs once so they would not be stiff beneath the covering material.

He did not know fear, for his faith in Ethyl was paramount. That which he did, he did for her. None would dare fault her, nor bring down her reputation as a bowwoman. He did not flinch as he saw the movement from afar that meant she was nocking her arrow.

A few seconds later he felt the tug at the crest of his hood that told him the arrow had landed true. Next a streak of fire touched his cheek and he heard a gasp from the crowd. He had been marked, but still he did not move.

The next arrows pinned the arms of his shirt, but did not touch his shrinking flesh, and the last framed his legs.

There was a cheer from the people as they rushed to crowd around Ethyl. Rory pushed his way through them to the now-vindicated man and pulled the arrows from their positions.

"You are free to go," he said. "You have been judged innocent."

The man said nothing, and without removing the cloak disappeared into the shadows.

Ethyl, too, made herself scarce. She graciously accepted the congratulations that were her due, listening for the voice of the man whose words would have made success complete, but they did not come.

It seemed that after he had revived his patient and sent him to be propped against the target, Drojan had stayed in his rooms, no doubt consulting the Runes as to the outcome of Ethyl's marksmanship.

She threw open the door and entered his abode.

"Drojan? Where are you? I succeeded without your help and without your bloody Runes!"

"There was no question in my mind that you would do so." His voice came from the back of the room, and she saw him standing in the deepest shadows.

"Hah! Had you believed in me you would have been there to share in my success."

"I believed in you, Ethyl. On my life, I believed."

"On your life, my foot. You believe in nothing but your silly Runes, and what have they told you?" She crossed the floor, moving toward him into the shadows. "Did they tell you of my fear? Did they tell you of the trepidation in my soul as I raised my bow to pass judgment? Did they tell you why I had to accept this position for the salvation of my eternal soul?"

"The Runes did not tell me, Ethyl, but perhaps it is time that you did." His voice was gentle, as were his hands as he guided her to a seat of soft skins and cushions.

She sat stiffly. "Why should I tell you, old man?"

"Because you want to tell me," he said.

She sighed. "You are right in that. I do want to tell you. It is time that someone be told."

A tiny flame trembled in the fireplace and grew in strength as she told her story.

"They said my mother was a witch, for she dabbled in herbs and was renowned as a healer. It wasn't until other healers came forth, trying to duplicate her herbal formula, that more harm than good was done and people became worse instead of better.

"One night the wife of a wealthy merchant died after taking what was said to be my mother's formula. Mother had never seen the woman and did not know how she could have come by the brew, but the harm was done. The merchant brought his friends and they burned my mother's cottage with her inside."

Drojan said nothing. He held her fine, strong hands as the flame flickered and grew.

"Had my mother not sent me on an errand, I would have perished with her. As it was, when I returned I was told I would face the test of the village archer.

"The man prepared me himself, lining me up against the tree and warning me not to lock my knees lest I faint and fall. All his arrows were spent, save one, when I remembered his warning. I bent my knees as his arrow left the bow. It struck me in the eye.

"The man took me to his home and brought me from the depths of despair. It was the archer who taught me to shoot so that I could conquer the weapon that had maimed me. I knew when I came to Corvus Croft I would be called upon to take up the gauntlet and serve as archer for the village. For this I have prepared throughout my life. My one wish was that you might be there to see my moment of triumph."

"I was there," he assured her.

The flame quivered and caught and from the far end of the log a second flame arose.

"You lie, seer. I scanned the crowd and saw you not."

"I was with you in every move you made."

"Why do you tell such falsehoods?" she demanded. "Think you I cannot believe what I see?"

"Then believe," he said as the two flames reached out and touched tentatively before grasping one another and bursting into brightness that slashed through the shadows. She took his face in her hands and saw the love and admiration in his eyes and the wound on his cheek.

His lips touched hers. And the flame kindled.

With her index finger she traced the bloodied line. A tinge of red reflected, more vibrant than the fire. She touched the tip of her finger to her tongue.

"I could have killed you, Seer. How did you know I would not? Because you are so great a seer?"

"No," he admitted. "Rather because I am a man, and I love you."

"And you jest with me and make mockery of my moment of triumph. I am a good archer. My arrows fall strong and true, but as a woman I have been the village joke for two decades. I came to Sheffield a girl with but one eye. I kept to myself and, until his death, my husband covered my infirmity as best he could. Since no one saw me clearly they believed me to be old. Before my time I was called old and will continue to be until I die. There is no place in your life for the likes of me. Why would you risk all for so little gain?"

"In my judgment the gain was immense, and the possible loss even greater. I was there with you, Ethyl, as I will continue to be there for you if you will have it so."

After years of revilement, Ethyl hesitated, savoring his words. "The fainting soldier was unable to stand his judgment, then?"

"Serine explained that the man was from Sheffield. Had his origins been revealed it would have been up to you to kill him, or yourself be killed. I could not allow that to happen."

"So you risked your life playing target to my arrows." Ethyl shook her head in disbelief. "What if I had *wanted* to kill him?"

"I can't believe you have ever *wanted* to kill anyone," he said as he raised first one of her hands then the other to his lips.

And while Ethyl knew she should challenge Drojan's assumption, she held her silence and allowed his kisses to climb past her wrist and up her strong right arm toward her neck. She pressed him to her and realized that the quickening of his body was in direct response to hers. She reassessed her opinion of the seer, and decided that perhaps he wasn't such an old fool after all. And, even if he was, he was *her* old fool and it was good and right.

For while Drojan was no longer in the prime of manhood, neither was Ethyl in the bloom of youth. If their bodies did not explode with passion at their initial contact, it gave them more time to enjoy the sensations neither had thought to know again.

The hair on Drojan's chest was silvery, with the least hint of gold in the firelight. Ethyl slipped her hand up his chest, allowing the hair to tug at her fingers. It pleased her to know that the things that pleasured her pleasured him, also. She was delighted when he squirmed beneath her hands, beneath her lips and finally beneath her solid, volatile body, as she took from him the job of giving pleasure and assumed a share of the giving herself.

He drew her close and buried his face in her firm breasts. Her lips fell on his forehead. She felt his pressure on her body intensify and wondered what delights she could set free in the perusal of a balding man's scalp.

"What is it?" she murmured. "How is it you enjoy this so greatly?"

He drew himself from the honeyed feast he had been anticipating and replied thoughtfully. "Your kisses awaken my senses and your breath is like the heat of the sun when it touches my head. It seeps through my body and arouses the most dormant feelings, some long forgotten, long unused, but willing, nay, anxious to bend to your wishes."

Ethyl's laugh was throaty and Drojan thought it the most exciting sound he had ever heard.

"It is not a thing that bends that will give me surcease," she purred.

And Drojan slid her from him, and with one last hungry look, covered her body with his own, murmuring words that came from his heart and touched her soul. Neither had thought love would ever come to them again. But it had come, and without more thought they were joined, one with the other. Their lovemaking was done with infinite care, drawing out each inimitable moment of sensual pleasure, giving all that each had ever dreamed during the long nights of aloneness. And as the fire died to its last embers, one single flame freed itself, bursting upward from the ashes of life for one last earthly glimpse of heaven.

* * *

"Ethyl!" Serine ran across the main room of their apartment. "I feared for you. Where have you been? Why did you not return when your duty as village archer had been done?"

"Drojan and I found there were matters we needed to discuss. It took longer than I had thought." Several days longer, she recalled with a smile.

Ethyl did not meet her lady's eyes and went toward the room she shared with Hendrick, hoping to avoid further questions.

It was not to be. Serine's eyes glowed with unnatural excitement. "Rory is gone hunting and I have convinced Damask to allow me to take the children on an outing to help me gather herbs."

"What herbs do you need?" Ethyl asked.

"I need no herbs, you goose," Serine admitted happily. "I have already contacted Ellis and Short Will and they will have a boat waiting to take us back to Sheffield. We are going *home,* Ethyl." Serine rejoiced. "We are going home."

Ethyl's heart sank. She no longer wished to return to Sheffield. She wanted to stay in Corvus Croft with Drojan.

"There is no time to waste. We must make ready. Hendrick is telling the children that they will be allowed to leave their tasks and gather herbs with us." Serine ran on as she laid the plans for the following day.

And although Ethyl had serious misgivings, she kept her thoughts to herself and trusted in the gods who had already rendered one miracle on her behalf.

Early the next morning Serine went through town gathering the children. It was a somber group that fol-

lowed her, with the younger children still yawning with
sleep and the older less than enthusiastic.

"Come, come," she chirped as she led them through
the streets. "You need not work today. Instead you will
spend a day of freedom."

"All our days in Corvus Croft are days of freedom," one of the boys grumbled loudly. He was apprentice to the town miller, and it was common
knowledge among his contemporaries that he lived for
market day when people from neighboring villages
came in to purchase supplies. It was the daughter of the
weaver of a nearby village who had caught his eye, and
his youthful heart, and held both tight in the vise of first
love.

Serine recognized the lad as the son of a serf from
Sheffield. He obviously enjoyed his new life. But his
place was at Sheffield, and, pray God, he would be well
on his way to that destination before another dawn.

The other children made no protest and took turns
looking for the herbs, flowers, berries and roots Serine
sought. Their search took them ever farther from the
village and closer to the cliffs above the water. It was at
the edge of the cliffs that she stopped to speak to them.

"Think how beautiful it must be in Sheffield today," she said dreamily. "Your parents are probably
looking up at this same blue sky and thinking how much
they miss you. Your brothers and sisters are thinking
how lovely it would be to have you back."

"Aye," came the reply, "they want me back to carry
my share of the drudge work. And half their share,
most like."

Many of the older children laughed, but the younger
ones blinked back tears.

Ethyl cast a baleful look in Serine's direction. She did not see where anything good would come from working on the emotions of babes.

"Wouldn't it be wonderful if we could sail back to Sheffield this very day."

One or two of the older boys began to look uncomfortable. What did their lady have in mind?

"With your forgiveness, m'lady," Tim, a tall, towheaded lad ventured, "I would dread the trip across the sea, and I doubt not that my family would be glad to see me again, but sorry to have another mouth to feed. I do not think you realize how it is sometimes in the village huts."

Tim saw that he had Serine's ear and quickly continued. "There are times when food and grain is scarce. If my mum or da became ill there was nothing to eat other than the scraps from the manor house, and it is always a fight to get those.

"Here in Corvus Croft I have plenty to eat and a warm house in which to sleep. My clothes are warm, and the material is made of new and strong yarn. I am learning a craft, as are the others here, and we are allowed to sell what extra we make and keep the money ourselves. Lady, I don't want to return to Sheffield to be your serf. I want to stay here and grow to be a free man."

Serine was shocked. "But Sheffield is your home. Your families are there! Surely you are alone in your opinion."

But other children stepped forward.

"I love my mum and da in Sheffield, but I love my new mum and da here in Corvus Croft, as well. I would not choose to go back," the miller's foster son told her.

Trying to mask her surprise and newly found apprehension, Serine passed out the crusty bread and rich cheese that she had brought and looked longingly over the sea. She had thought it would be so easy. She would no more than suggest that they take a boat and run away and they would all but race to the waiting vessel. It was not to be. These children had known a taste of freedom and found serfdom bitter on their tongues. The mere fact that they had spoken their feelings was enough to show Serine that they no longer thought as serfs, giving humble obeisance to their overlord. Like the other people of Corvus Croft they spoke their minds.

Somehow Serine knew she must get as many as possible down the cliff and onto the boat waiting in the cove below. If some of the older children did not want to go along, Serine would take them to some point down the coast and let them return to Corvus Croft.

She was certain she could get them onto the boat by insisting that they gather water lichen. Hopefully, it would not occur to them to suspect that the boat was ready to set sail as soon as all were aboard.

She was about to suggest they venture down the cliff when Hendrick came running toward her. "There is a ship in the cove below, Mother," he gasped, "and men with weapons."

Serine stood and shielded her eyes from the sun. She wished she dared place her hand firmly over Hendrick's mouth. It was unlike Hendrick to blurt out information that would alarm his companions and thwart Serine's plans. She was about to chastise him when she realized all was not as she had expected. From her vantage point she could see not only the men, but several little boats bobbing some distance from the coast.

She could only hope that Ellis and Short Will would run for cover. Serine shooed the smallest children away from the edge so they would not be seen and started back toward the cliff, but Ethyl's firm hand stopped her.

"Send the swiftest of the boys running to warn the village. Take the little ones and follow as quickly as you can. I will hold the marauders below as long as I have arrows."

Hendrick lost no time in following Ethyl's orders, but Tim and some of the older boys began rolling rocks and clods down the path and dropping them over the cliffs. They would not be dissuaded, and Serine realized that her plans had come to naught. The boys were willing to fight for their new families and their freedom.

"Serine. This is not the time to argue. Take the babes and return to Corvus Croft else you'll see these children taken again." Ethyl nocked her arrow and carefully let it fly.

She did not look back to see if Serine heeded her advice. While the boys created a diversion, she shot an arrow and ran quickly to another spot in the hope that the men would be tricked into thinking there was more than one archer on the cliffs. It was the same ruse that had fooled the Celts. There was no reason it should not fool the Celts' enemies.

Before a dozen arrows had flown Ethyl saw the little skiff that was to have been their escape move quickly into the water. Ellis and Short Will had escaped. Now it was up to Ethyl and her aspiring army to hold the enemy at the bottom of the cliff until help could arrive.

Her arrows were all but spent, and she reserved the precious few she had remaining to pick off the men who made their way to the top of the cliff. Soon there would be no choice but to run, for she knew neither herself nor the brave lads who stayed with her could fight them hand to hand.

She made her way back toward the trees, motioning to the youths to follow. It was then she felt the earth tremble. With shouts of anger, challenge and the pure joy of a fight the Celts came thundering in on their ponies.

They rode without saddles and clung to the shaggy little horses as though a part of them. Ethyl could not help but admire their ability. As she loosed one last arrow and made to slide out of sight among the trees, Rory called to her.

"Are you all right?" he asked as he pulled his horse to a stop beside her.

"Of course." She bristled. "Those men are soldiers, not archers. I doubt they could hit a tree with a spear. And our lads did an admirable job of holding them down the face of the cliff where they could do me no harm."

Rory laughed. "I will give them the chance to fight." He kicked his horse into action but his voice floated back, and the words "Drojan is coming" brought both joy and dread to Ethyl's heart.

The sounds of fighting were far behind her when Ethyl saw a cart rumbling through the meadow. Her heart lurched as she recognized Drojan leading the horses.

They stopped with some twenty feet between them, moving together again but one step at a time. They had not seen each other since they had bade farewell after spending a night of amazing lovemaking.

"I feared for you, Ethyl," Drojan said, breaking the silence.

"Did your Runes not tell you where I'd be, Seer?" Ethyl's words were softened by the quaver in her voice.

"I saw men and boats near the water. I saw you and Serine and many children. I thought you meant to escape, and could not bring myself to believe you would leave me."

She moved closer...so slowly. "I am here," she reminded him.

"As is a band of invaders," he countered.

"I held them until the men of your village could come. No man could have done more." Again the challenge.

"Had they not come you would have been on your way to Sheffield with your lady." It was an accusation, but the sadness in his voice touched her heart.

She took the last steps, though he did not move, even when she stood before him.

"I would not leave you, Drojan. And if you are but half the seer you claim to be you must see that."

"I can see nothing when my eyes are blinded with your brilliance."

Ethyl slipped her arms around him and rested her head against his shoulder. There was a smile on her lips. At least the man was a realist. Even in the first throes of love he had not said she was beautiful, which she was not, and most like had never been. He had said she was brilliant, and that she would not deny, for her newly found love for Drojan made her feel as though she glowed from within.

She felt his lips press against her forehead. A gentle, wonderful kiss that demanded nothing more than love returned in kind.

"Come," he said, "show me where they fight. By the time we reach them there will be wounded who will need to be taken back to the village."

Ethyl squared her shoulders. What did he think she had been doing while the others were sounding the alarm? How did he think the men had been kept from reaching the village?

"There are already wounded men," she said somewhat sourly, "albeit they are the enemy."

"Your enemy, or mine?" Drojan asked.

"Ours," came the reply.

Chapter Ten

Even as he fought, Rory could not ignore the suspicion that Serine and the children had been on the cliffs above the sea for reasons far removed from gathering herbs and lichen. His heart sank as he realized that even as she proclaimed her love for him through the actions of her lovely body, in her heart she longed to return to her own land.

He wondered if she had sent the children with the warning, or if they had come on their own accord. There was no way of knowing, for she concealed from him her innermost thoughts even though she could not conceal her desires.

An ax whistled past his ear and he knew that he would do well to concentrate on the battle that surrounded him and put aside his affair of the heart with Serine.

His sword slashed faster and the enemy backed away, knowing instinctively that their adversary was possessed by more than the simple love of battle.

With his men behind him, Rory chased the retreating marauders over the side of the cliffs, where they tumbled to the ground below, dragging their wounded comrades. Insults and threats sounded across the water as Rory and his men chased the boats out to sea. Defeated, the invaders were more than anxious to be well away from the Celtic madman who continued to threaten their lives.

It wasn't until they were well gone that Rory had time to notice that Drojan had stopped beside him.

"Well done, warlord. Your brother will be pleased with your work, though he be disappointed in not having returned in time to enjoy the battle himself." The seer clapped Rory on the back.

"Why did you not warn us?" Rory demanded. "Surely you must have seen danger of this magnitude."

"I saw the woman and children near the water. I saw boats and confusion. I felt a threat, but thought it might be but the inner battle of the Lady Serine torn between her desire to return to her own country and her desire for you."

Rory raised his eyebrows and Drojan shrugged. "As you can see," the seer said, "my heart overruled my head."

Now it was Rory's turn to shrug. "I know the feeling," he admitted as the two men laughed at their own failings.

Rory returned to the village amid shouts of jubilation. The celebration was twofold. Not only had Rory conquered the Viking pirates, but the woman he had brought to Corvus Croft had sounded the alarm that had saved the village.

The excitement of the moment had sent all thought of Serine's desire to return to Sheffield from the minds of the children. They were being hailed as heroes and unwilling to cast any aspersions on the festivities.

Serine, however, was unaware of their silence. She retired to her rooms, waiting for the summons from Guthrie that would most likely herald the end of her freedom. She would be allowed no second chance to whisk the children away and could only pray that the opportunity would present itself so she could escape with Hendrick sometime in the future.

She watched listlessly for Rory and his warriors to return. Her heart lurched at the sight of him, and lurched again when she realized he had been bloodied. She longed to go to him, before he was told of her failed escape, and explain that her desire to leave Corvus Croft had nothing to do with her love for him.

She wanted to tend his hurts and keep him from being hurt more. But it was not to be. He went directly to the hall where Guthrie waited and it was but a few minutes before Serine heard a knock on the door and knew she was summoned to account for her actions.

With heavy heart Serine left the questionable security of her rooms. Somehow she must salvage custody of her son. They would not take him away from her. She would not let them. Regardless of her attempted escape, she had saved the life of the headman's brother and lost her own heart in the bargain. They owed her a debt of honor and she vowed not to let them forget. She vowed they would not take Hendrick from her.

Voices called out to her as she passed the crowd. A cheer went up as she entered the hall. Perhaps all was not lost, she thought as she approached the dais where Guthrie and Rory stood. Hendrick was talking animatedly with several of the other children, the excitement of the day obviously still upon him.

Serine stopped before the men and stared boldly at them, daring them to punish her for what she knew was right and just.

Another cheer went up and Serine looked around to see Ethyl enter the hall. Serine was relieved to see that Ethyl looked none the worse for wear. In fact, she glowed with happiness and excitement. Probably having to do with the fact that Drojan stood at her side.

For a moment Serine felt a surge of envy. How she would have loved to have known Rory was beside her, but it was not to be. Serine stood alone, as she had always stood alone. Even her husband had done little to succor or defend, leaving her much to her own devices as he had gone about fighting in the Crusades.

Perhaps it was her fate to stand alone, but somewhere in her heart was a deep desire to be loved and protected. To pass the scepter of authority and let someone else take the responsibility from her shoulders.

Her eyes met Rory's. As though reading her mind, he stepped from the platform and drew her toward his brother.

That Serine's husband was no longer among the living had made a difference. The wanting, the needing to love and be loved was still the same, but the reason for denial had been removed and Rory looked upon Serine with a gaze fired by desire. Even when he felt deep in his heart that she had gone to the sea to take the children and escape, he still could not give voice to his doubts, nor brand her with his accusations before his brother and the council.

He could only hope that Serine had sense enough to do likewise. A well-meant confession would have been folly.

"I assume the invaders were routed?" Her words were directed more to Rory than to his brother.

A smile of pride and satisfaction brightened Guthrie's face. "Rory has rid us of the invaders, and I have rid our people of the wolf that plagued our livestock. It has been a most satisfying day."

"I am pleased for you, my lord," Serine said politely, still wondering how much the man guessed of her thwarted plans.

"How lucky it was that you chose to take the children toward the water," he probed gently.

"I had hoped to add lichen to my supplies," she replied in a voice as cool as if she told the truth.

"One of the men who arrived early thought he saw a lone ship running along the shore, away from its fellows. Did you happen to notice it?"

"I believe there may have been such a ship. In the confusion I imagine it might have been separated from the rest." What a cool liar she was becoming, Serine mused silently.

"One of our captives says he knows nothing of the ship and swears it did not belong to his people."

"Perhaps it was an errant fisherman," she suggested blandly. "I have never been knowledgeable in the identification of boats and was in no position to bid them stop and give account of their presence."

Guthrie looked at his brother. It was obvious that further questioning was useless. Serine would admit nothing. "So be it," he said aloud. "This is not a time for questions. It is a time for celebration. It is the time to reward those who have served us so admirably this day."

He raised his arms above his head and the people cheered. "Thanks to the Lady Serine, our village has been spared invasion. And thanks to my brother, Rory, the invader has been driven from our shores." Again the people cheered. "They must be rewarded for their services," he proclaimed above the shouts of the throng.

Now he held out his hands for silence and was accorded his appeal. The townsfolk quieted, some of them silently reaching out to lay their hands on the children they claimed and loved as their own. Would Guthrie's gratitude strip them of their newly found families?

His face told them nothing, but he smiled upon all with confidence and they trusted him to do what was best for all involved.

He signaled to Drojan, and the seer led them away from the boisterous crowd where they could talk without easily being overheard.

"It has not escaped me that very likely you deceived us by asking to take the children on an outing," he said quietly. "Not being used to devious women, Damask granted your request. There is no way for me to prove my belated apprehensions. Regardless of the reasons for your presence on that cliff, your subsequent actions were done at great risk to yourself and for the benefit of the people of Corvus Croft. If our women could bear children I would gladly release both you and your son, and any of the children of Sheffield who chose to go with you, and allow you to return to your home. However, such is not the case. You will, however, be allowed the continued custody of your son, with Rory as your—"

"Jailer." She finished the sentence for him. "And you have a very shallow concept of how to show your gratitude."

Guthrie refused to take offense at her accusations. "Your son will have every opportunity here in Corvus Croft...."

"Except that of his birthright as hereditary lord of Sheffield," Serine retorted.

"If Sheffield is more important to you than Hendrick, you are welcome to return to your estate, alone." It was Rory's voice that issued the challenge.

"Your memory is very short, it seems." She flung the words at him.

"If you wish to compare memories, or the lack thereof, I will be more than happy to do so...but privately." He turned to his brother. "There is no sense in trading insults for the entertainment of the entire village. I'm sure Serine and I can work out some sort of amicable agreement between ourselves. And right now I am weary from riding and fighting and feel encrusted with the blood of my enemies."

"Of course," Guthrie agreed. Actually, he had been enjoying the sparring match with Serine, but saw Rory's point. It was better to allow the woman to leave than to have her somehow best him before the townsfolk. "Go and refresh yourself." He glanced meaningfully at Serine and concluded, "And take your woman with you."

Serine gasped aloud, but Rory had taken her arm and was propelling her through the crowd toward the door. "Hold your tongue, lest you lose what little advantage you have left." He thrust her ahead of him toward their apartments.

"Advantage! Every advantage should be offered me," Serine protested as they reached the door. "First I saved your miserable life, and now I have saved your village from invasion. In my country a personage with

such recommendation would be honored and rewarded."

He closed the door behind him before answering.
"The very fact that you were at the water's edge when
the invaders arrived has given question as to whether
they were there on your bequest. Until my brother can
ascertain the truth of the matter you will do well to tread
lightly."

"Old Ethyl risked her life to keep the men from
reaching the top of the cliff," Serine noted.

"Ethyl's actions are not in question," Rory told her
bluntly. "Nor are the actions of the children. It is only
yourself and your intentions."

"How can you accuse me?" she demanded.

"Because I know what I would do in like circumstances, Serine. Now, send for the servants to bring
water. I need to cleanse myself of the blood and sweat
of battle as well as the shadows of doubt. Perhaps when
the haze of weariness is washed away I will see things
more clearly and more to your benefit."

Serine caught her breath, but did not argue. She knew
Rory had tried to save her from admitting more than
need be through the baiting of his brother. She also realized he was fully aware that she had planned to leave
him without so much as a fare-you-well. But he did not
know that it would have broken her heart to do so, and
somewhere deep in her soul she thanked the marauders
for their untimely approach, for it gave her more time
to spend with Rory.

The servants arrived bearing bread and meat along
with the water for bathing. Serine watched as they prepared the bath, and quickly added some preparations of

her own. Deftly she added a bit of the bitter brew; she knew well it would help his wounds to heal more quickly, as well as soak the aches from his weary bones. Rory sank into the water, a look of blissful relaxation on his face.

Serine took a soft cloth and squeezed the water over his shoulders. She remembered how she had wondered if he had a wife when first she had ministered to him thusly, so long ago at Sheffield. She had allowed her imagination full rein and her jealousy for a wife who no longer existed had all but choked her. Now there was neither wife nor husband between them—only the discord caused by her desperate need to return with her son to Sheffield, and his pigheaded stubbornness in keeping her from doing so.

She watched the water slither over his broad shoulders. She took marigold soap and rubbed it over his back. He sighed in contentment. The soap dropped into the water. She reached for it, her hands brushing the water-slick flesh of his thighs. The soap was in her hand, but she did not draw it from the water.

He leaned back and cupped her chin in his large, water-warmed hand. His eyes held hers and then coasted over her face and centered on her lips. They parted and the tip of her pink tongue slipped across. He reached forward and caught it in his mouth and the match was met.

She had removed her rich outer garments and wore only a light smock as wont when assisting with a bath. Water dripped from Rory's knuckles and fell on her lush breasts, disappearing enticingly down the front of the garment. She wriggled as each drop found a new pathway across her breasts and down her body.

Rory released her lips and followed the moisture his hand had left on her chin, in unerring pursuit until his lips approached their goal. He pushed the smock from her shoulders and down her arms until her breasts were freed. His mouth explored them in joyous torture. Her garments dropped to the floor as his mouth pillaged her warm, inviting contours, and his hands unerringly drew her onto his waiting body where they undulated together, mindless of the time or the cooling of the water or the waves of passion that swept over them and extended itself to the waves of bathwater that sloshed unheeded onto the floor.

And still, even with the first heated thrill of euphoria behind them, even with their bodies sated with the pleasure of the other, it was not enough.

He lifted her against him, and she clasped her legs about his hips, as unwilling to release him as he was to let her slip away. Thusly, he carried her to the bed and they rolled themselves dry, lost in the throes of passion and pleasure until neither could bring themselves to move.

Rory cradled Serine in his arms. His lips touched her forehead as he spoke. "At this moment I cannot bring myself to believe that you really meant to leave me." There was a wondering tone to his voice and she knew he wanted her to deny that she had planned to leave, and in so doing, now at this most precious moment, he would believe her. But she could not bring herself to do so.

"At this moment I cannot believe it, either. After all, my lord Rory, it was you and your brother who came out with the tale of my proposed escape. I have admitted nothing, other than the obvious fact that I was on the cliffs at a time when I was able to alert your village to attack."

"And if I asked you to swear on your precious Sheffield that you did not plan to escape, would you do so?"

"If you asked me to swear I would be hurt and the love we have so recently shared would be a mockery." She would have rolled away, but he held her fast.

"Our love is not a mockery," he said, forcing her to look into the depths of his eyes. "The world is a mockery and the circumstances that have brought us together and governed our relationship are a mockery, but our love is a gift from the gods."

"Which gods?" she asked. "Yours, or mine?"

"When we are together, like this, there is only one god that matters, the god of love."

"And is it that you expect me to sacrifice all that I hold dear on his altar while you offer nothing but the act of indulging your body?"

She had struck true. In giving her pleasure, he took equal pleasure himself. He took her body, he took her love, just as he had taken her child and, most like, her precious Sheffield should she not return within a reasonable period of time.

"I offer you all that I have, Serine. My love, my lands, my help in raising your son."

"It is a selfish promise," she murmured, knowing he would not agree. "It is not enough. It will never be enough until you are willing to allow me to return and claim my son's birthright."

"That I cannot do." His voice was sad and seemed far away.

"Then it will never be enough."

And though the full length of their naked bodies touched, still tingling with the memory of love, their souls had once again been forced apart.

Serine tasted the salt of the tears that trickled down her cheeks and realized they were not hers alone. With a little cry she turned and buried herself in his arms. Despite the harsh words, and the even harsher truth, she would hold him for this little time, and pray God that when the time came, she would have the strength to go.

On the other side of the stronghold, Guthrie pulled his wife against him and rested his head on her breast. He knew nothing of miracles, nor of the torment storming about the two people who dared to love one another against all odds. He only knew the peace and satisfaction he had when with his wife.

Damask had come from another country and had looked askance on him when first they had met, but her doubts had soon turned to love and her questions to laughter as she sparkled like the sunshine and lit the corners of his world. He dared not think what life would be without her. And even though she was child-less, he would not have traded her for all the women in the world.

It did not take a seer like Drojan to know that Rory felt the same love for Serine, and she returned it in kind. It was only her determination to return to her own land that held them apart.

Guthrie, as headman, must think of a way to over-come this obstacle. He would reward Serine in such a way that she could not refuse, and in doing so, bind her to Corvus Croft and to Rory, now and forever. Surely, if he was able to pull off such a coup, luck would shine upon him, and his people would know peace, prosperity, and possibly parenthood, once again.

There was a smile on his lips as he drifted into slumber, determined to put his plan into motion as soon as possible.

Chapter Eleven

The dawn had hardly broken when Guthrie called for a meeting of the council. Rory left his bed with reluctance, not only at having to leave Serine's loving warmth, but at the singular dread in his heart that his brother might destroy the spark of trust that had been kindled between Serine and himself.

He knew his worst fears were to be realized as soon as Guthrie opened his mouth, and despite his arguments, the council agreed enthusiastically with Guthrie.

With the sun high in the sky the council sent for Serine.

There was concern in her eyes as she took her place before them, although she saw nothing but acceptance in their faces. They all seemed quite pleased with themselves, and somehow Serine did not feel comfortable with their pleasure. She looked to Rory for assurance. He met her eyes and looked away, his face a mask, telling nothing.

Her heart began to beat in her head, blocking out even Guthrie's voice. It took all her concentration to make out his words. Words that might well seal her fate and that of her son.

"In addressing the council, the Lady Serine has recently proclaimed herself a widow," Guthrie reminded them. "And while she has our deepest sympathy, we deem to lessen her sorrow with our judgment and grant her dearest wish."

A glimmer of hope lit Serine's eyes.

"It has come to the attention of the council that the Lady Serine has had deep concerns about the future of her son, Hendrick. We, therefore, propose to alleviate her fears and provide that which she lacks." He smiled, and the council nodded in approval.

"As reward for your efforts on the behalf of the people of Corvus Croft, it is the pleasure of the council that you be given in wedlock to my brother, Rory, who is, next to myself, the most powerful man in Corvus Croft. As a result of this union you need not fear having your son taken from you, for Hendrick will surely be son to both of you, as would any issue from your marriage."

He paused, waiting for Serine to agree.

But Serine did not agree.

"Has Rory consented to this?" she asked. She knew the answer. Of course he had concurred. It mattered little who the woman was, as long as he had his son, or in this case, *her* son.

"Rory will be a good husband to you and a good father to Hendrick," Guthrie assured her. "The wedding will take place—"

"The wedding will not take place," Serine's voice called out over that of the overlord. "I must spend my year of mourning for my dead husband and cannot consider your proposal until the prescribed time has passed."

Her words held only a smattering of truth. According to Dame Margot's message, Elreath had been dead these many months, but the promise of a full year of mourning would buy her the time she needed to take Hendrick and escape. By seeming to go along with Guthrie's plea Serine would lull their suspicions, and when the opportunity presented itself she would go, leaving Rory and her heart behind.

Guthrie opened his mouth in protest. He was not accustomed to having his gifts refused, but Serine gave the man no time to argue.

"I am not your prisoner. I came here to see that your brother, who is, by your own admission, the most powerful man in the village save yourself, be returned to you hale and healthy after I saved him from the jaws of death. Although he had, by his actions, shown himself to be my enemy, I did not ask ransom, only a trade, like for like. My son for your brother. You, Lord Guthrie, have chosen to disregard my petition and treat me unfairly."

"What could be more fair than to give you in marriage to Rory, wherein all that he has is yours?" Guthrie asked. "There is nothing left for you in England. Your son is here. My brother is here. You are offered a whole new life of riches, comfort and respect. What is there in England to compare to that?"

"There is Sheffield," came the answer. "If Rory would be such a solicitous and devoted provider, then let him come with me to Sheffield and raise Hendrick to his majority."

The council buzzed at her suggestion. Guthrie bent to confer with the other men.

"We understand your love of your home in England," Guthrie conceded, "and, in truth, if our women were not barren we would most likely consider your request. But our women are barren and each child, as well as each man, is necessary to the survival of our community. You may stay here as Rory's betrothed until your year of mourning is ended, or you may return to Sheffield, without your son."

It seemed as though the whole fate of the village hung on the premise that the women were barren and the men would never willingly agree to give up the children they had taken. When she spoke it was as though she but reflected her thoughts aloud. "In other words, my lord, if your women proved fertile and began producing children you would allow me to take my son and return to Sheffield."

Guthrie looked up in surprise. He had not given the matter thought, for the women *were* barren, and there was no promise of children other than the ones they had taken. Still, Serine had the knowledge to heal Rory and bring him back from the jaws of death.

"Have you the knowledge to make this happen?" he asked.

Before Serine could open her mouth, Ethyl stepped forward. "My lady has nothing more than the ordinary knowledge of any chatelaine regarding the use of herbs for the welfare of her people."

Guthrie gave the woman a piercing look. He understood that she was trying to protect her lady from any accusations of witchcraft, for it would surely take a witch to charm the barren women of Corvus Croft into producing children.

He deemed it prudent not to question Ethyl's words, and turned instead to Serine. "What say you?"

She looked into Rory's eyes and saw the pain. He wanted her to stay in Corvus Croft, to love his home as he did, and that was impossible when Sheffield lay in peril.

"I would be happy to use what knowledge I have of the herbal remedies to try to release the women of Corvus Croft from their barrenness."

Guthrie did not even bother to discuss the matter with the council, or with his brother. "Very well. You will be allowed your year of mourning to obtain results. If, at the end of that time, our women are still barren and show no sign of pregnancy, you will marry my brother. Should our women respond to your treatment and bear issue, you will be free to leave and take your son with you."

"What of the other children of Sheffield?" Serine asked.

"Those who wish to return with you would be allowed to do so. Drojan will oversee your efforts." He got to his feet, indicating that he had made his final offer.

Serine sighed. She could not fight the men of Corvus Croft and her love for Rory at the same time. A year was a long time. Many things could come to pass, and should she find a way to return to Sheffield with her son, she would do so.

She raised her eyes to meet those of the man she so undeniably loved. Could he see the love that permeated her soul? Love that blurred her judgment and fogged her good sense. But no, only in the songs of minstrels did people see into the souls of their beloved. Rory only saw that she did not want to marry him, and that was not true.

For a moment she thought of returning alone to Sheffield and raising an army to invade Corvus Croft

and take back the children, but how could she initiate
an attack that might mean the life of the man she loved?

The year would give her time. Time to weave her
plans, and time to spend with Rory, for if she had to
squeeze a lifetime of loving into that little year, she was
determined to do so. And although she felt very little
faith that her herbs would make fertile the women of
Corvus Croft, it gave her the time she needed to find
another means of escape.

She looked at Guthrie and then at each of the council, but it was to Rory that she gave her answer.

"I will accept your offer."

To the Celts a betrothal was much the same as the
handfast marriage. Rory and Serine would live as husband and wife for the year and at the end of that time
they would marry.

Guthrie gleefully reminded them that any issue from
the union would be deemed legitimate and eligible to
inherit. Rory took a ring from his finger to seal the
promise.

And so it was done . . . quickly. With no preparation
and little fanfare. But it was enough to irrevocably
change their lives. Within a week Rory told Serine to
make ready, for they were moving out of the castle and
onto his estates nearby.

To her surprise, Serine found another of her serfs
when she arrived at McLir Manor with Rory.

They had but entered the courtyard when a baby's
gurgling laughter came to them above the sounds of
carts and horses.

"I thought there were no infants in Corvus Croft,"
Serine challenged as the laughter sounded again.
"Surely you will not ask me to believe that sound is a

figment of my imagination, or perhaps a wandering spirit?'' She had said her words in jest, but Rory paled noticeably.

"Take the lady and her party into the hall," he ordered the steward. "I will see to the laughter myself."

"M'lord, it is but the lass and her babe that was brought from the Sheffield raid. My lord Guthrie felt she would be safe here until she was ready to make a choice as to which man she would take as husband."

"Husband?" Rory repeated.

"Taken from Sheffield?" Serine stopped in her tracks and looked toward the gardens at the rear of the house. "You mean Gerta and her babe are here?"

She had given up all hope of finding the girl, for there had been no sign of her during all the days Serine had been at Corvus Croft.

She turned to Ethyl, who had just passed through the houseyard gate. "Did you know of this?"

"Know of what, my lady?" Ethyl took in the scene and decided it boded ill for someone. Serine was in a temper.

"Did you know that Gerta the milkmaid from Sheffield was here?"

"I do not know it yet," Ethyl said bluntly. "I see no Sheffield face other than your own and Hendrick's."

Serine wanted to scream at the woman's indifference. Instead she turned on her heel and started after Rory, who was already rounding the corner of the house. "Are you coming?" she called to Ethyl without looking back.

"I would not miss this for all the world," Ethyl admitted as she picked up her pace. For it appeared to Ethyl that, having found another woman in residence, Serine had been bitten by the green dragon of jealousy.

Rory did not pause until he entered the well-kept kitchen garden. The scent of herbs mingled with the sweet-smelling flowers. As bright and golden as the blooms themselves were the heads that bobbed among the tall stems as the woman scooped up her child and lifted him toward the sky.

The baby's delighted laughter ceased midgiggle when he saw the new arrivals.

Gerta caught the expression on her son's face and turned slowly, bringing him into her arms, where she held him close against her. Her eyes widened.

At first Serine thought the young woman recognized her. However, the next moments gave reasonable doubt that Gerta had seen her at all.

In a flurry of motion the steward brushed past them and rushed to Gerta. She turned to the man in pretty confusion.

"Make your bow, lass. 'Tis the master himself who stands before you."

The girl dropped gracefully in an exaggerated curtsy and raised clear blue eyes to gaze in wonder on Rory's face.

"Thank you, my lord, for giving us the shelter of your home."

Rory stared at the woman, who bloomed with the health and vigor of youth. His eyes went from her to the chubby babe she held in her arms. The child grinned and held out his arms. But it was to the steward that the boy wanted to go.

"And this be Master Jamie," the steward announced proudly. "A fine lad he is, too." He took the baby from the woman and helped her to her feet.

And, although the baby was content with the attention of the steward, the mother could not take her eyes from Rory. Her admiration was almost palatable, and, in Serine's opinion, only a fool would not have seen it. Rory paid the woman little mind, his attention on the boy in the steward's arms.

"Gerta." Serine stepped from behind Rory and into the girl's view. "I am glad to see you here. I was unable to learn of your whereabouts at the castle and feared you were lost. Are you well?"

"Oh, most well, Lady Serine." The girl smiled, covering well any surprise she might have felt at seeing the Lady of Sheffield in these surroundings. She dropped a little curtsy and returned to staring at Rory.

"We did not know whether you would be coming back," the steward explained swiftly. "This seemed the best place for the young woman. She has been a great help with the house. I was hoping that if you did not wish to keep her for yourself you would allow me to ask for her. My woman has been dead these many years, and I would welcome a wife and son."

The man looked hopefully at his overlord, but Rory did not reply. He was watching Serine, and had come to the same conclusion as Ethyl. The Lady of Sheffield was surely upset by the appearance of the young woman.

Perhaps there was hope, after all.

"I will give thought to your request," Rory assured him. "Right now, I'm sure Serine and Ethyl wish to be taken to their rooms." He turned to Gerta. "Can you see to that, mistress?"

"Most gladly." Gerta breezed past the steward. "Come this way."

Serine walked stiffly toward the house. This had not been the sort of reception she had expected. Not only was there another woman in residence but Rory was obviously interested in her, and reluctant to allow his steward to make a commitment.

Ethyl stepped up beside her. "How convenient that Rory comes home to both woman and babe. He is doubly blessed to have such a harem available to him."

Serine glared at Ethyl and bit her lip, choking back angry words.

"Now that he has found a willing and available woman, and one with a child, at that, perhaps he will join in my petition to the council to allow me to leave with Hendrick," Serine suggested.

Ethyl looked back at Rory, who was following them, holding Hendrick's hand. "I doubt he sees it that way," she said wryly.

Serine took a deep breath. "Ethyl, somehow I must turn this situation to my advantage."

"And that, too, may be a real challenge," Ethyl said as she followed her mistress into the house.

Serine found that life at McLir Manor was much the same as it had been at Sheffield. Except that there were men to go out and hunt for game, which kept the domestic flocks from being depleted to feed the castle during the winter months.

Winter officially began on the feast of Michaelmas at the end of September and was a harbinger of the hard months ahead. By the time the blossoms of spring thrust their heads through the ground, hunger and deprivation would be found at all levels of life. But Serine was a good chatelaine and immediately began taking stock of the supplies of Rory's holdings.

The days were filled with the supervision of the household and listing all that would be needed against what was available for the hard months ahead. The nights were filled with love. Rory was openly pleased with Serine's willingness to work beside him for the betterment of his estate. He could not help but hope that she would grow to love it and forget her insistence on returning to Sheffield.

Hendrick found that he enjoyed the life so very much like the one he had left behind in England.

"It is much the same, is it not?" he asked his mother as she supervised the storing of supplies. "We did this at Sheffield."

"It is *not* the same," she admonished him. "Rory's holdings are not your heritage. You belong at Sheffield and I intend to see that you are allowed to return."

The boy wandered about the room, peering into bags and baskets. "When I go home I will see that all my serfs learn a trade they can ply in the winter. Then, in the spring, they can market their wares."

Serine shook her head. "The serfs will want to neglect their estate pledge and go to every fair in the countryside. Your estate will suffer."

"The people here do so and their land is lush and well tended," Hendrick said.

"The people here are not serfs," Serine reminded him.

"Perhaps that, too, should be changed," Hendrick said thoughtfully. "Tim and the other boys from the village are happy here. They do not wish to return to England."

"They are happy because this is still new to them. Once they are no longer spoiled and feted they will want to return to Sheffield where they belong." Serine's voice was firm, but in her heart she wondered if her words rang true.

Hendrick did not argue. He did not understand his mother's indignation, but he knew that it was directed at the circumstances, and not at himself.

With the aid of Ethyl and a reluctant Drojan, Serine had reviewed every aspect she could think of in an effort to discover where the problem lay in the inability of the women of Corvus Croft to become pregnant.

"It cannot be their diet." She sighed as she went over a list she had made as to what the women ate. "The food is much like what we have in Sheffield, and, in truth, even the poorest villager here eats as well as the castle folk in England."

Together they made certain the women were not taking motherwort, which was believed to prevent pregnancy. Nor were they using undo amounts of nutmeg or rue, which were known to cause miscarriage.

"And it can't be due to the indifference of the men." Serine paced back and forth across the herb kitchen. "Each woman swears that her man could not be more attentive in doing his part."

"And that is surely a miracle in itself," Ethyl said sourly. "Men are renowned to enjoy that part of a relationship above all else. Why would they not be attentive?" Ethyl crumbled a mixture of dried herbs and rubbed her hands together before brushing them over her garments. "It seems to me it is the men who are not doing their part, else the women would be pregnant."

Serine took immediate offense. "That is not so. Rory could not be more solicitous of my feelings."

"Is it disappointment I hear in your voice?" Ethyl probed. "Perhaps you think he will let Hendrick go should you give him a child of his own. I tell you, it would not be so. He would keep all of you here forever.''

Serine had not thought what might happen should she become pregnant. She had not done so even though the love they shared had progressed to a point where it sometimes threatened her sanity. This must be one of the times, for surely Ethyl's words smacked of truth.

Serine did not reply. There was no need. Ethyl was correct in her premise and they both knew it.

Rory fought his own battle. He did not want Serine to leave, but, for the good of his people and his village, he wanted the women to become pregnant. Invariably, when pondering the subject, his thoughts returned to Serine's reaction when she had learned of the presence of Gerta in his home. Had it been relief that there was another woman with a boy child who might take the place of Serine and her son, or had it been jealousy that had caused the sharpness in her voice?

He could not pretend to know, but he would do all in his power to find out. And if it meant forcing Serine into admitting she did not wish to share him with another woman, he would do so. He might even enjoy the game, he thought with some amusement.

Gerta did not bother to hide her pleasure at Rory's attention. She proudly displayed her son, loudly singing the praises of the boy whenever possible.

Through the steward's favor, Gerta had found a place at the table above the salt, as well as having a room of her own. And while she did her share of work around the manor house under the careful tutelage of the steward, there were also maidservants who kept and cleaned Gerta's rooms, as well as varlets who cooked and served the food. Her life in general was a far cry from that of a milkmaid at Sheffield.

From what she had been told when she arrived in Corvus Croft, her little son would be raised a free man, no less in importance and respect than the steward himself.

And now it seemed even Rory found Gerta and her babe of interest. Perhaps Rory McLir himself would decide to adopt the child. As she watched the chubby cherub crawling around on the garden lawn she reflected on what his life would be like should he grow up with the advantages she envisioned.

"So, here you are."

Serine's voice jarred the girl from her daydreams. Gerta jumped to her feet and bobbed a curtsy. "The steward has given me some free time to feed my child and let him play a bit in the sun," she explained.

Serine sat on the bench, drawing the girl down beside her. "There's no problem," she assured her. "It was just that you looked so pensive. I wanted you to know that I understand, and I'll do everything possible to see that we return to Sheffield where we belong."

Gerta jumped to her feet, her face reflecting her horror at seeing her plans for her son suddenly shattered.

"Oh, no, m'lady," she managed to say. "It wasn't longing for Sheffield that I was thinking on. I bless the day that the men of Corvus Croft brought me and my babe here."

"How can you say such a thing?" Serine demanded, all sympathy washed away with the girl's words. "Sheffield is your home."

"In Sheffield I was but the milkmaid and of such little note that no one paid me any mind until I was made May Queen and became pregnant by the Stag Lord."

Gerta shook her head. "I do not wish to leave Corvus Croft. Here my child is accepted and, as a woman obviously able to bear children, I am accepted, too."

Serine paused thoughtfully. This was not the first time she had been told that one of her Sheffield serfs did not want to return to their home. "I will not try to force you, nor will I try to convince you to return to Sheffield. But I will give you the opportunity to return should you change your mind."

"I have no wish to return to Sheffield and live as a milkmaid when I can have a man who will love and care for me right here in Corvus Croft."

Before Serine could answer, Gerta's face brightened. Serine saw Rory cross the garden, nonchalantly lifting the baby boy when he saw the child's upraised arms. And while there was little more than a greeting between Rory and the baby's mother, Serine felt an unsettling pang over Rory's interest in the little boy.

Serine went about the village talking to the women, making suggestions under the watchful eye of Drojan, who, in turn, was under the equally watchful eye of Ethyl.

And while the older couple never kissed or caressed in public, there was no question of their relationship. Their eyes touched with understanding and affection no matter the distance between their bodies.

Damask, with her easy laughter, was a welcome friend, and Serine found herself falling into easy camaraderie with the woman.

With the arrival of October, Serine, with the assistance of Damask and Ethyl, gathered mistletoe and gleaned away the berries, cutting the leaves and small twigs. From this they extracted the fresh juice, and the village women drank it in a cup of warm water both morning and evening, but the holidays were upon them and there was still no sign of issue.

Serine wrung her hands, but Damask continued her tasks as wife of the headman, while Ethyl said nothing.

"I don't understand either of you," Serine scolded as they sat before the fire in her solar. She was on the final stitching of a wimple for Ethyl as a Christmas gift. It was no secret, and Ethyl contemplated it with the pride of future possession.

"What is it you don't understand?" Ethyl asked, her eye centered on the wimple.

"No one except myself seems to care that none of the women is with child." She jabbed the needle through the linen and caught her finger with the point.

"We all care, Serine," Damask assured her. "But those of us who live here have become immune to disappointment when it comes to childbearing. We no longer cry in public."

Serine accepted her explanation and turned to Ethyl instead. "And what about you? You seem not to care that we are not to be allowed to return to our home."

"I feel very much at home here," Ethyl said quietly.

"You can't mean that! Why, everything here is different from England. Even the preparations for the holidays are steeped in the ways of the Druids rather than in the holy mother church."

"The holidays are the same. The feasting is the same, and Christmas is still the Christ child's birthday," Ethyl assured her mistress. "The only difference is that these people admit that festivities took place long before the priests came with their robes wrapped about them and their hands held out for alms."

" 'Tis true." Damask backed up the older woman. "The yule log came from the Druids and even 'blood month,' when the animals are slaughtered, reaches back deep into the past."

Serine looked on the days between All Hallows' Eve and Christmas as a dark time, filled with the mourning cries of doomed animals. This was the time of winter slaughter when the meat was butchered and smoked or salted to keep it eatable as long as possible. And while she did her part to preserve the meat, she looked forward to the time when work was suspended over the fortnight from Christmas Eve to Twelfth Day and festivities took full reign.

"I guess I am a bit out of sorts," she admitted apologetically. "I had so hoped that the mistletoe would prove to be the miracle we have awaited."

Damask shook her head. "We no longer believe in miracles," she said sadly. "But we have held more hope in our hearts since you agreed to try to help us. Surely if your knowledge of herbs could save Rory when he was so close to death, you will come upon the elixir that would allow us to bear children. You cannot imagine how much I envy you Hendrick." She sighed and laid her embroidery in the basket. Her eyes took on a dreamy glaze as she continued to speak. "To carry within my body the child of my husband would be to me the greatest of miracles. I have prayed and sacrificed and even made pilgrimages, but perhaps the old ones are right and the village is truly cursed."

"That's ridiculous," Ethyl grunted. "The cows calf, the chickens hatch their eggs, the pigs reproduce. It is not the village that is at fault."

"Are you casting blame on the men because they stole the children from your village?" It was more an accusation than a question, and Ethyl took it as such.

"It is not for me to cast blame. I say that only the people of Corvus Croft are barren. The animals, the fowl and even the land is fertile and productive."

"Then what is the answer?" Damask asked, but tears formed in her eyes before Ethyl could reply. "Nay, never mind. There is no answer. We will go on as we have and I shall live a long, prosperous and barren life."

Blinded by tears, she rushed from the hall.

Chapter Twelve

To all the people of Corvus Croft it seemed the union between Rory McLir and Serine of Sheffield was made in heaven . . . to all save two.

Serine loved Rory. And while she went through the motions of a good and loyal woman, betrothed to a man who was honored and revered in his own land, she knew that when the time came she would take her son and leave, and she knew that time would come.

Despite this knowledge, it pained Serine to see Gerta with Rory. It pained Serine when the fair young woman scurried across the courtyard, the hall or the garden to present her son to the lord of the manor . . . Rory.

It hurt to see Rory take the child and swing the bouncing boy about in his arms, answering the infant's laughter with his own.

Rory's demeanor with Hendrick was always so much more restrained. There was never any display of the lightheartedness Rory showed Gerta's child. And while it was doubtful if Rory could have picked Gerta out in a crowd, despite the fact that she lived in Rory's house and ate the food he provided, it hurt, nonetheless, when Serine was forced to witness Rory's uninhibited displays of affection for the woman's infant son.

"Why does he not marry Gerta?" Serine scolded as Ethyl tried to arrange her hair. "Why does he not allow me to take my son and return home?"

"He doesn't love her." Ethyl gave Serine's hair a jerk. "He loves you, and you throw his love in his face."

"What do you expect me to do?" Serine demanded. "Should I give in to his demands and tell him I will stay in Corvus Croft? If you were lady of Sheffield Manor, is that what you would do?"

Ethyl paused thoughtfully before answering. "I would give serious thought to my actions, but there is no doubt in my mind that, knowing what I now know of life, I would not throw back the love Rory McLir offers, for someday you will surely blame the people of Sheffield for your loss, you will blame Hendrick and, more than that, you will blame yourself."

"That's ridiculous. Sheffield has been in my family for generations. I would never willingly give up Sheffield. Rory must understand, and once he does, he will support me in my pledge to return to England."

"Is that what you believe?" Ethyl asked, her one eye penetrating Serine's fragile shell.

"It is what must be." Serine's eyes filled with tears as she said the words.

"Only the gods say what will or will not be," Ethyl returned, "and even they can be wrong once in a while."

"Ethyl, why do you oppose me on this?" Serine asked the woman who had been her main means of support throughout this ordeal. "Why have you deserted me?"

Ethyl stared at Serine for several seconds before speaking. "Because, Serine, you are wrong. I cannot support you."

Serine's breath caught in her throat. "Will you try to stop me?"

"I will not stop you," Ethyl assured her. "But on your own head will rest the outcome of your actions. With this understood, I will help you in any way I can."

Serine felt hysteria rising in her throat. "Do you condemn me because you no longer wish to leave your paramour?"

"No more than you wish to leave yours," Ethyl retorted. "I will be here when you need me, but do not try me too far, Serine, for in my opinion you are being heady and selfish. You will destroy yourself and those who love you with your obsession for Sheffield. If I cannot help you, I vow I shall not hinder you. But do not ask me to go against my beliefs, for I will not."

"I shall ask for nothing that is not for the benefit of my people and my village. The majority must be served," Serine promised self-righteously.

It was only after Serine had left the room that Ethyl had time to wonder to which majority she referred.

The more time Rory spent with Gerta and her little son, the more he was beset by conflicting emotions. How much better it would have been for all concerned had the Celts taken Gerta and her babe and left Hendrick behind. For, in all truth, Gerta's station in life in Corvus Croft was far more promising than it would ever have been in Sheffield. And although Gerta had not the petite figure or the graceful movements of the Lady of Sheffield, the former milkmaid fit in physically with the women of Corvus Croft. Only Serine and Damask were noticeably different. Dainty and slim, they both looked to be exactly what they were. Ladies to the manor born. Gerta and most of the women of the Celts were larger in proportion, with generous bodies that bespoke an ease in bearing children. Yet no children were born.

Once Serine and Rory had taken up residence at Rory's manor, Gerta was no longer sequestered. Men and women alike flocked to the young mother to admire her babe, the youngest child to appear in Corvus Croft for over a decade.

Gerta basked in the admiration for her little boy and welcomed their comments and advice. It was obvious that any single man in the village would have gladly taken Gerta to wife, and there was some grumbling that a woman, obviously fertile and of childbearing age, should be kept single through the whim of one man. But Rory was oblivious to their complaints. He would not force Gerta to wed any man and it never occurred to him that she hesitated in her choice due to the hope that she might become the wife of Rory himself.

With Ethyl's help, Serine continued to dose the women with her herbal concoctions. Hope sprang and failed with each passing month, and still there was no sign of issue. But it wasn't until Damask appeared at her door in tears that Serine reached the depths of despair.

"My monthly flux is on me," Damask sobbed. "I had so hoped this time it would not come." She buried her face in her hands. "It is not that I do not love my husband. He is everything to me. I live only for his love. Being his wife and bearing his children is all I wish in life."

"But surely it cannot be time for your monthly tides so soon," Serine objected. "Perhaps you have started early and it is a good sign."

"'Tis not early. It is late," Damask wailed. "And I had so hoped." Again a sob overtook her, but Serine paid little mind, absently patting her friend's shoulder.

It seemed only yesterday that both women had been within days of each other in their monthly tides, and now Damask had run late enough that she had hoped hers would not appear, while Serine had lost track of time, for her own flux had yet to materialize.

In an effort to quiet Damask's sobs, Serine began to question the other woman. "Perhaps there was some medication given during the plague that has caused this infertility. What do you remember of that time?"

"I know no more of it than you." Damask wiped her eyes. "I came to Corvus Croft long after the plague had struck."

Serine's head snapped up. "And there was no plague in the village from whence you came?"

"None." Damask sniffled. "Indeed, my younger sister has two children and is expecting a third, and she has been wed but four years."

Serine stared at the distraught woman, remembering how it had been with herself. She had hardly become a bride when she had learned she was to be a mother. That was her duty and a woman's lot. Had her husband not gone off on crusade it was likely Hendrick would have had several siblings despite the advanced age of his sire. Serine had not complained about her husband's absence, nor had she objected to him ignoring her when he was in residence. An heir was what she had wanted, and an heir she had, until the Celts had come and taken him from her.

"Guthrie would have been far better served had he married my sister," Damask observed morosely. "He would have had the son he so desires."

"Has he ever reprimanded you for your lack?" Serine asked suspiciously.

"Guthrie loves me, just as Rory loves you, but even I can see the longing in his eyes when he looks upon Gerta and her babe." Again the tears flowed from her eyes. "I would do anything to give him a son, yet there seems to be nothing I can do."

Serine slipped her arm around Damask's shoulders. There seemed to be little either of them could do, for Serine was completely out of remedies. She knew of no potion that the women had not tried. And all had failed.

Unable to give more than comfort to Guthrie's wife, Serine sent Gerta to bring food and wine, and the women sat close to the huge fireplace trying to shut out the pervading chill that had entered both their bodies and their hearts.

It was there Ethyl joined them. Seeing that Serine had her hands full with the despondent Damask, Ethyl poured the mulled wine and placed the warm, sweet bread on a low table before the hearth.

"Thank you, Ethyl." Serine smiled as she served her guest and lifted her own cup, relishing the warmth against her hands. The spicy vapors wafted toward Serine's face and she breathed deeply of the fragrance.

Without warning her stomach lurched. Her hands trembled and her throat constricted. "Do not drink," she cried as she ran into the courtyard, where she was instantly ill.

By the time she returned, wan and shaking, Gerta was proclaiming her innocence. "I swear I did nothing but bring the wine from the kitchens. I only brought what was given me. I wouldn't harm my lady. What good would it bring me to do so?"

"Perhaps it would bring you a rich and powerful husband," Damask suggested. "With Serine gone, Rory might look upon you and your son with favor."

"I look no higher than the steward," Gerta declared
with downcast eyes. And, at that moment, her statement became truth. If Serine was, indeed, sick by some
unknown cause, Gerta knew it would be worth her life
to look on Rory McLir with marriage in mind.

"Then it's the steward you should wed, and soon,"
Ethyl said flatly. "For unless I miss my guess, Rory will
wed no one but the mother of his own child."

All the women looked at her askance.

"And have you gained the power of a seer simply by
your association with Drojan?" Serine asked, wondering at the smug look on her companion's face.

"It does not take a seer to suspect that Serine's vapors have nothing to do with the wine in her cup, but
rather having partaken fully of the wine of love." Ethyl
suppressed a smile at the looks of disbelief on the faces
of the other women.

The next moment Damask was on her feet. "Oh,
Serine, can it be so? If you are pregnant there is hope
for all of us. I cannot wait to tell—"

"Tell no one," Serine ordered. "Ethyl only specu-
lates. She has no proof that my indisposition is anything more than a bad piece of fish from breakfast.
Until we have some reason other than an upset stomach to believe I am with child, no one is to say anything."

"But—" Damask tried again.

"No one!" Serine reiterated, and Damask bowed her
head in agreement. But the women knew that if, indeed, Serine was carrying Rory's child the news would
be all over the village in less than no time.

"What will you do?" Ethyl asked once Damask had
gone.

"I do not know," Serine admitted. "It was my plan that the women become pregnant so that I could return to Sheffield, but I did not think to become pregnant myself."

"Then you should have stayed out of Rory McLir's bed," Ethyl told her.

"As you stay out of Drojan's bed?" Serine returned.

"I would welcome Drojan's child were it possible for me to bear one. But my childbearing days are past. It is not Drojan's child I crave, but his love."

"I wish you luck, Ethyl. Love is an elusive thing, for if Rory loved me as Drojan loves you, he would let me go."

"And if you loved Rory as I love Drojan, you would not wish to leave him."

The two women stared at each other. No further words were spoken, for there was nothing left to say. Each had expressed her opinion and each believed herself to be right. Only time would tell which spoke the truth.

Ethyl broke the silence. "What will you do now?" she asked.

But Serine was mulling over the information she had gleaned from Damask, and paid little heed to the question.

"Did you know that Damask was not in Corvus Croft during the plague?" she asked.

"Damask seldom confides in me," Ethyl told her.

"Her sister has borne several children, though she is younger than Damask, and married less time." Serine expressed her thoughts aloud, neither expecting nor requesting an answer. "For a moment I thought I knew the answer. It seemed as though perhaps the lack was not in the women, but in the men, instead. But how could that be if I carry Rory's child?''

Ethyl tore off a piece of bread and popped it into her mouth. "Perhaps you have been dosing the wrong prospective parent."

"That cannot be." Serine sighed. "Rory was here during the plague. His wife and child died of plague and he was sorely taken himself. There is no difference in Rory's life-style and that of every other man in Corvus Croft. I must look elsewhere for my answer, and do it quickly, for Guthrie may decide to go back on his promise when he learns there will finally be a baby born in Corvus Croft, and the child is mine." She slammed her hands on the table in frustration. "Why could it not have been Damask who conceived? Now I must find a way to take Hendrick and leave here, with or without permission, and I must break the heart of the man I love by taking his child with me, or allow my own heart to be broken by leaving the babe, and that I cannot do." She covered her face with her hands. "It is indeed a bitter, bitter decision."

The fire snapped, and the wind howled about the thick stone walls. Serine closed her eyes behind her fingers and allowed the sounds to engulf her. Unwilling to face the future, she allowed herself to drift back, remembering all the precious moments that had brought her to this time and place.

She remembered how she had fought the powers of darkness for Rory's life, and how his fever had soared to the point where the poisons had caught in his body. She remembered the way his skin burned as she and Ethyl had somehow managed to place him in the tub of tepid water, forcing the herbs into the very pores of his body.

She would have lost him had it not been for Old Ethyl's knowledge of the ancient potion that cleansed the blood and washed away the poisons, making him whole and able to function normally once more.

Serine remembered how quickly Rory's body had healed under her care. How she had delighted in seeing him return to health. How strongly she had believed that all she would have to do was return him strong and healthy to his people and they would grant her request and allow her to take the children and leave. Now it seemed that not only some of the children but the adults as well wanted to stay with the Celts in Corvus Croft. But staying was not an option open to Serine. She must return to Sheffield, and Hendrick with her.

In her heart she blessed the brew that had restored Rory to life and health, and yet, she could not help but despair in the fact that the brew had done its job all too well, for there would be the very devil to pay when Rory learned she carried his child. Yes, there was no doubt the brew had done its job too well.

Her eyes flew open behind her fingers. "The brew!" The words erupted from her mouth, and Ethyl jumped at the sound of her voice.

"What about the brew?" Ethyl asked as she settled herself again on the chair.

"It was the brew!" Serine was on her feet. "Don't you see? The only difference between Rory and the other men of Corvus Croft is that Rory has been liberally dosed with the bitter brew."

"But what has that to do with—"

"Ethyl, it's not the women who lack the ability to produce children, 'tis the men." Serine pulled Ethyl to her feet and embraced the woman. "All we need do is

tell the men to drink the brew, and the women will soon
be with child and we will be able to go home.''

She gave Ethyl a second hug and was about to dance
away when Ethyl took the younger woman's shoulders
and held her fast.

''I told you the brew that is bitter to the tongue has
been forbidden in many parts of the country. To make
it here would be to court disaster. Should anyone suspect it is the bitter brew we make, we would be killed.''

''Ethyl, that's ridiculous. These people want children. Once I explain to them that the brew will heal
them they will be anxious to test its powers.'' She
paused, midstep. ''Do you doubt this?''

''I think your hopes have overpowered your common sense. And while it is entirely possible that you are
correct in thinking it due to the brew that Rory may
have sired your child, there was great risk in making the
brew at Sheffield. To make it here would be to court
disaster. I beg you to reconsider, Serine, if not for your
own sake, then for Hendrick's.''

''It is for Hendrick's sake I must take the chance. I
think you are overly protective of the brew, and not
without cause, from what you have told me, but I have
no other option and I will not be thwarted by superstition.''

''You are in a land that is entrenched in superstition.
If you succeed they will hail you as their hero and sing
your praises, but should you fail, they will have your
life, Serine, and likely mine, as well.''

Serine placed her hand on her friend's arm. ''No one
could have been a better friend, Ethyl. Should my plan
go awry I will not implicate you in any way. But I shall
make the brew and see to it that the men use it.''

''And I shall pray for both of us,'' Ethyl said.

* * *

Serine went to the storeroom off the kitchens, where she stored her herbs. Distraught with worry, Ethyl went up the stairs to the peace and quiet of her own room.

Neither woman saw the figure in the far shadows of the hall. And though all the words had not been clear at such a distance, Gerta had heard enough to understand the seriousness of what might happen. She slipped from the room wondering how best she could use her information to enhance her position, and that of her own little son.

Right now she would wait to see how Serine's plan progressed. The last thing she wanted to do was to make an enemy of her former mistress. Still, she would do what she must to insure her son's future.

She lifted her skirts and swung her hips provocatively as she walked toward the kitchen. Humming a little tune, she blessed the day she had been snatched from her drafty little hut in Sheffield and brought to the comfort and luxury she had found here. She had been living in fear that Serine would find a potion that would help the women to conceive and take the unmarried Gerta back to Sheffield to be relegated to milkmaid once again.

Now, thanks to the conversation she had overheard, Gerta knew she had the wherewithal to stop Serine from forcing her to return to Sheffield.

Gerta thanked God for her sharp ears, and her light tread. But most of all she thanked him for giving her the information she needed to allow her to stay.

Serine was in the room where she stored her herbs when Rory found her. She looked up when he opened the door. He stepped into the room but did not come to her.

"Ethyl said you were here," he said. His voice was flat, without inflection. "She said you believe you have the solution to our problems."

"I believe I know why there are no children in Corvus Croft. Oh, Rory, just think of it. If I'm correct, within a year there may be babies again in your village." Her smile was tremulous as she waited for him to respond.

"And when the babies come, you will go. Is that why you are so excited? The thought that you will be able to leave with Guthrie's blessing?" He searched her face, hoping she would deny the truth of his words.

"I am excited because I believe I know what is wrong."

"Wrong!" Rory slammed his fist against the worktable. The dried herbs rattled in protest. "Even I know what is wrong. Our women are barren."

Serine's temper flared. "The women! Always the women!" She swung around the table and confronted him, head-on. "Let me tell you, Rory McLir, 'tis not the women who are at fault. Most like 'tis the men."

"Hah!" His well-formed lips curved into a sneer. "There's not a man in this village who does not love his woman often and well. It's not the men, I say."

"Then they should be happy to participate in a little experiment to see if they can help their wives."

"What is it you want them to do?" His question echoed his skepticism.

"I want them to take the bitter brew that you took when you were healing from Ethyl's arrow."

Rory threw back his head and laughed. It was a warm, rich sound and sent chills of anticipation rushing down Serine's back. "A fine chance you have of getting the men to do that. Not even for their women would they drink a potion that tastes like spoiled wine."

"There is no other choice," Serine told him. "If the men want to father children they must allow the bitter brew to help them."

"And if the brew could perform this miracle, and the fault is within the man and not the woman, then why are you not with child? God knows, we have loved one another to the very depths of our being, and still there is no issue."

"And if there were a child, would you allow me to return to Sheffield with Hendrick, or would you poison Guthrie against me and make him go back on his word?"

"Guthrie never goes back on his word. Neither myself nor any man alive could hope to force him to do such a thing. But I will not lie to you and pretend I would not ask him to reconsider due to the change in circumstances."

Serine drew a deep breath. This was not the time to admit her suspicions. "Rory, there is no other answer. Damask came to me today. She told me she was nowhere near Corvus Croft during the plague. It cannot be the plague that has interfered with her ability to conceive." She laid her hand against his chest and looked up into his face, taking in his strong jaw, his dark eyes and his raven black hair. God, how she loved him. "Help me to get the men to drink the brew, Rory. At least give me the chance to prove whether I am right or wrong."

"If you are wrong, the village loses the last chance to produce children, but if you are right, I will lose you." He took her into his arms and crushed her against him.

"Serine, Serine, it need not be this way. Stay with me. Sheffield will survive with Dame Margot in charge. When Hendrick reaches his majority, he can claim his rights."

"Sheffield will be distributed to friends of the king, and Hendrick will have nothing. No matter how much I love you, I cannot shirk my duty to my child and my heritage."

"You are betrothed to me," Rory reminded her. "Will you shirk your duty to me?"

"My duty is to love you, as well as to try to use my simple skills to assist the women of your village to bear children."

"Forget about the women and their children, or lack thereof. Just think about my love for you." His mouth moved across her forehead and pressed against her hair as he breathed in the clean, herb-kissed scent that was hers alone. "Forget everything except how it feels when I touch you, and how it feels when you touch me."

He pressed the palm of her hand against his mouth, and her legs went weak as longing overcame every conscious thought.

His tongue, warm and moist, caressed her palm before his lips traveled up her arm, hovering momentarily at her wrist, and again at the soft skin at her elbow.

Serine lay back in his arms, her fingers entwined in his thick hair. She closed her eyes and made a little purring sound deep in her throat. "When you kiss me like that I forget everything . . . everything in the world except you, and how much I love you."

"How much I love you." He repeated her words, but it was a statement in itself, and there was an element of wonder in his voice as he realized the depth of his caring for her. It seemed a miracle to him. Just as she was a miracle come to life. Her hair, her skin, the generous curve of her lips. The way she laughed and the way she sighed with pleasure when they made love. He wanted to hold her, to protect her, to love her forever, and all she could think of was leaving him and returning to Sheffield.

The thought angered him, and he tightened his grip on her lithe body. Unaware of his anger, she responded by sealing herself against him, molding her curves to his muscles in delightful abandonment.

In his arms Serine was able to forget everything. There was only Rory, with his enticing kisses, his persuasive touch and his ability to sweep all thought from her mind. Even Sheffield became but a shadow.

His kisses filled her with the magic of love. A magic long denied, and she was propelled like a leaf caught up in a storm of passion and desire.

It was only when he was no longer with her that she was able to bring herself back to reality and separate what must be from what might have been. Only when his arms were no longer around her could she divorce duty from desire.

Now her whole being responded to his hungry kisses and she met him with a hunger of her own that would not be assuaged with less than complete possession.

Their love became a banquet of physical delights, as decadent as the richest dessert, and as heady as the strongest wine. Together they sank to the herb-strewn floor. Each movement released the fragrance of the herbs, surrounding them in an aroma as pure and clean as love itself. The love they bore each other that would not be denied.

Chapter Thirteen

"Seer, look to your Runes and tell me what you see." Ethyl spoke the words as she opened the door to Drojan's dwelling.

The man gave her a disparaging look. "I do not take kindly to being ordered about," he reminded her. "You would do better to ask me to use my abilities rather than demand that I do so at your inclination."

"Inclination or no, you would do well to draw your circle and consult your Runes, for Lady Serine believes she has discovered the reason behind the women's barrenness, and she thinks the fault lies with the men."

Ethyl almost laughed to see the look on Drojan's face. He gaped at her in disbelief. "That cannot be," he protested. "It is the women who bear the children."

"And the men who plant the seed," Ethyl said. "If a seed is not planted, the sprout does not grow."

"The men have labored long and hard to plant their seeds both in the soil and in the bellies of their wives. Your mistress is at fault in her premise. There is nothing wrong with the men."

Ethyl shook her head and laughed. "Old man, you are wrong. Open your eyes and use your wisdom. Cast your Runes and believe what they tell you, then come to me and we will see if, together, we can keep the husbands and wives of the village from one another's throats."

"If Serine insists on blaming the men for the lack of children there is surely nothing I can do to rectify the situation. You must speak to her and tell her to mend her way of thinking. No man in the village will accept her mad assumption."

Nonetheless, he took the pouch that contained his Runes from inside his tunic and carefully drew a circle on the floor. Once inside the circle he purified himself with incantations while Ethyl went to the far side of the room and settled down to watch in silence.

With great concentration he took forth the Runes and laid them before him. His face brightened, clouded and brightened again. He looked up and motioned Ethyl to come to him.

"It is just as I said," he assured her with pompous surety. "There will be children born in our village. The Runes clearly state it to be so."

"Do they clearly name the parents?" Ethyl asked.

"Runes do not concern themselves with such menial matters. It is enough that they have informed us of this wonder of the future. I shall go and inform Guthrie. He will rejoice at the news, as will the rest of the village."

Drojan reached out to sweep up the Runes, but Ethyl stayed his hands. "Wait, Seer, there is more you should know that may give meaning to what you see."

He looked at her askance. "What do you know, woman, and why do you test rather than tell?"

"I have reason to believe that Serine is carrying Rory's child," she said.

"Aha!" Drojan hooted the word as he jumped to his feet. "See! It is just as I said. The men are not at fault.

Rory has planted his seed in a woman from another village and she is fertile.''

"Damask is from another village," Ethyl reminded him, "yet she bears no babe."

"Damask is young," Drojan hedged. Damask's inability to conceive had long been a puzzlement to him.

"Your theory is without merit. Damask's sister is even younger and already has several children of which to boast," Ethyl returned. "There is only one conclusion that can be reached, and one experiment yet untried. It is the men who must be dosed."

"With what? They are not impotent. What can you possibly give them that might make a difference?"

Ethyl took a deep breath and sank onto a bench. "When Rory was sore wounded we thought him to be lost to the powers of darkness. His fever soared and his body swelled from the poisons therein. It was then Serine remembered the elixir of herbs that is bitter to the tongue. I knew how to prepare it and she begged me to do so. The task done, we were able to save the man's life. Now Serine feels that if all the men were given the same brew, they, too, would find themselves able to father children."

Drojan looked from the woman to the Runes. The message was written clearly there. A woman carried the knowledge that might save the village, but only through the sacrifice of "self." Fear gripped his heart. Never had he felt so strongly about another human being as he did for Ethyl. She seemed part and parcel of his conscious mind. He could not think, having found her, how he would survive if she was taken from him.

He swallowed the dryness in his throat, foreboding permeating his bones. "What is the brew of which you speak?"

"It is the brew of bitter herbs, outlawed for use by those who cannot understand its goodness."

"As I feared." He turned away, looking through the window toward the sky. "Must you involve yourself in this? It is the Lady Serine who wishes to challenge the gods. Let her concoct the brew and take the blame or the blessing as the case may be."

"That I cannot do," Ethyl told him. "The secret of the brew is mine and mine is the responsibility to see that it is done correctly and without deviation."

"Should it be discovered that you use a potion reputed to have poisoned many, even I cannot save you," he told her.

"I know that, and I do not ask. I can but tell you that the bitter brew has never harmed a soul in this world. It was made for the good of others, and was used for same."

"Rethink this, Ethyl." He tried to keep his voice steady, to reason with her and talk her out of assisting in this dangerous pursuit. "There is no reason for you to become involved. Serine is knowledgeable about herbs. She does not need your help. It is dangerous...."

But Ethyl chose to misinterpret his words. "Never fear, old man. I will die silent before I involve you. No one will ever know that I so much as spoke to you of the brew. You have nothing to fear."

She turned toward the door, but he was there before her, blocking her way.

"But I *do* fear," he confessed. "I fear for you. There is danger here. Danger for you."

"Then you should not be concerned." She ignored his concern. "I have lived with danger as my companion all my life, and survived. It is no different now."

"Ethyl, I ask you not to become part of this." He blocked the door, his face a mask of anxiety. "The people of the village are a superstitious lot. The men must always rebel at any hint of disparagement on their virility. They will try to discredit you in any way that they can, and mistrust all that you propose to do, regardless of your noble intentions."

"I should not have come." She sighed, realizing the truth in his words. "I thought perhaps you would be of help, but you give me nothing but empty warnings." Again she stepped toward the door. "Let me go, old man. You ask too much."

He took her words into his heart and turned them back onto hers. "It is because I am an old man that I ask this of you, Ethyl. All my life I have been alone, living the solitary existence of a seer. Now, when my life is almost over, I have found someone with whom I wish to share my last years." He held out his hands, palms upward in supplication. "Ethyl, I don't want to lose you. I want to spend these last years with you. I want us to be together."

She closed her eye and blinked back the tears. It had been so long, so very long since she had heard the need and love in another person's voice. "When I was chosen as archer for the village, you risked your life before my arrows. You did not ask my permission, nor did you tell me of your plan. Had I mis-shot, I would have lost you and all true meaning for living. Once more you must place your trust in me, Drojan. Grant my knowledge the same trust you put in my skill."

She placed her hands in his and moved willingly into the comfort of his embrace. But even as his kiss lifted her from the cocoon of years, she heard him grumble, "It is not you I distrust, my love. It is everyone else."

* * *

Since there was only a small amount of the potion left that Serine had brought from Sheffield, the women set to work to produce a copious amount, which would serve the whole village. Once the herbs were in the vats, they would age for a fortnight. During that time Serine and Ethyl set about in an effort to make the men drink the brew.

It was Damask who had given them the idea. Joining them in the herbal workroom, she had shuddered when Serine suggested she taste the liquid.

"I would almost rather remain childless than take such a potion." She shivered visibly and stamped her foot after swallowing. "If this is what brought Rory back to life I have no doubt he got better only to keep from having to take more. 'Tis truly nasty!"

"We plan on asking the men to drink it." Serine tried to sound nonchalant.

Damask, still suffering from the aftertaste, shook again. "I cannot imagine getting Guthrie to swallow even a mouthful. He would spit it out before the smallest drop could find its way down his throat."

"Would he not drink it if he knew it would enhance his chances of becoming a father?" Serine persisted.

"He wouldn't believe anything that nasty could provide positive results," Damask told her friend. "No, Serine, you must come up with a better excuse to get that vile potion down any man in this village. In truth, it looks as bad as it tastes, and any man who took a mouthful would swear he'd been poisoned."

"Think you the women would drink it?" Serine asked hesitantly, feeling her last hope slipping away.

"Are you certain it is to drink, and not a poultice for a boil?" Damask suggested.

"I am sure that this bitter brew is the last hope for children for Corvus Croft," Serine said, holding the last of the brew against her breast. "I would think a brave man would have the courage to swallow even if it is not palatable."

"Guthrie would have to drink it first before I would take more," Damask contended.

Serine's eyes lit with joy. "That's it. As soon as the new batch of brew is ready you will both take it, and all the other husbands and wives, as well. And the men will take the first draft to set the brave example for their wives. What think you?" Serine directed her question to Ethyl, who had remained silent throughout the discussion.

"I think you'll be very lucky if anyone takes more than one swig of the brew, but even one swig is worth a try. And, God knows, some of the spirits men drink smell as bad and taste worse." She turned back to her pestle, ending her portion of the conversation.

Serine honored the older woman's feelings and turned her attention to Damask, who was still trying to think of some way wherein she could entice Guthrie to agree to take the brew so that she would be spared.

By the end of the month it was evident that Serine's plans had gone awry. With each woman to whom she spoke it became more obvious that the men had refused to take the brew, and would continue to do so. Any hint that they might be responsible for the lack of children was met with disbelief bordering on thoughts of heresy.

"I dare not approach him again," a well-endowed matron announced. "He's never had a harsh word for me, until I hinted that it might be of benefit to us both if he would take the brew." She straightened the sleeves of her tunic and tugged at her skirt. "I shall not attempt it again." And, giving Serine a self-righteous glance she pranced off across the green toward her home and her uncooperative husband.

Serine wrung her hands in frustration. She looked to Damask for support, but Guthrie's wife had no support to give.

"It is the same with Guthrie. He won't touch the herbal brew. I have tried slipping it into his gruel, as well as his mead and ale, but he always sniffs it out and bellows at me as though I'm trying to poison him."

" 'Tis not poison," Serine insisted. "I've told you a hundred times the brew has no ill effects."

"Except that it looks and smells terrible," Damask asserted. "I cannot abide the sight of it myself, and my stomach turns if the carafe passes beneath my nose."

"You are too squeamish," Serine scolded. "If you find yourself with child you'll think yourself half dead before you recover from the earliest stages of discomfort."

"If I find myself with child I will be too happy to care about physical discomfort," Damask asserted, oblivious to the expression of disbelief on Ethyl's face.

The young woman left, her small supply of bitters replenished. It was then Serine turned to Ethyl.

"We need to make more of the brew," she said as she assessed the supply in her jars. "It seems they waste more than they use, and—"

Ethyl bent over the jar. "You are right on all counts," she agreed, "but I refuse to jeopardize your life and my own by making more of the brew. There has already been talk likening it to poison. I will not do more than I have already done. You have become addleheaded in your quest to return to Sheffield. If the women are so dull witted that they cannot think of an inventive way to make their men drink of the brew, perhaps they don't deserve children.''

Serine gasped. "How can you say such a thing?'' she asked. "You know as well as I that the women have much love to give.''

"Not if they are too dull to invent a way to make their men swallow but a small drink, no worse than green ale.''

"It is not their intelligence that is at fault,'' Serine declared. "It is their honesty. They are too honest to deceive their husbands.''

"And you are too gullible to be believed,'' Ethyl snorted. "I'll leave you to your dreams of honest women. I'm going to Drojan. He, at least, has no illusions about the human race.''

Serine followed the woman to the door. "But, Ethyl, I need help. I cannot manage a brew of such proportions by myself.''

"Then give the herbs to each of the would-be mothers and let them brew it themselves. Perhaps their men will drink of it when they know it was made in their own abode.''

"You have at least the beginning of a good idea,'' Serine told her. "I will give each woman a vial of her own to be kept in her home, and I will ask them to help me prepare the mixture so they can see that the concoction is but a harmless blend of herbs that most of us use every day.''

Serine prepared for her project, even though, true to her word, Ethyl did not offer to help and went on about her own business. By the time Rory came home, Serine was well on her way to completing the task of measur-

ing out the ingredients for each of the women to take
their own container of brew.

The day was cold and blustery. Rory entered the room
bringing with him a blast of wintry air. He grabbed
Serine's arm and buried his cold nose in the warmth of
her neck. She wriggled against him, objecting in jest
only, for she enjoyed the love play involved in the
warming of his chilled body.

"Leave off," she objected. "You will muss my herbs
and ruin all that I have achieved this day."

"And what have you achieved that is so important?" He continued nuzzling, but his face now
searched for warmer, more intimate areas, and he bur-
rowed into the warmth of her breasts.

"I am going to give the village women the herbs they
need to get them with child. It is up to them to get the
men to use it."

"And am I allowed to use this potion also?" he
teased as he relished her warmth.

"You have used it and well," she told him. "If you
were any more healthy or virile there would be no holding you."

"You can hold me, and as often as you like," he
teased, his fingers plucking at the strands of her hair
that fell about her face when she worked.

She slipped her arms beneath his heavy fur cloak and
nestled against him. How she wished his words were
prophecy, for she longed to lose herself in his embrace,
but there was more to life than the dictates of love, and
she had blood promises that must be kept. Promises
that were in direct opposition to the man she loved.

"I will hold you," she murmured. "Hold you close
and often." And their love bloomed once again.

* * *

By the time winter was full upon them the main topic of discussion among the women was their imaginative ways of ingesting the bitter brew into their unknowing husbands.

"I slip but a few drops into each cup of ale. He never notices the slight change in taste, and he drinks so much ale that he takes the required amount," one of the women said with a laugh.

"I take it into my own mouth and let it flow into his when we kiss. He claims now that my kisses are bitter, and he must sweeten them with his own. We always end up making love, so I have been forced to dispense the brew to him during the evening, else he does not open the smithy until the morning is half spent." The woman giggled at her boast, while another began telling a story of her own.

Serine listened to all their tales and complimented them on their ingenuity. But privately her heart was heavy. She stood at the window, looking out over the countryside, when Rory joined her.

"Tell me, Serine, what is wrong? Have the men refused to take your concoction?"

"'Tis not that, Rory." She crossed the room and joined him at the fire. "I am needed to see that the planting is begun in Sheffield. In a few weeks it will be too late to assure the crop, and I will still be here, for although the people of Corvus Croft are taking the brew, the women show no sign of bearing children."

Rory could not hide his pleasure. "Perhaps you are destined to stay here with me." He reached out and took her hand, drawing her to him. He no longer argued when she spoke of returning to her estates. The decision was no longer with him. It was in the hands of the gods, and even Drojan had no answer.

If the women proved quick with child, Serine would take her son and leave. And if the bitter brew failed to provide the necessary ingredients that brought forth children, Serine would stay and most likely continue in her quest. Until the women either became impregnated or grew too old to have it matter, the men of the village would be happy, for all of them, including Rory, would see that the women bore them children, or literally die trying.

He laughed and pulled Serine down onto his lap. "Do not fret yourself. No matter what happens, one of us will be happy and the other sad."

"It need not be that way," Serine protested. "If you would only come back to Sheffield with me. It would only be until Hendrick reaches his majority, and—"

"You know that is out of the question, Serine," Rory chastised. "My brother needs me. I am his most trusted general and leader of his forces. My responsibility lies here, and here I will remain."

Serine leaned toward him and touched his lips with her own. "I understand," she said. But in her heart she would never understand, for if she understood his position, she might be forced to reconsider the validity of her own. But there was no confrontation in kissing, and the urgency of their love forced all mitigating thoughts from their minds, as need overcame actuality, and their passion deepened.

Yet the sadness in her grew, for even now she deceived him, for she had not yet told him that while the women of the village had not quickened, Serine herself carried Rory's child.

Shortly after the winter holidays, unrest pervaded Corvus Croft. All through the days of celebration there had been a feeling of anticipation, but when the villagers returned to their daily tasks, gloom pervaded, as dark and dank as the winter months.

And while the women apparently continued to ply their men with the brew, they no longer came to Serine with the tales of their cleverness.

It was during this time that Ethyl vacated her room in the manor to live with Drojan. She made no excuses or apologies. She did not ask. She simply told Serine that she would return to perform her daily tasks, but her nights belonged to Drojan.

It did not surprise Serine that Ethyl was so open about her relationship with the seer, for Ethyl had never cared for the opinions of others. But Serine did give much thought to the changes in the older woman, who had taken her place as an intelligent woman acclaimed by the people of Corvus Croft, while in Sheffield she had been defamed as an old crone.

"What sort of love is this that you share with Drojan?" Damask asked as the women sat before the fire in the solar. "Is it some sort of magic spell that the seer has done to rejuvenate you?" Damask leaned forward as she asked the questions.

Ethyl fought to keep the smile from her face. Either of these women was young enough to be her daughter, yet the love she knew was as fresh and exciting as if she were their contemporary. "Love is love. There is little difference whether it comes with youth or with age," she said philosophically. "What you and Guthrie do to have a child, Drojan and I do for the enjoyment of each other." Ethyl said the words in such an offhand manner that it took a moment before their meaning reached either of the other women.

"You mean he still can..." Damask found herself unable to finish the sentence. Drojan looked to be as old as any man in the village with his white hair and balding pate. And while he was not hobbled by age, and seemed able to join the rest of the men in their activities, even Guthrie did not remember Drojan being involved with any woman.

Ethyl sighed and rested the wool she was carding on her lap. "There is little difference between a young man and one that has lived long enough to be considered old. I have known both and I can assure you that the quick, heated passion of youth is nothing when measured against the lasting embers of age. I have no doubt that you and Guthrie have delved, planted and found slumber before Drojan and I have more than begun our quest for fulfillment, but then you have your whole lives ahead of you and must hurry to meet your destiny, while Drojan and I have nothing but time to give and take the pleasures saved up throughout a lifetime."

Her words would have silenced a lesser woman, but Damask was nothing if not inquisitive, and having gone so far, was determined to have her answer. "I had not thought a man of such age could pleasure a woman," she said.

"It is the younger man who often has no idea of pleasure. His forte is passion, and release. I, too, believed as you when I was young, but I, too, was wrong."

"In what way?" Serine voiced a question for the first time. Desiring a word of hope that there could still be something to look to between herself and Rory after Hendrick was grown.

"The driving force of young love is no longer prevalent. Sometimes nearness is enough. To reach out in the silence of the night and feel his hand close over mine gives me as much joy as ever I knew in the impromptu couplings of my youthful marriage." Ethyl looked into the fire and fought the tears that threatened to stain her cheek. "It is late." She rose abruptly. "I must go. Our supply of herbs is sadly depleted. I will go out and see what I can find. I'll see you when I return."

Without further ado, Ethyl took up her cloak and walked out the door.

Damask glanced at the windows. "Surely it cannot be all that late," she ventured. "The sun is still high in the sky. There is still much to be done."

"She needed to be with Drojan for this little while," Serine said quietly, "and I cannot tell her nay."

"Think you Guthrie will still love me when I am old?" Damask sat up straight and smoothed her tunic over her finely molded body.

"I pray that every woman might know a love like the love shared by Drojan and Ethyl."

But Serine's words did not comfort Damask. She slumped in her chair. "Surely Guthrie will not love me if I do not give him a child."

"Are you still giving him the brew?" Serine inquired.

"Of course I am. We both take the vile concoction, but summer is all but upon us and still nothing. Oh, Serine, how much longer must we wait?"

"We will wait until the brew can cleanse the body of the evil that keeps you from having a child. It will come in time, just as love has come to Ethyl."

"But surely the brew cannot ask credit for the love between Ethyl and Drojan," Damask said coyly.

"Who are we to say that it is not in some way responsible? Had Rory not taken the brew it is unlikely Ethyl and Drojan would have met." Serine's eyes sparkled as she saw Damask's mood lift.

"Perhaps I will give it more time," she said. "And I, like Ethyl, think it is time I returned to my husband."

The women bade one another farewell, but Serine returned to her seat by the fire and rethought all she had learned that day. For she knew that as long as she lived she would never be happy unless she could be with Rory, and she was willing to wait until his hair was white and his skin leathery with age, if only she could spend the remainder of her life in his arms.

Did Rory, she wondered, feel the same about her? Or when he aged would he prefer a younger, more beautiful woman?

As if in answer to her question, Gerta's laughter floated up into the room, accompanied by the deep tones of Rory's voice complimenting the girl on her child.

Gerta had cleverly managed to keep from accepting the proposals of the village men. From the steward to the lowliest plowboy, she continued to stall when they asked for her hand.

Serine knew she must leave Corvus Croft soon and Gerta must be well married or return to Sheffield with her, for Serine would not allow Gerta to stay, alone, with Rory. Serine might give Rory up, but she'd be damned if she would allow another woman to take him away from her. She would speak to Gerta to see if she had a preference, and the sooner the better.

Chapter Fourteen

The day dawned to the sound of drums and horns. The men rushed to the castle.

Once again ships had been sighted off the coast. Rory would meet them on the sea, and Guthrie would take his men and guard the shore.

"Do not fear," Rory told Serine as he changed his clothing. "We will drive them back, and chase them from our shores. Ethyl will protect you."

"Ethyl is not here," Serine said quietly. She didn't want him to go. She couldn't bear to think of him risking his life again. What if something happened and he did not return to her? What if he never knew that his line would endure through the fragile life that even now grew within her belly?

"Ethyl has gone? Where?" Rory paused. He had counted on Ethyl being there to take care of Serine. Ethyl seemed formidable, and even though Serine might have the spirit of a Valkyrie, she was soft and beautiful.

"She has gone out to search for herbs. Our supply is all but spent and there seemed no reason why she should not go." Serine did not want Rory to be angry with Ethyl.

"That would explain Drojan's absence at the council meeting." Rory slammed his fist against the bench. "He has gone off with her. Together they are skipping through the forest like a pair of wood sprites while our village is left unguarded."

"Surely they could not have known," Serine protested.

"Drojan has the power to know, when his mind is not muddled by a woman. He should have read the Runes. He could not have missed what was right before his eyes." Rory swung his leather cloak about his shoulders.

Serine's eyes were filled with tears. "Men don't always see what is before their eyes. They rush out to follow their hearts and their eyes see nothing."

"What do you mean?" His fingers paused in fastening the clip.

"What do you see when you look at me?"

"I see the woman I love. A woman who insists on spurning all that I stand for and wishes only to return to the musty castle of her childhood."

"And, in your eyes, has that woman not changed during the time you have known her?" Serine searched his face.

His eyes ran over her body. "Changed? I think not. Except you have waxed plumper, somewhat. When first I saw you I beheld a graceful sylph, but now your body is lush and even more enticing. If you do not stop tempting me with your questions I, like Drojan, will forget my duty and take you back to bed."

"There is no need," she replied vaguely.

"Between you and me there is always a need." Rory's eyes burned bright and he stepped toward her. Surely the enemy was not so close that he might not love Serine once more before he left.

"There is no need because the deed is done." She saw the confusion in his expression. "That which you hope to achieve by making love to me has become reality."

Still he did not take her meaning. "I make love to you because I love you and, for all our differences, believe you love me in return."

"And there is nothing more you want from me, save my love?" She turned, wrapping her arms against her middle. Holding the linen gown so that it outlined her body.

In that instant Rory realized the extent of physical changes that had taken place. Serine's breasts were full and lush, and her belly, so flat and firm when first they met, was now rounded with the promise of...

"A child!" He stepped before her, arms outstretched, but could not make contact. "Our child! Yours and mine!"

Still he dared not move, as the fear he had fought for most of his adult life all but overwhelmed him.

Serine carried his child. A miracle in itself. But Serine wanted to leave Corvus Croft. To leave Corvus Croft, and Rory McLir.

Surely the fates could not be so cruel that twice in one lifetime they would rob him of both wife and child.

All thought, all words of love froze in his heart and he could only express his deepest desire as he dropped to his knees and wrapped his arms about her hips while he buried his face against her stomach. "Promise," he gasped through tears of utter desperation, "promise you will not leave me."

Her hands tangled in his hair as she pressed his head close against the new life that grew within. "Oh, Rory,

I love you so much." She felt the tears drop from her eyes onto his raven hair, like diamonds in the night. "I will not leave you now."

And it was not until Rory was well out to sea that he realized Serine had mentioned only the present, and left the future to the gods.

Serine's heart was filled with happiness as she wended her way down the stairs. She had planned to go to the room where she stored her herbs, but paused when she noticed Gerta and her babe near the kitchen hearth, and went to join the girl.

"It was a long winter, was it not?" she asked as she teased the baby with a piece of wool.

"It was indeed," Gerta agreed.

"But now that summer is all but upon us it is fair time that you should have a father for your little son, and a husband for yourself." She smiled as she spoke, but Gerta did not return the gesture.

"I have not found a man who pleases me," Gerta objected.

"When did you become so difficult to please?" Serine watched the girl closely, aware of her discomfort. "I do not recall you being overly particular at Sheffield."

"I doubt that you recall me at all when we were at Sheffield," Gerta said sourly. "I was the milkmaid and you the lady. Why would you notice me?"

"Because you were part of Sheffield and it is my business to see to your welfare. How do you think you came into possession of the hut in which you lived? Had it not been for my intervention, you would have been homeless when your mother turned you out, heavy with child."

"The hut was mine by right," Gerta declared. "I was May Queen at Beltaine a year past, and my son is the issue of the mating of the maiden with Stag Lord. It is because of my fertility that Sheffield proved prosperous over the past years."

Serine did not bother to hide her dismay at the girl's admission. The Beltaine ceremony was an ancient one and took place on May Eve. One of the village lads ran with the deer and killed the stag. After this fete he would return, triumphant, to his village and, during the ensuing celebration, would mate with the maiden, the chosen May Queen. If this mating proved productive, it was believed the land would be fertile and the harvest bountiful.

"Gerta, you know the ancient rites are forbidden at Sheffield."

"And you know that they are observed," Gerta countered. "I have a right to be particular. I must give thought to the future of my son."

"And the best possible situation for the child is to give him a father of whom he can be proud. Or would you rather return to Sheffield and resume your life there?"

"The Celts will never allow my child to leave Corvus Croft," Gerta scoffed, "as we both know."

"When the women begin to bear children there will no longer be any reason for you to remain here. Unless you are a woman wed and carrying your weight in the community, you will be free to leave."

"By the time these women bear children I will be more ancient than Old Ethyl and it will no longer matter where I live."

"The men are allowed but one wife each. If you will not wed, where do you plan to live?" Serine felt a tightness in her chest as she realized she already knew the answer to her question.

"I plan to remain right here," Gerta said boldly. "Perhaps your luck will change and it will be you who returns to Sheffield."

"Whether I return to Sheffield or not, I will see you well married before I go. Several of the men have spoken for you. Since you have no preference, I will make the choice myself, and don't jerk your chin at me," Serine scolded, "for you'll not go to Rory with your complaints. He has gone to defend Corvus Croft from invaders and when he returns he will be pleased to learn of your betrothal."

Gerta pulled her mouth into a tight line. "We'll see about that," she mumbled as she scooped up her baby and hurried from the room.

Serine sighed and stared after her. There was no doubt in her mind that Gerta had set her heart on Rory, and would not willingly give him up.

When he returned, Serine would ask him to reinforce her declaration and explain to the girl why her aspirations to become Rory's wife, or leman, were impossible.

Serine remembered how Rory had embraced her, and the expression on his face when he had begged her not to leave him. And the tug on her heart as she had admitted to herself that, despite her love for Sheffield, she could not abandon the man she loved even more. Somehow she must find a way to secure her son's inheritance and still keep close the man she loved.

The sea lay before them, lost in a thick gray mist that wove a pattern of light and shadows across the gleaming surface of the water.

"We cannot hope to find the enemy in this gruel," Guthrie complained. "They will land and be upon the village while we search the shore."

Rory studied the patterns of the fog as it parted and closed like a living thing, thwarting their every plan to keep the invaders from attacking their village.

It was as though the hand of the fog had closed around Rory's heart. Somehow he must find a way to keep these men from Corvus Croft and Serine.

They will not have her. They will not take her from him, he vowed in silent desperation.

"We will split the men into small patrols to guard the coastline and hope we are lucky enough to discover where the invaders land and stop them before they are able to regroup," Guthrie declared.

"Wait." Rory placed his hand on his brother's arm. "I think I see a way to force the marauders into our hands."

The hope in Rory's eyes was transmitted to Guthrie as Rory explained his plan. "The fog is our friend," Rory explained. "We will sail out and around the enemy and push his ships toward the rocky shore. When they realize they are too close to turn back, they will be forced to find a place to land, and since there are but two, and those only a short distance apart, you will be there waiting. The enemy will be trapped between us and forced to surrender."

"And what if the fog is not our friend?" Guthrie asked. "What if it dissolves, leaving us exposed?"

"Then we will no longer need guess their location." He slapped his brother on the shoulder, knowing his plan had been accepted.

Through the fog they skimmed, slowly herding the enemy ships like errant sheep. The voices floated eerily through the mist as the men veered too near the rocks and called down curses on one another for poor seamanship. The landing took place where Rory had said it would, and Guthrie's men neatly captured the would-be invaders as they came ashore.

Rory heard the cries of distress from his enemy mingled with the shouts of triumph from his allies and his heart swelled with relief. Corvus Croft was no longer in danger. Serine was safe. In a few hours Rory would hold her in his arms again and know that no danger would befall her. And it was well and good, but it was not enough.

Twice in the short time since Serine had come she had been endangered by invaders. The first time Rory had been gone and she had been forced to fight them herself. Only a stroke of luck had sent him back from the hunt in time to save her.

Fate dared not be tempted too far. Sooner or later the men would be tardy in protecting their women and their homes, and all would be taken from them.

And, even as the fog parted before him, Rory saw what he must do in order to protect Serine from a fate far worse than that which she had already endured. The men of Corvus Croft had invaded Sheffield out of desperate need to repopulate their village. They did not plunder, rape or kill. It behooved them to deal as gently as possible with the families of the children they appropriated so the youngsters would think kindly of their captors and learn to live in Corvus Croft without fear or hatred.

But the men who were intent on invading Corvus Croft came for slaves and plunder. What they did not steal they would kill after all usefulness had been destroyed.

Rory slammed his fists against the rail of his ship. He must put a stop to this senseless cycle.

Once before, with the help of the women, they had driven the marauders back into the sea, but each one they had driven out now returned tenfold. And, as long as conditions remained the same, they would continue to return, for it was the way of war and survival. It was up to Rory to stop them. To stop the enemy and keep Serine as safe in his home as she was in his arms. If she realized that only he could keep her safe, perhaps she would put aside her insistence on leaving him. For while Rory could defeat the enemy, he found the spirit of Serine of Sheffield undefeatable and for that spirit he loved her all the more.

With his plan in mind and the vision of Serine in his heart, Rory brought his ship to anchor and went to find his brother.

"Kill them!" Guthrie gestured his sword toward the prisoners that were being dragged from the water.

"That is senseless," Rory admonished, placing himself between his men and the invaders.

"Senseless?" Guthrie found it impossible to believe his ears. "Senseless? Rory, it is the way of the victor. For what purpose should they be allowed to live?"

"To remind others that we are a force to be reckoned with and that if they will pay homage to us and become our liege men, we will allow them to live and return to their homes, free men."

"You've gone soft in the head," Guthrie chided. "Such a plan would surely be our demise."

"Such a plan would be our victory," Rory proclaimed. "Do you want to live in fear, wondering each time we must leave our village if we are to be invaded by such as these? Or would it be better if they were to pledge themselves to us and never dare invade our shores again?"

"They would lie to save themselves," Guthrie declared.

"And to attack their sworn liege lords would be to defame themselves. They would be outcasts and unworthy of alliance. To prove themselves untrustworthy would be to open themselves to attack and invasion by any and all without recourse."

Guthrie stroked his beard. "What you say holds merit, but how can we be certain they will not say we lie when we say they have pledged themselves to us?"

"We will call in the headmen from the rest of the villages along the coast. They will stand with us and witness the truth of our treaty," Rory told him.

"It could be done," Guthrie admitted as the guards forced the enemy to their knees. He held up his hand and stepped forward. "Hold your swords," he called out. "We will first speak with our invaders."

Side by side Guthrie and Rory walked toward the condemned men.

"I think your herb woman has made you soft," Guthrie grumbled. "We should kill them and be done with it."

"My woman has made me clever," Rory growled back. "If we kill them, their children and their children's children will come after us until we are no more. I look to the future. To kill these men, here and now, but protects the present. Look to tomorrow and you will see that I am right."

"We will call a council of all the tribes who inhabit these shores. If they concur and the invaders agree, they shall swear themselves to us and we will allow them to go from our shores, but if they object to your plan, they will die." Guthrie's long stride took him toward the prisoners.

The prisoners were rough men, golden of skin and hair. Their clothing was coarse and worn and they came from the sea. Except for their coloring, Rory knew that they looked much as his own men had looked when they had landed on the shores of England and made their way toward the peaceful village of Sheffield.

He could imagine the terror that would appear on the faces of the women should these marauders reach them. He could imagine the screams, and the pleas, for he still heard them in his dreams. And he could imagine Serine being torn from yet another child...his child...and he could not allow that to happen. Somehow he must outsmart not only the invaders but his own brother, as well. Somehow Rory must find a way to safeguard his woman and his children, if not through brute force and death, then through fear of deserved retribution brought about by the code by which they all lived.

Somehow he must beat these men at their own game, for he knew how easy it was to conquer, and how hollow the victory. As long as there was a breath left in his body, or a thought in his mind, Rory would never allow Serine to be threatened or hurt again.

"Be at peace, brother," he said. "I know what I am about."

"I would be more at peace if Drojan were here." Guthrie glanced over the landscape as though he could conjure up the man from sheer willpower.

"But Drojan is not here," Rory reminded him, "and if he were, he would support my plan. How many times have we ignored his pleas for temperance?"

"And why should we not ignore such ideas now?" Guthrie asked. "Do we change our ways simply because you decide it is the thing to do?"

"We change our ways because for the first time in many years we have something more to protect than ourselves. Our land will live and prosper and I intend to see that every person living there has the opportunity to do so. Would you see these men come back and take Damask from you?"

"They could not take her if they were dead!" Guthrie noted.

"But their sons and brothers could. If a treaty is signed and an oath taken, all will be pledged to live under its rules." Rory came to a halt and glared at his brother.

Seeing the determination in his brother's eyes, and hearing the truth of his words, Guthrie gave in. "So be it," he said. "But, by the gods, you had better hope you are right, for if you are wrong, brother or no, you are a dead man, for it is no secret that, even now, the men are against you. They conquer to kill the enemy, and you will take the euphoria of victory from them. They will not take kindly to my order, or to your plan."

"Whether they take kindly to it or not, they will obey, for they are our liege men, and once our enemies have given their oath to support rather than fight us, our people will learn acceptance." Rory tried to put into his voice assurance that he did not feel.

Once more Guthrie stopped as the last of the prisoners were brought ashore. "What if they refuse our offer?" he asked.

"Then we have no choice but to kill them," Rory said despondently. "To kill them and to wait until their kin learn of what we have done and come in even larger numbers to destroy us and those we love.''

Rory's words brought up the image of Damask being carried away by one of these fair-haired warlords from across the sea while Guthrie lay dead. He felt the sweat of fear slicken his hand as it rested on his sword.

"Tell the prisoners our demands," he ordered, "and if they agree, send runners to the heads of all the nearby clans. We want as many witnesses as possible if this is to work. And, for the love of Woden, will someone find Drojan!"

"Think you Drojan can give you better direction than I?" Rory asked cryptically.

"If Drojan is wrong we can blame the gods, the Runes or the elements, but if you are wrong, little brother, the blame will fall on you and, more than that, on myself for being fool enough to let you take me into your wild scheme. Now ferret out the leader of this group and tell him of our demands before I lose the last remnants of my temper and regain my common sense and kill him myself."

The air was fraught with anticipation as news filtered back to the village.

Tim, the weaver's adopted son, was by far the swiftest of foot and ran back and forth between the battle and the village with the news.

"And Rory McLir went far out into the sea and came up behind the invaders, moving them toward the shore where Guthrie sent fiery boulders from the catapults. The enemy ships were broken and their men captured."

"Then it is over." Serine rejoiced. "When will our men return? How soon will they arrive?"

"We will have a great celebration, with food and winter ale for all," Damask added. "I will give the orders to butcher the cattle and sheep, and..." Her face paled and she steadied herself, grasping Serine's hand. "It is not something I enjoy," she apologized, "but we must honor those who have defended us so bravely."

"Come." Serine took her friend's arm. "I will help you." She turned again to Tim. "Go and see when they return while we make ready their welcome."

The two women went toward the kitchens while the boy ran back toward the coast. It was well after dark when he returned, and the excitement on his face had been replaced by weariness. He went directly to the manor and Serine, for she had been his lady in Sheffield and old habits die hard.

"Most of the men are on their way," he told her, "but your lord will not come, nor will his brother."

Serine jumped to her feet. "He is hurt," she gasped.

"No, no, Lady, it is not the case. The overlords have chosen to remain behind to negotiate a treaty with the marauders. 'Tis Corvus Croft that holds the advantage and must make clear to those who would invade our land that their antics will not be tolerated."

"Did they not kill them and send their bodies back to their homeland?" Gerta came forth to ask.

"Rory chose to negotiate a lasting peace, rather than to continue the killing. We have the upper hand and therefore the ability to name our own terms." There was pride in Tim's voice as he spoke of his new home, a pride echoed in Serine's heart. But even Serine did not guess what those negotiations would cost.

Chapter Fifteen

The birds called and fluttered from branch to branch. Drojan walked well ahead, while Ethyl moved from the forest path to inspect the new growth that might prove useful in Serine's medications.

The rays of the sun cut a slanted line through the trees and Ethyl glared indignantly at its plane.

"Seer!" she called. "We have come too far. It will be dark soon. We cannot make the village before nightfall."

Drojan stopped and waited for her to reach him. "On the contrary, woman. We have not gone far enough. There is a place I would have you see before we return."

With one last skeptical look at the sun, Ethyl fell into step beside him. "This place you speak of had best have a warm fire and plentiful food, for there is a chill in the air and my stomach is empty."

"The fire is no problem," Drojan told her. "As to the food, we have bread and cheese. Should you want meat I suggest you shoot your dinner and I will prepare it for you."

Ethyl allowed satisfaction to illuminate her face. Her sharp eye searched the shadows as she nocked her arrow. One shaft flew, and then another. In the next moment Ethyl returned with two small birds skewered on her arrows.

"Think you this will be enough?" she asked.

"More than enough," Drojan replied, "for it is not only meat and wine for which I hunger."

Their eyes met and held until he offered his hand and escorted her through the trees. The path veered to the left, but Drojan guided her through a dense thicket of rock and brush opening into a secluded glen.

A thin shaft of water fell gently from the cliff high above. The grass was lush and thick, like green velvet against the azure water. Rocks of coral jutted upward enclosing them within their rosy warmth, and above, those same rocks parted to disclose the darkening sky.

The birds slipped in and out of the trees, curious at the appearance of their guests.

Ethyl looked with wonder as the last rays of the sun turned the stone to golden rose that deepened as though lighted from within. "I am glad that I was allowed one eye with which to see this beauty," she said breathlessly.

"And I am glad to be able to share the beauty of this place with you." Drojan slipped his arm about her and held her close, absorbing her warmth with the beauty of the moment.

Before the night's chill could reach them, Drojan lighted a fire and cleaned and skinned the grouse Ethyl gave him.

He spread the bread and cheese on a flattened rock and brought forth a skin of wine.

Ethyl fidgeted restlessly. "It is I who should prepare our repast for you," she insisted, but he stopped her protest with a light kiss.

"No, Ethyl, tonight you will relax and watch while I do for you. It is the way I wish it."

And she relaxed under his gentle persuasion. His attention pleased her and she was glad she had decided to discard the black patch she had worn over her blind eye for so long and replace it with a patch of neutral color covered with silk. She removed the leather jerkin she wore and allowed herself the comfort of the loose tunic, for with the fire holding the warmth of the sun-heated rocks, their bower was fair comfortable.

She pulled her hair from the tight laces and allowed one side to fall over her face. In the rosy light her skin took on the warmth of youth, as did his, and in the flickering firelight they could not see the imperfections of age.

The meal was finished, the wine gone and the problems of the day behind them as they settled back on the velvet rug of grasses.

"And how did you conjure this place into being, Seer?" Ethyl asked. "It is so lovely I cannot believe it is not a magic place that will disappear with the dawn of a new day."

"I found this glade long ago, and have often come here to reflect on life and to renew myself. I have never brought another person with me, nor have I seen one here," he told her. "You are the first, and the last, with whom I will share this beauty."

"And for that I thank you, with all my heart." Ethyl wondered at the happiness they shared here. The peace of mind and soul she had never before experienced. "I would I had something of equal value to offer in return."

"Your love is of far greater value to me," Drojan told her. "It is a miracle of the gods that I never hoped to know. There is nothing, not even my reputation as a seer, that I would trade for what we have found together."

"Nor I," Ethyl admitted, "but I had little before we met, and now I have everything. I only wish, sometimes, that we could have found this love in our youth and experienced its joys throughout these many years."

"Had we found our love in our youth we would have squandered it, as youth squanders all riches. It is only now that we can truly appreciate what we have and glory in that which we find together." He lifted her hand to his lips.

He believed as did she, and his words were but the echo of her thoughts. Together they would hold fast to the time they had left to spend together and find happiness in each other's arms.

Their sighs joined the serenade of the falling water in a symphony of the senses as they moved through discovery toward passion and finally fulfillment of the soul as well as the body. And as the rosy glow of the rocks dimmed to a dusky glimmer, they slept and dreamed not of youth but of the promise of spending the rest of their years together.

Dawn struggled through the clouds. A heavy mist covered the land. Drojan and Ethyl broke their fast on bread and cheese and bathed in the spring at the foot of the waterfall as they had each day of the time they had spent in their hidden glade of happiness.

"Must we go?" Ethyl turned to him as she readjusted her eye patch. "Can we not stay a while longer?"

Drojan put the last of the cheese into his pack and scattered the crusts of bread to the fowl. "We will come

again," he promised, "but it is time we returned. I
awakened with an unsettling feeling I cannot explain."

"Should you read the Runes?" Ethyl asked.

But Drojan had already started toward the entrance
of the grotto. "There is no time. We must go back, and
swiftly."

Ethyl did not argue. She picked up her bow and
quiver of arrows and followed him into the woods.

They were less than half a day's walk from the village when they came upon Tim.

"Praise God!" the boy exclaimed. "I thought I
would never find you, and my lady would be lost for
certain."

"Lady? Lady Serine? What are you saying?" Ethyl
demanded. "What has befallen her?"

"The breath of the harpies has fallen upon our village since you have been gone," the boy said breathlessly. "First, ships were seen off our coast. Guthrie and
Rory took the men and went out to meet the enemy."

"And...?" Drojan urged the breathless boy to speak.

"The invader was soundly beaten and brought to
shore to be executed, but my lord Rory had a change of
heart. Instead of killing, he chose to negotiate a treaty
wherein the men would pledge themselves to Guthrie
and swear never again to invade our land or threaten
those who live therein."

"A fine plan and one I have often advocated," Drojan said. "It seems they did not need a seer to follow the
correct path."

"Not so." The boy swallowed and regained his
breath. "The treaty is taking a great deal longer than
expected. Rory and Guthrie have stayed with their prisoners, but the majority of our men returned to the village only to find everyone in the throes of violent

illness. They blame Lady Serine, saying she has poisoned them with her brew."

Ethyl's brow furrowed with concern. "I must go to her."

Drojan drew her away from the boy, where they could speak more privately. "If you go this way they will associate you with Serine and accuse you, too. Wait until I can go into the village alone and assess the humor of the people."

But Ethyl was not to be waylaid. "You do not understand," she told him. "I warned her that this could happen when first the brew was mentioned. She insisted on taking the chance."

"Did she so greatly wish to return to Sheffield, then?" he asked.

"Sheffield?" Ethyl exclaimed in frustration that she was not understood. "It was at Sheffield that Serine insisted she be allowed to make the brew to save Rory McLir's life. Had she let him die, none would have been the wiser." Ethyl shook her head and pulled away from her lover. "If Rory loved her as she does him he would be there at her side."

"Rory does not know his lady is in danger," interrupted the boy, who had followed them. "Even now he wrests with the council and the headmen of the other clans. He would come if he knew of the danger, but I was told to come after you, and have done so, leaving Rory to complete his mission."

"Tell us all you know." Ethyl urged the boy along as they hurried down the dirt road.

"The battle was—"

"To the devil with the battle," Ethyl exploded with impatience. "Tell me what you know of the sickness that has struck the village. Everything! And quickly."

Subdued at not being allowed to expound on the merits of the battle, the boy recited what little he knew about the sickness that had struck the village and could not be quelled.

The men were gathering in little clumps, their faces drawn with worry, as Drojan and Ethyl moved swiftly through the streets. When they neared McLir Manor they went their separate ways.

Ethyl slipped through the gate near the kitchen garden, while Drojan walked boldly to the great door and demanded admittance.

Serine greeted them with pleasure, oblivious to the danger that waited outside.

"What news?" Ethyl asked as Serine came toward her, hands extended in greeting.

"I have done it," she exulted. "I found the courage just before the men went off to face the invader."

"Speak, woman," Drojan ordered. "What is it you have done?"

"Why, I told Rory that I was with child." She looked from one face to the other. "And promised I would not leave him until we could try to find a solution to our dilemma."

"A promise you must now break," Ethyl told her.

"Surely not, Ethyl," Serine protested. "It is you who have urged me not to be so anxious to leave the man I love. Now that I have come to grips with myself, you change your perspective and suggest that I go back on my word. I do not understand you. I thought that when you returned from your time with Drojan you would be gentler and less quarrelsome."

"It is not Ethyl who is looking for a quarrel," Drojan told her, "but the men of Corvus Croft. From what we can learn there is sickness in the village and they blame it on you.''

"What do you mean?" Serine hurried toward the window of the solar and looked across the farmland toward the castle. From her position she could see the villagers forming into groups, their arms gesturing toward McLir Manor, their voices raised in anger and fear. "What has happened?" She looked from one face to the other. "Who is ill and why was I not told? I could have—"

"You have done enough, Lady." Gerta's voice came from the open doorway. "It is because of you and your bitter herbs that half the village is near death. 'Tis worse than the plague and the people will be satisfied with nothing less than your death."

"That cannot be." Serine looked around in confusion. "I have given them nothing that would make them ill. Surely there must be some mistake."

"The mistake was that they believed you would help them when all you wanted was to leave and take your son with you." Gerta warmed to her theme. She knew that Serine had not felt well herself and had allowed things to slide as she waited for news of Rory.

"Gerta, you know I have not meant to harm the people. Do you not stand on my behalf?" Serine asked as she saw the hatred on the girl's face.

"You care nothing for anyone but yourself, your son and your precious Sheffield." Gerta fired the words at her former mistress. "You care nothing for me or for my welfare and would have wed me to a man twice my age."

"The man is the steward of McLir Manor," Serine noted. "Yours would have been a place of honor and respect. No milkmaid could hope to improve her lot to such an extent in other circumstances.''

But Gerta hoped for far more than that. And with Serine gone she knew her hopes could become reality. For it was not the elderly, strait-laced steward she wanted in her bed, but the virile, handsome Rory McLir himself, and Serine had played into Gerta's hands.

''My lot is no longer your concern,'' Gerta told her. ''If you are wise you will take your son, your one-eyed harpy and her paramour and flee for your lives, for if the illness rages through the night those able to walk will come for you with the dawn and it will be your life that is at stake.''

''But I know nothing of their sickness.'' Serine fought to keep the desperation from her voice as they watched the girl flounce out of the room. ''How can they place the blame on me?''

Ethyl went to Serine and took her arm. ''They blame you because if they did not they would be forced to blame themselves. It does no good to quibble. They will not listen to reason, and I will not stay here and watch you burn.'' She turned to Drojan. ''Does your skiff still nestle in the small harbor?''

''It does, and both the boat and myself are at your service.''

''You would come with us?'' Ethyl searched his face.

''I told you I intend to spend the rest of my life with you. I cannot do so if you are in Sheffield and I am here. We will take Serine and Hendrick back to their home and return here when I deem it safe.''

''If you leave these people in their hour of need, it may never be safe again,'' Ethyl reminded him. Her thoughts reflected the memory of the magical hours they had spent in the grotto. He could see the sadness she felt at the possibility that they would never be free to go there again.

"Woden's woman, I know what you are thinking and share in your moment of sorrow, but this sorrow is for a moment only. We will know many days of happiness as long as we can be together. Why do you cry?"

Ethyl swallowed the lump that came to her throat and fought back the remainder of her tears. "Seer, unless you are as blind as my useless eye you must see that I do not wish to be known as Woden's woman. I want only to be Drojan's woman, in what is left of this life, and the next."

His hand closed over hers. "So be it," he whispered. "Now go and tell the Lady Serine of our plans... Drojan's Woman."

The joy in her face rendered her ageless.

Yes, she and Drojan would know great happiness together, but there would be no such happiness for Serine, as she would leave behind the man she loved. The man who loved her in return.

She straightened her back and brought her head up, turning to face Serine. "Rejoice," Ethyl said, "for your prayers have been answered. You and Hendrick will be returned to Sheffield and no one the wiser until it is too late."

Serine wrung her hands. She could see Rory's face as it had looked when he had begged her not to leave him. "But I do not wish to leave now," she protested.

"Then you should have been more careful in what you asked for," Drojan said cryptically, "for the gods grant only what they hear. Now, get your things together, and Hendrick's, as well. We must be away with the tide."

Serine looked into their faces and saw the silent resolve. She had no choice. The village men would mill around the countryside until darkness fell and then, pray God, go to their homes. Even if the indisposition that afflicted them had subsided by morning, Serine and the bitter brew would be under suspicion. Without Rory to protect her, she was lost.

A sob escaped her lips. Without Rory she was lost, but she had just realized the depth of the loss. How different it was to be forced to leave the man she loved, rather than endeavoring to return to Sheffield of her own volition. Still, to stay was to invite disaster, not only for herself but for Ethyl, as well.

She would slip away in the dark of night as she had imagined so many times before. Now that the time had come, however, it was the last thing she wanted to do.

It seemed so unfair that after all the months of wanting to be away, now, more than anything in the world, Serine wanted to see Rory once more. With aching heart she choked back her tears and went to find her son.

There was a smile of satisfaction on the face of Rory McLir as he rode beside his brother toward home. They had gathered the leaders of all the nearby clans and forced the invaders to pledge fidelity with all as witness. It had taken longer than Rory had thought, but was well worth the time, for it had been a moment of great achievement. He had managed to secure the coastline and in so doing, Serine and his unborn child were protected.

As he thought of her, a tender smile touched his lips. How he looked forward to returning to Serine's arms. Arms that would now open to his embrace without hesitation. No longer must he wonder whether she gave of herself to gain his trust until she could take her son and escape. She had willingly told him of her condition and had given her word that she would stay. Together, after the birth of their child, they would find a way to secure Sheffield for Hendrick, since it was of such importance to Serine, for he could deny her nothing now that she had given him her love.

His thoughts were interrupted by his brother. Guthrie was still grumbling over the outcome of the invasion.

"It is not the way of the Celt to allow an enemy to go off without chastisement after they have invaded our shores," he complained.

"Has there not been enough bloodshed without initiating it needlessly?" Rory asked.

"It is not needless when it teaches a well-deserved lesson," Guthrie replied shortly. "Our enemies remember their defeats by their fallen comrades. They grudgingly give us their respect when they look to their ranks and count the missing faces. We had the opportunity to send naught but dead bodies back to their cursed shores. What more powerful statement could be sent?"

"The statement that our enemies had come and were humbled and defeated. The statement that they agreed to swear fealty and agree never again to invade our shores on pain of certain death. Dead men would not have the ability to make such a statement." Rory refused to allow his brother to spoil his triumph.

"Should they decide not to honor their pledge of fidelity we may all be dead men," Guthrie reminded him, "and we are no better off than we were the day they invaded."

"And no worse." Rory clapped his brother on the shoulder.

"Drojan would—"

"Drojan would agree with me. He has counseled temperance many times, as well you know."

Guthrie could not deny the truth of his brother's words. "What you say is true." He sighed. "Still, I have a feeling of unrest, as though something is not right."

"Are you planning on usurping Drojan's position as seer?" Rory teased.

"Perhaps we will be forced to rely more on our own instincts if Drojan continues to frisk about like an amorous sheep."

Rory laughed at his brother's analogy, but, in truth, it bothered him that the seer had not come to give his advice and encouragement on their enterprise toward peace. "The old man has found love," Rory said lightly. "Do not begrudge him happiness. He has known little enough in his lifetime."

"How say you that?" Guthrie challenged. "The man has a position of respect and is welcome at any table and in any village. He has power and no doubt considerable wealth. Why do you think he has not had a lifetime of happiness?"

"I only think how lonely I was before I found Serine. Even when my fevered mind feared that she would slay rather than save me, I could not help but look forward to the sound of her voice and the touch of her hand. I would hope Drojan has found that same happiness with Ethyl."

Guthrie bowed his head. "I had not thought of it in that way," he admitted, "and I hope you are correct, brother." Then his laughter rang through the air. "And

I wish to again experience the happiness of which you speak so eloquently. Let us ride.''

They put heels to their horses and all conversation ceased, but Rory found it difficult to put aside Guthrie's misgivings. It *was* strange that Drojan had not answered their call and come immediately to their side. Especially since the seer had so often championed exactly that which they had achieved.

But the feeling of accomplishment overpowered all else and Rory set aside any anxiety he might experience, attributing it to the excitement of the moment and his anticipation of telling Serine of his achievements.

The brothers reached home in the late afternoon. Few people were in the fields. Instead the villagers milled about the town clumped in small groups, their faces furrowed with frowns of worry and anger.

There were no cheers of welcome as Guthrie and Rory approached with their small entourage. As they neared the castle they slowed their horses to a walk. Several of the shops were closed, the craftsmen nowhere in sight. A group of men broke from a heated discussion, and one of the crusty old warriors led the way toward the brothers.

"What news?" Guthrie called out as the men marched purposefully toward them.

"It is good you are back." The leader halted in front of the horses, forcing them to stop.

"How so?" Guthrie fought to control his horse, who wanted nothing more than to reach his own shed and manger.

"There be more trouble here in the Croft than what you left behind, I vow," the man proclaimed, while the others grunted in agreement.

"What trouble?" This time it was Rory who asked, as the serpent of fear awoke and writhed in his stomach.

The man turned on the headman's brother. "The foreign witch has poisoned our women."

Chapter Sixteen

Rory stared at the old warrior in disbelief. His first instinct was to throttle the man, to make him retract his accusations against the woman he loved. But the hostility on the faces of the other men told him that the soldier was not alone.

Rory dismounted and stood eye-to-eye with Serine's accusers. "What has happened? Tell me, now!"

"We returned to find those left behind purging and puking, too ill to do more than lie abed. At first we thought it might be some tainted food or a piece of bad fish, but it has not lessened and even more are afflicted."

"You were gone and your Sheffield lady saw her chance to destroy us all out of revenge for taking the children from her village," another added.

"Where is Serine? What have you done to her?"

"She hides in McLir Manor and dares not show her face," the soldier boasted. "Go to your home, Rory McLir, and tell your foreign witch to give us the antidote or we will march on your house and force her to do so."

"You will stay away from both my house and my woman or you will answer to me." Rory jumped back

onto his horse. "Guthrie, are you with me?" Rory
asked his brother.

"I would not be so quick to go," the man told Guthrie, "for your own wife is sore taken and has scarce
gone from her bed since you left."

"See to Damask," Rory called. "I must go to Serine." And he urged his horse to a gallop, scattering the
groups of people like feathers in the wind.

The house yard seemed unearthly silent. This was not
the welcome he had anticipated throughout the long
days and longer nights since he had left. He tossed his
reins to the groom and went swiftly to the door.

This time it was the servants who scattered, disappearing into the nether regions of the house rather than
face their master.

"Serine! Serine, answer me! Where are you?" Rory
took the stairs two at a time and burst into the apartments they shared. Within moments he was on his way
back down the stairs. "Hendrick! Where are you, lad?
Answer me!"

There was a scuffling below the staircase, but by the
time Rory reached the area it was empty.

He paused in the center of the room. It was obvious
that something was amiss and the servants wanted no
part of telling him. "Wine!" he bellowed. "By the
gods, I will have wine and have it now, or I will put
every man, woman and child to the whip."

A serving girl was shoved into the room from the security of the kitchens. She stumbled forward clutching
a pitcher and goblet in her hands.

"Here, m'lord." She thrust the goblet at him and
sloshed wine into the cup. The pitcher thumped down

on the table and the girl would have been gone had Rory
not stopped her.

"Where is the Lady Serine?"

The girl crumpled to her knees. "I do not know," she
cried. "I swear I do not know."

There was a rustle of clothing and Rory looked up
expectantly, but it was Gerta who came toward him. A
Gerta he hardly recognized.

"I will serve my lord," she said, dismissing the unfortunate girl. Even in the dim light he noted the pow-
der caked on her face, covering her usual ruddy
complexion. The dress she wore belonged to Serine, and
although it was not uncommon for a lady to reward her
servants with remnants of her own clothing, this particular dress had been but lately obtained. It seemed out
of place that Serine would part with it so readily.

Gerta came to stand before Rory. Close, far too close
for a servant and a lord. His eyes moved over the girl's
attire and she preened herself. It was when she turned
that he heard the jingle of metal and realized she wore
the keys of the chatelaine.

"Where is Serine, and why do you wear her keys?"

"Lady Serine is gone." Gerta fingered the coveted
keys uncomfortably. "As for the keys, who else would
have them? No one is here to play the part of chatelaine."

Rory swallowed his anger. The girl had said the word
and given away the ruse, for to Gerta it was but play. A
village milkmaid playing the part of a great lady of the
manor, but the play was at an end. "Again, Gerta, I ask
you where the Lady Serine has gone and why she is not
here to greet me."

"She crept off in the night," the girl blubbered as he
grasped her wrist firmly. "And well that she did, for it

is only a matter of time before they come here looking
for her."

"Who are *they?*" he asked, but he already knew what
her answer would be.

"The villagers, of course." Gerta retrieved her wrist
and rubbed it gingerly. "'Tis common knowledge she
poisoned us all with her brew."

"Has anyone died from this malady?" Rory inquired.

"Not that I've heard, but it is only a matter of time.
The sick get no better as the days go on." The girl
leaned against him. "Why, I can hardly walk myself
and only your arrival brought me from my bed." She
gave him a meaningful look that said had he been willing to go to her bed she would never have left it.

"What of your child?"

"Jamie?" She looked around, assuring herself that
the child was nowhere in sight.

"Is *he* ill?" Rory demanded. "Who cares for him
while you are incapacitated?"

"Jamie is just fine. Serine would never harm a child.
But she has taken Hendrick and gone. You cannot want
her, my lord. She is most like too old for childbearing.
I can give you a number of fine, healthy sons and
daughters. Beyond that, I can care for your house and
warm your bed. You need not look for the Lady Serine
when you can have me."

Rory stared at the girl. He hardly heard her words. It
was Serine's words he remembered. He had left in the
hope of bringing about a better, safer life for Serine and
his people. Instead, his absence had taken from him the
thing he desired most in life. Serine and the child she
cradled within her body.

"You needn't hide your desire any longer," Gerta was saying as she twisted a thick plait of her maize-colored hair. "I know you have longed for me from afar and that gratitude to Serine for saving your life is the only reason you did not present your suit. I waited, though. I would not have any other man. Had Serine not been jealous, she might not have reached such dire straits that she had to resort to poison to be rid of me."

"And what makes you think Serine wanted to be rid of you?" Rory pulled himself from his reverie in time to grasp the girl's last words.

"Why, she threatened to force me to wed with the steward. I knew you would not wish it to be so." She batted her eyes as she had seen the ladies do when they passed her as she milked cows in the fields of Sheffield.

Gerta was hiding something, but Rory could not imagine what it might be. "Come." He grabbed her arm and propelled her along with him. "We will go to Guthrie. Perhaps he will be able to sort this out."

They had but reached the door when they were aware of deep voices raised in anger. The noise followed them from McLir Manor through the town. An odious sound that permeated the air and caused the heart to swell like the bloat of fear until they reached the castle, where Guthrie met them with an anxious expression on his face.

"Where is Serine?" he asked once he realized it was Gerta who accompanied his brother.

"According to Gerta, Serine has been driven away by the very people she sought to help."

Gerta bowed her head and tried to look penitent, but the joy of her success was too great for complete achievement.

"What have you discovered?" Rory asked his brother.

"Only that some of what is rumored may be true." Guthrie rubbed his head in frustration. "Damask is indeed ill. She was unable to do more than greet me and tell me not to fear."

Gerta realized that the men paid her no mind, and doubled up as though in pain. "I can go no farther. Pain grips my belly. I know the poison again does its work."

Because they stood just within the doors of the great hall, the crowd that had gathered in the bailey were able to observe Gerta's actions. Voices of anger rose and fell until a spokesman took his place before the crowd.

"Give us the foreign witch and we will make her tell the antidote." His cry was taken up by the others as they moved toward the brothers.

"There is another foreign woman here," a man called out, pointing an accusing finger at Gerta. "Perhaps she knows something."

Gerta cowered against the stairs leading to the solar, forgetting her supposed illness in her haste to put herself as far as possible from the angry mob.

Rory and Guthrie conferred for a moment before coming forward.

"Are there any new cases of this malady today?" Guthrie asked.

"My wife took ill this morning," one of the men volunteered.

"And no one shows any sign of recovery," another man complained.

"*You* all look to be in good health," Rory observed. He knew the bitter brew did nothing but good. Rory himself was living proof of the benefits. More than that,

Serine would never have sought to harm his people. They must look to another source for the cause of the illness.

"Liam!" Rory challenged. "How was this poison dispensed and by whom, and how do you know, since you admit you were not here?"

"It was your English lady," Liam said doggedly.

"When and how?" Guthrie reinforced his brother's question.

"When I was gone, and no doubt through that nasty brew the witch urged us to take. She promised children and has given us sickness and, most like, death."

Rory turned to Tavish, who leaned on his crutch near the edge of the crowd. The man had been injured several weeks before the invasion and had not been able to join the other men. "Are you ill, Tavish?" Rory asked.

"Except for my leg I feel fine," the man declared. "'Tis my wife who is sick. I came to find the Lady Serine and ask for something to ease her."

Serine was gone. The moment opportunity had presented itself, she had taken her son and returned to the land of her birth. And, try as he would, he could not find it in his heart to blame her, for he knew the demeanor of the mob and the fear they would send into the heart of a woman.

He should have given up his plan for a lasting peace, killed the invaders and returned home. Had he been here none of this would have been allowed to happen. He cursed himself and his misplaced loyalties. Once again he had lost his woman and child. Was he destined to live alone forever without wife and family?

His eyes swept the hall and he imagined it ringing with the laughter of children. Guthrie's children, but not his own. That hope had sailed across the sea with

Serine, and he knew there would never be another woman in his life or in his heart. Still, he felt he must defend her.

"I cannot believe that Serine did anything to cause you pain. You accuse her falsely and without proof. Until you can show me something other than your blind accusations, I will not believe you."

"If she is not guilty, then where is she?" Liam asked. "Why has she fled if she is innocent?"

"She has fled to save herself from your stupidity." Damask appeared in the open doorway, a shimmering flame against the darkness of the hall. As always, the men were silenced by the presence of her bright beauty.

It was the old soldier who first found his voice. "It is not stupidity to suspect treachery when we return from battle and find our women sick unto death. They are poisoned, I tell you, and the witch must be made to pay!"

"Your wives have taken to their beds not from poison, but from pregnancy," Damask told them. "I myself suffer from the same malady."

She looked up at Guthrie and saw the amazement and joy reflected in his face. Without a word he reached out and took her into his great arms, holding her as gently as if she were a crystal chalice of immeasurable value.

"Are you certain?" he managed to say.

"I am most certain, my lord husband." She took his face in her hands and lightly kissed his lips.

"If my woman is with child, why has she not told me?" one of the men demanded.

Damask reluctantly disengaged herself from her husband's arms. "It has been so long since there was a woman pregnant in this village I doubt anyone remembered the discomfort of the early months."

"What our lady says is true," another man declared. "My woman kept nothing in her stomach when our first child was conceived, but in the grief of his loss and the years of waiting for another I had put it out of my mind."

"I would believe you, but for one thing." Liam lumbered forward. "How can so many women become pregnant at the same time, and why are they not all with child if this be true?"

"Perhaps some of you men did not take the brew," Damask suggested. "It is your wives who have failed to conceive because you would not cooperate."

Several of the men looked at the ground, and Damask knew she had spoken true. "Go to your homes," she urged. "Ask your wives if what I say is not true. In a few months our village will ring with the laughter and cries of children and all will be right with the world."

She again turned to her husband. "This was not the way I wished to tell you, but I was not aware of the accusations of the villagers until I heard them shouting outside our walls. I could not allow them to speak ill of Serine." She turned now to Rory. "She must be terrified. Why did she not come to me?"

Rory could not meet Damask's eyes. He looked instead out over the darkening fields. "Drojan and Ethyl have taken Serine and returned to England." He took a deep breath and tried to steady his voice. "I wish you joy in your news. I hope you will bring forth a healthy child to grace your halls and fill your hearts and lives, but my house will remain silent. The laughter, the joy and the children will be yours."

He brushed past them toward the door but Gerta rushed forth and blocked his path.

"It need not be so, my lord," she gushed. "I would gladly share your home and bear your children. You know I am well able."

"You claimed you were ill," he reminded her. "How can that be when the other women are with child and you have no husband?" His eyes narrowed and perused her body. "Would you have me wed with you and make you mistress of McLir Manor and then pawn off another man's child on the pretense it is mine? Is that the pledge of honor you bring to your husband?"

"Oh, no!" Gerta declared, dropping to her knees in supplication. "My illness is nothing more than a slight indisposition. I have known no man other than the father of my son, Jamie."

Rory looked at her, long and hard. She squirmed under his eyes.

"Please believe me," she urged. "I am young and strong. I will be a good wife and mother and take great care of McLir Manor."

Still Rory did not speak.

"And I will be an honest and loyal wife. You will never have reason to complain." She hurried on, hoping to find the right ploy with which to win him. "Can you not believe me?"

"I do believe you, Gerta." Rory finally spoke. "And, in truth, you deserve the chance to become a good and loyal wife. Your son, Jamie, is a fine, healthy lad and one of which any man would be proud. Therefore, I will give you in wedlock to the steward, for I know he cares for both you and your child. As wife to my steward you will have the care of the house and keep it in good condition whether I am in residence or not."

"But I do not wish to wed the ste—"

Her words were cut off midsentence as the steward of McLir Manor himself came bearing down on them carrying little Jamie on his shoulder. "I could not help but overhear, and I will take her, my lord," he announced. "I will take her with a heart full of gladness, and I care not whether she be with child this day or no. For if it is so I will love the child as my own, and if not, she will be soon, I'll vow."

A cheer of laughter went up from the remaining crowd as the steward led his wife-to-be off toward the church.

"What will you do?" Guthrie asked as they watched the exuberant steward lead away the reluctant young woman who stood half a head taller than her proposed husband.

"I do not know," Rory told them. "I have not yet decided. In my heart I believe that Serine left to insure her own safety and that of our unborn child. The threat was too great. Drojan and Ethyl are with her, I know she will be safe, but I wish to God she had not gone."

"You heard the men," Guthrie said. "They might have killed her in their false belief that she had poisoned their women. Had Damask not come forth we would still be worrying the problem as to what had caused the outbreak."

"Go after her, Rory," Damask urged from the safety of her husband's arms. "Tell her it is safe to return. By the time you bring her back she will be a hero among our people. Do not let her break both your hearts because of a misunderstanding that was not of your making."

"And what do I tell her? That I was unable to guarantee her safety the moment she was out of my sight?" He pressed the heels of his hands to his eyes. "Do I admit that I was unable to control my own people? That I am such a poor leader and hold such a lack of respect that they would threaten those I hold most dear?''

"You fled Sheffield when Serine believed her overlord was coming to take you as his prisoner. There is but little difference from this situation to that. Serine would understand your dilemma,'' Damask assured him gently.

"Ah, but there is a difference,'' Rory told them. "Serine never left me. She placed her frail body between me and my enemies. But when she had need of me, I was not here.''

"You are a man. You cannot be expected to be here all the time.'' This time it was Guthrie who tried to reason with his brother. "Can you not see that perhaps it is best this way? The women are with child. Serine has won the right to ask to be returned to Sheffield and take her son with her. She has done so. And, as headman, I will not give the order to have her brought back. If you wish to go and talk to her you must do it on your own, and should you bring her back it must be of her own free will.''

Rory nodded his head. "It will be as you say,'' he murmured, and without looking back he started walking toward McLir Manor.

All around him voices called out in greeting. He could hear the cries and laughter of men and women to whom hope had been returned. The faces that met him were filled with happiness, and the tears that lined their cheeks, tears of joy.

"What a fool I was not to have remembered...'' a woman's voice chortled.

"Forgive me for worrying you so,'' another crooned as Rory passed the door of the cottage.

"I cannot believe this has come to pass," a man admitted.

"Believe it, and give me the slop jar," his wife answered.

How Rory would have loved to have been able to share these tidbits of information with Serine. How he would have loved to hold her in his arms and tell her that all was well and that his people revered her as did Rory himself.

How wonderful it would have been had he been able to tell her that they now knew what had caused the sickness in the women, and how they would have laughed together.

Surely Serine would not have gone from him. Surely she would have held to the promise she had given when she told him of the child she carried. Their child... hers... and his... the child he had waited for so long.

The servants were setting up the tables for the evening meal when Rory reached the manor. This time they greeted him with effusive warmth, welcoming him to his home and going out of their way to be of service.

"Do not fear, master." The cook came from the kitchens to assure him. "Drojan and Ethyl went with your lady. They'll not let her come to harm."

"I know," Rory told the old man. "I know." But knowing did not ease the pain and he could not eat the food they placed before him. Instead he drank but little of the wine and went to his room, where he fell into the bed that still carried her sweet, fresh scent, praying for sleep while bitter tears of hopelessness streamed down his cheeks.

Chapter Seventeen

After a seemingly endless time at sea, Serine approached Sheffield castle with dragging steps. Despite her weariness she was pleased to see the courtyard was neat and obviously well cared for.

Domestic servants rushed back and forth emptying basins and chamber pots, while others carried fresh rushes they had gathered to be placed on the floors. She could hear the sound of the smith working his forge and the steady slosh of water as the laundress pounded linens in a wooden trough containing the mixture of wood ashes and soda.

Before she reached the hall Serine was also aware that the cook was hard at work. The scent of onions and garlic, mixed with that of boiling meat and spices, permeated the air.

Serine's bedraggled appearance had kept the serfs from recognizing her, and since it was market day there were many strange persons in the village. Consequently, Serine's presence went unremarked.

It was only when Ethyl and Drojan reached the outskirts of the village, accompanied by Hendrick, that the serfs left their tasks and ran to see what was happening.

In their haste to reach Hendrick and his escort, they bypassed the bedraggled Serine without a second look. It wasn't until she came face-to-face with Dame Margot that she gained recognition.

Margot started through the door to the hall just as Serine mounted the stairs.

The woman came to an abrupt halt, almost overbalancing in the shock. "Serine!" she managed to gasp. "Is it truly you?" Her momentum took her down the stairs. "By all that's holy, Serine, we thought you dead. Lord Baneford was about to send an emissary to learn of your fate and that of Hendrick. How did you manage to gain your freedom?" She looked fearfully toward the outskirts of the village as though the invader might have followed.

"There is just myself, Hendrick, Ethyl and Drojan, the seer," Serine told her. "The others will be along soon. Their presence must have been discovered."

Margot smiled. "If so, they will have many questions to answer." Margot put her arm about Serine's shoulders and led her into the hall. "But even before you satisfy my curiosity you must have food and wine and a comfortable place to rest. Your room is ready and waiting. I never stopped hoping you would return."

Serine gave the woman a grateful smile. "You have cared for Sheffield admirably," she said. "It looks as though I had never been away." But a sudden quiver within her belly reminded Serine that she had, indeed, been away, and the fruits of her visit remained with her. "But what is this about Lord Baneford?" she asked as she sank into a chair. "I feared he planned to overtake Sheffield and place his own man as master."

Margot called for the servants and fussed over their tardiness, finally moving a stool herself so that Serine could place her feet upon it. "I thought the same, but it turned out to be the selfish hope of a dissatisfied knight. When you did not return I went personally to Baneford to beg his protection for Sheffield, that it be held for Hendrick."

"And did Baneford agree?" Serine asked, somewhat shocked at the turn of events.

"Not only did he agree, but he has promised to take Hendrick into his household to be tutored with his own children and subsequently serve as squire prior to receiving knighthood. He gave as reason the loyalty of the lords of Sheffield, including Elreath's service to the crown."

Margot was so obviously proud of herself that Serine found it impossible to tell the woman she did not want Hendrick going to any other household. She wished to teach him herself until she was forced to allow him to squire. But she was relieved that Sheffield would be held safe for her son, and that the devotion to the king's cause that had taken Elreath from his family and finally cost him his life would be properly rewarded. Elreath had been a good man and deserved as much.

"We will speak of this later," Serine said as the wine arrived.

"As you wish," Margot agreed, handing Serine a pewter goblet.

The sound of voices came closer, and although Serine recognized the cries of happy greetings, the very thought of the mob from which she had fled sent chills down her spine.

Suddenly Dame Margot's voice trilled through the vast hall. "And here is Hendrick and... Merciful God! Old Ethyl, is that you?"

A man, exuding dignity and wisdom, placed his hand on Ethyl's arm. "It is Ethyl, indeed, but she no longer carries the stigma of age."

"No, no, of course she doesn't," Margot managed to say. "I can see that now." She moved closer to the woman who had been her contemporary for so many years. "What have you done to yourself?" she whispered. "Have you discovered a fountain of youth that has changed you so?"

Ethyl glanced at Drojan before answering. "I am the same as I have always been," she said. "It is only that I have found love and am loved in return. I find it to be the most powerful of potions."

Margot looked from one to the other. "How sad that Serine could not have sipped from the same draft for I vow she looks the worse for wear."

Ethyl's unobtrusive movement silenced the other woman. Margot looked abashed at having been called for a faux pas she did not understand. In an effort to change the subject Margot asked, "And what of the handsome young man we fought so hard to heal? Did he not have the grace to escort you back home after you saved his life?"

This time Ethyl was hard put to keep from slapping her hand over Margot's mouth. She stepped forward just in time to hear Serine give a little cry and slide from the chair onto the rushes.

"What do you mean, they will take Hendrick from you and you will be left with nothing?" Ethyl paced back and forth across the solar. "You have accomplished much these past weeks since your return. You have Sheffield, and possession is assured you by the king himself. Besides, it is Hendrick's right to go and prepare himself for knighthood. Surely you would not make him go to his knightly vows ill prepared?''

"But he is so young," Serine protested. "He need not leave me for several more years."

"He is well beyond the age when most boys are given into the care of their sponsors, as well you know," Ethyl returned. "Had his father been here to see to the lad's welfare, Hendrick would have gone long ago. Now, cease your fussing or you'll upset your unborn child."

Serine crossed her arms against her breast and glared at the older woman.

"What is it?" Ethyl asked. "Your face is red with outrage."

"'Tis that sometimes I think I liked you best when you were still Old Ethyl and knew your place." Serine softened her words with a smile.

"When I was Old Ethyl I had no place and my words were given little heed. You resent them now because you know I speak the truth and it is not a truth you wish to hear."

"There is only one truth I wish to hear," Serine burst out as her eyes suddenly swam with tears.

"No! Do not ask." Ethyl shook her head. "I will not again entreat Drojan to read the Runes on your behalf. He has told you that he has no clue of Rory's whereabouts."

"But Drojan is a seer. It is his business to know," Serine noted.

"He can tell you only that Rory misses you and is as miserably unhappy as are you," Ethyl said with finality. "Now, ply your needle or your child will be forced to live in this world as naked as when he enters it." She picked up the tiny garment on which Serine had been stitching and thrust it into her hands.

Serine tossed it back at Ethyl. "Sew it yourself, for I cannot see to do it now." She rubbed at her eyes, pretending the redness came from working in the dim light rather than from the ever-present tears. "I wish—"

But this time Ethyl actually clapped her hand over the younger woman's mouth. "I have told you before. Be careful what you wish for. Learn to control your tongue, for you may find that you have been given that for which you asked."

Serine hung her head. "Why is it I am cursed to bear and raise children without the comfort and love of husband and father?" she asked, rebelling against that which seemed always to be her fate.

"Probably for the same reason that I was known for the better part of my life as *Old* Ethyl and seen as a creature of ridicule and fear." The words were blunt, but not bitter. "God does not give us more than we can bear, but there are times when certain people refuse to accept their trials," she said more gently. "Had I given in to despair and thrown my fate back into the face of the gods, I would never have lived to know Drojan and the love we have found."

"And I am happy for you, Ethyl." Serine tried to apologize, but her own misery was too great. "It is just that I gave up everything to bring my son back to Sheffield so that he could be raised on his own lands. Now Hendrick is to go into guardianship and it is the babe I carry who will be denied the right of growing up in his rightful environment."

"Do you wish to leave the management of Sheffield to Dame Margot and return to Corvus Croft?" Ethyl asked.

Serine's eyes reflected her anguish. "What awaits me there? A pyre and fire? The accusation of witchcraft?

Death to myself and my child? I think not! If Rory is to
see his child, he must come to me!" Again her voice
broke as she admitted, "And I cannot understand why
he has not done so."

"Can you not?" Ethyl asked.

"What do you mean?"

"You never made a secret that everything you did was
toward the end that would bring both you and Hendrick back to Sheffield. You tried to escape and were
thwarted by the invaders. You tried to shame Guthrie
into giving you permission to leave, more than one time,
and it was only with his agreement to allow you safe-conduct to your home should the women become pregnant under your ministrations that you agreed to betrothal with Rory McLir."

"But I did agree," Serine reminded her.

"Think you a man wants to be second in his woman's heart or, in Rory's case, possibly even third after
Hendrick and Sheffield, depending on what you
thought carried priority that day?"

"How can you say such things?" Serine's hackles
rose. "Rory was always first in my heart and in my
mind."

"So you say now, but during the time you spent with
him you certainly had a strange way of showing your
devotion to him." Ethyl gave a little sniff of distaste.
"Think on my words, Serine, and then we will talk
again. You are correct in only one thing you say. It
would be unwise for you to return to Corvus Croft until you know the disposition of the villagers, but do not
expect Rory to come racing to Sheffield after you, for
in his mind you have attained your desire and he is no
part of it."

"He is all of it," Serine protested. "Without him there is nothing worth having."

"Then perhaps instead of crying over what you cannot have and dare not do, you should expend your strength on what you might do to let Rory know how much you love him." And with that Ethyl walked out of the solar, closing the door behind her, satisfied that she had exhausted the subject and covered all possibilities. It was only after she was well on her way home that Ethyl realized there was one situation that she had not considered. In her efforts to make Serine understand her own motivation, Ethyl had forgotten that if Rory McLir returned to Sheffield his life was forfeit. For it was Rory who had led the original raid and stolen the children of Sheffield.

Corvus Croft was a village transformed. The women hummed as they performed their chores. The men whistled and sang in their work. There was laughter and good-natured joking, and even those who had not yet conceived held hope in their hearts that it would soon be so.

For, even before the haste of forced departure, Serine had made certain that Damask knew the formula for the brew and was able to make it should the need arise. In Serine's heart it had been not only for the people of Corvus Croft, but also on the off chance that something might happen to Rory and he would again need the relief only the bitter brew could give. Although Serine had warned Damask to follow the directions exactly, she had come to realize that this brew was associated with herself, and there was little chance it would ever be associated with the concoction outlawed so long ago. The success or failure of the brew rested on

Serine's shoulders, and she had done what she felt she must to insure the life and continued health of the man she loved.

But Rory had no notion of Serine's devotion, and only at McLir Manor was there less than jocularity. Rory would not allow anything that had belonged to Serine to be touched. It was as though he expected her to come through the door, her arms filled with sweet smelling herbs and her face wreathed in a smile.

However, it was Gerta, not Serine, who came through the door. Gerta had accepted her fate, if not with joy, at least with silence and a modicum of compliance. She was pleased with her new status in life and the respect gleaned from being the wife of the steward. She could not, however, keep from imagining the amount of respect and honor, not to mention the sexual gratification, she would have known had she managed to coax Rory into wedding her. And there were times when her disappointment showed in her demeanor.

Today the dejection on Rory's face was so obvious that even Gerta was able to read his thoughts.

"'Twould be best if you forgot about Lady Serine and found a new woman. I vow there's some who'd be willing to leave their husbands should you give the least encouragement." Gerta kicked at the rushes as she spoke. The maids would rue the day for not having swept them out.

"Gerta, you do an acceptable job managing the housemaids. Do not cry for the impossible," he warned. It irritated Rory that his feelings should be so obvious that even the unschooled girl could easily guess what was in his heart. "You should be proud to be the wife of a man like the steward. He is revered and honored."

"And old and short!" Gerta added.

"His age and height should have nothing to do with the man or his love for you," Rory counseled. "Stand straight and hold your head high."

"And when I do so I am taller than he is," Gerta complained. "I hear the people tittering when we pass by."

"Perhaps it is but the women commenting on the richness of your gowns," Rory suggested.

"Perhaps." Gerta sniffed derisively. "But listen yourself, my lord, for sooner or later you will hear how the people jest over your undying love for the woman who left you without looking back."

Rory's eyes hardened. He would have liked to refute her words, but knew there was a grain of truth in them.

"'Tis surely too bad you cannot make your peace with Lady Serine, once and for all," Gerta commented as she inspected the sideboard for any sign of dust or grime on her way from the room. "Of course, we all know it would mean your life to return to Sheffield. And since lady Serine has no way of knowing she is free to return here without fear of reprisal, it seems to me your plight is as hopeless as mine." Her back stiff with indignation, Gerta made her way out of the room, leaving Rory to his thoughts.

So they laughed at him, did they? He had given his all for the welfare of the village. Risked his life numerous times. Put the good of the people above his own wishes. And to what purpose? That they would laugh at him in his hour of need? That his own people would jest behind his back over the fact that he must spend the rest of his life without the woman he loved?

No! It would not be so! There had to be a way to reach Serine. To talk to her. To hold her in his arms.

There had to be a way, and, by the gods, he would find it!

The anger, the despair grew within him like a canker. Each time the sound of laughter reached his ears, Rory could not help but wonder if it was at his expense.

In their own euphoria the villagers joked about those less fortunate, forgetting that had it not been for Rory and Serine their laughter would have been shallow and their lives bleak.

When they laughed at Rory they laughed at Serine, also, and, as the summer came upon them and the women waxed plump and round, Rory decided he had had enough. On a perfect summer's morn Rory McLir went to confront his brother.

"Rory, what brings you here this fine morning?" Guthrie left his place at Damask's side and came toward the younger man.

"I am going on a voyage," Rory told him. "I need some men to accompany me."

"I see no problem with that," Guthrie agreed without bothering to question further. "I only ask that the men go of their own free will. I do not think any man should be away from his wife when the long-awaited children are born."

"I could not agree more," Rory told him. "And I give my word that not one soul will accompany me unless that person truly wants to go."

Guthrie slipped his arm about his wife, his attention taken again by the woman who carried his child. This time he did not think of his brother's plight. Guthrie's thoughts hovered more and more about Damask and his own happiness.

Rory directed his next comment to Damask. "Should I not return in time to see your child born, I wish you luck and an easy birth."

"But surely you cannot plan to be gone any great length of time," Damask objected. "Where would you go?"

"I'm going to Sheffield," he said, "and I do not know when I will return." He swung about on his heel and was gone before the astonished couple could collect themselves enough to call him back.

"You must stop him," Damask warned her husband. "He will be killed if he sets foot on English soil, and the men with him, also. 'Tis a great price to pay just to see the woman you love."

But Guthrie would not budge. "Think, woman! There is no man here who will risk life and limb to join Rory in his journey at this time. When my brother learns the demeanor of the men, he will give this folly second thought."

"Or he may go alone," Damask suggested.

"That would be foolhardy," Guthrie declared, "and I doubt Rory would do such a thing, even for love."

Damask would have said more, but her husband silenced her with a kiss. "Should we have any reason to believe Rory plans to go to Sheffield alone, I will speak to him," he promised, and Damask had to be satisfied with his decision.

Throughout the next days Rory mingled with his people, trying to ferret out anyone who would make the commitment of going to Sheffield with him. At the end of the week he had spoken to every man in the village and not a one was willing to go.

"I know you are grieving for your lady, but she will surely be at Sheffield no matter when you arrive. There is no need for such haste, since it cannot be more than a clandestine meeting at best," Tavish observed. "Besides, there's not a one of us wants to be away from the Croft when the women start birthing their babes. It's too long we've waited and we'll not be denied."

As Rory was leaving one of the cottages, he felt a tug on his cloak. He looked down and recognized one of the children stolen from Sheffield.

"What is it, lad?" he asked as he gazed into the child's solemn face.

"I would go with you," the little boy said. "The people here are good to me, but I miss my mum and da. I long to see my brothers and sisters again and I want to go home to Sheffield."

"Is your family here not kind to you?" Rory asked.

"Aye, they are kind, but soon there will be a new babe and they will forget about me in their excitement." He rubbed a grubby hand across his eyes. "Truly, my lord, they do not need me anymore, and I want to go home."

Rory contemplated the child for a long time. The boy was too young to appreciate the distinction of being a freeman rather than a serf. His thoughts were those of loneliness, and he clung to the memory of the family he knew and loved.

"Are there other children who feel as you do?" Rory asked gently.

The boy nodded. "You won't punish them if I tell you who they are?"

"You won't be punished and neither will they," Rory promised.

The boy gave the names of several other children and told Rory where they lived. There were four altogether. They were about the same age. The older children had seen the advantages of living here, while the younger children were little more than babes and had adapted well to their new environment, bonding quickly to their adopted families.

The children who wanted to return and a grown man would fit comfortably into one skiff. It took but a knowledgeable seaman to handle such a small craft. The greatest danger was the sea itself and the ever-threatening storms that might overtake them. Still, it was worth a chance. Besides, it was the only chance he had.

Rory had already spoken to the men in the households into which the children had been placed and knew that all but one of their wives was pregnant. Since the barren couple was somewhat older, there was the chance that the woman would not conceive regardless of how scrupulously she administered the bitter brew. Rory decided not to tempt fate. He would leave the young Sheffield child with the older couple. The other three children he would return to Sheffield in the hope they would buy him the right to see Serine.

There was no other choice. The men of the Croft would not consider accompanying him in the fear they would miss the long-awaited births of their children. It concerned them not that Rory's child would be born in a foreign land, away from his paternal heritage. It seemed to matter little that Rory himself had given his all to see to it that the wishes of his people came to pass.

Serine had been correct in her wry assessment of the situation. Unless there was a funeral or a celebration, the people of Corvus Croft cared little for anything other than their own endeavors.

Not one of the men for whom Rory had risked his life was willing to give his time and strength to try to allow Rory to find fulfillment in his own life, even though Rory had given his all for those who denied him in this, his hour of need.

Rory had no question in his mind, nor hesitation in his heart. He would take the youngsters who wished to return to the families of their birth and leave those who chose to remain. He set about to put his plan into motion. He would go to Serine and lay his heart and his life at her feet. If she had meant what she'd told him the day he left to face the invader, and she had not left of her own free will, she would welcome him and see the truth and the sacrifice of his offering.

If Serine had no desire other than to remain unhampered in Sheffield, Rory would most like die, and gladly. For denied the woman he loved and the child she carried, life was without meaning.

His own people would not share his misery, nor would they help to alleviate it. He owed them nothing. Serine and Rory had given his people all they said they desired, and now those same people offered nothing in return. Instead they but looked into their own selfishness and gave thought to naught but their personal desires.

Strengthened by his own resolve, Rory began to set his plans into motion. Before the waning of the moon, he vowed he would see his beloved Serine once again.

Chapter Eighteen

A light mist enveloped the shore as the little skiff touched English land. The children clambered over the side, anxious to be free of the confines of the vessel.

Rory packed up a bundle of food and secured the boat, hiding it lest his plans went awry and he had need to escape. When he was ready, he called the children together and they began their journey across the countryside toward Sheffield.

How different this was from the first time he had made the journey. Instead of desperate men intent on stealing what they must have to survive, he was now accompanied by the squeals and laughter of children who delighted in pointing out places they remembered as they went on their way.

This was not a forced march. Indeed, in consideration of the children's ages, the little group moved slowly, the children running in circles most of the time. When evening fell they were still a good distance from their goal, and Rory decided to stop for the night.

"We will leave early in the morning," he promised them. "It is far better to arrive in Sheffield with the dawn than to come in the middle of the night when everyone is sleeping."

In truth, it might have been better for Rory to arrive at night. He could slip into Sheffield, deliver the children and see Serine, and none would be the wiser. But that was not his plan. To achieve his goal he must have the support of at least some of the people of Sheffield, and he could not gain support by stealth or force.

Rory and the children talked and laughed together, then, huddling close, the children slept while Rory kept watch. His thoughts slipped over the sea to his home, and he wondered how his brother fared when faced with the wrath of the villagers who awoke to find some of their children gone.

Would Guthrie guess that it was Rory who had taken them? Or would he believe the ploy that Rory had devised while the children were still with their adopted families?

Life would undoubtedly be much easier for everyone involved if it was believed that some outsider had come and stolen them away. His eyes grew heavy and he was lulled by the rhythmic breathing of the young ones, until at last he joined them in sleep.

The first rays of light crept through the trees when Rory again opened his eyes. The children slept deeply and he nudged them until they awoke. It was important that they stay together, for if he could not prove that he had returned them freely, his life would be forfeit indeed.

"This is the last of the bread and cheese," he told them as he divided it between them, "but soon you will again eat good English food, prepared by your own mothers."

The children ate what they were given, washing the fare down with water from a nearby stream. They did not bother to tell him that bread and cheese was often a treat in Sheffield and gruel the most usual fare of the day. Their footsteps lagged as they remembered the meat and eggs that accompanied the meals they had come to expect in Corvus Croft. But anticipation is a great energizer and excitement erased all else by the time the sun had climbed into the morning sky.

They had no more than stepped onto Sheffield land when one of the children gave a screech and raced toward a plump woman carrying a large basket. Vegetables went flying as she recognized the child and embraced him amid the falling produce.

Her cries of joy attracted the other serfs, and by the time they reached the village a procession had formed.

At first Rory was surprised that the people accepted him without question. Then it came to him that they had never seen him, with the exception of the few who had helped carry him to Sheffield when he was sore wounded.

The rough, unruly Celt was gone, and in his place was a man who could walk the English countryside without question. He allowed a swagger to his gait as they approached the manor house that was Serine's home.

If she loved him, she would not give his identity away, and if she did not, it would matter little what happened to him.

The doors of the keep opened and Serine stepped into the light. She had blossomed in the expectation of motherhood and looked like a full-blown rose, lovely and fragrant and filled with life.

"What is it?" she asked. The people all cried out at once in answer to her question. "What has happened?"

"The Celts..." The alewife shouted above the rest. "'Tis the Celts!"

Serine's eyes opened wide. She looked to Ethyl and Drojan for verification but received only a reflection of her own confusion. Surely Rory would not again raid Sheffield. Had they not suffered enough at his hand?

"What about the Celts?" She managed to hold her voice steady and her head high, though her heart sank within her breast and her child kicked mightily in protest.

"The Celts have returned our childer," came the reply as a woman rushed forward and thrust a five-year-old child in Serine's face.

"And mine, also," Hildegard chortled, hugging her little girl.

Serine passed among her people. It did not take her long to realize that there were but two or three children from the dozen or so that had been taken. She also recognized them as having wished to return to England the day of her ill-timed attempt to escape.

"But who...? Who is responsible for this miracle and how has it come to pass?"

"A great lord, come from afar," the alewife declared. "A true champion of our people." She gestured toward the crowd. The people stepped aside, and Serine found herself looking into the blue-black eyes of Rory McLir.

But this was a Rory that only Serine could recognize. No more the rough warrior, for the man had done away with his facial hair and stood before her clean shaven and dressed as a proper English gentleman.

Her spirit raced toward him, but her body would not move. Her breath caught in her throat and her words with it. She dared not speak. Dared not say his name aloud in the fear that someone would discover his identity and take him from her.

She moved toward him regally, as behooved the Lady of Sheffield, and held out her hand. "We thank you for what you have done for our village. You are welcome in Sheffield. Please come into my home.''

He took her hand and placed it on his as he allowed her to usher him into the hall.

Servants scurried to see to the comfort of the man who had returned their children. There was no time alone, nor moment of conversation free from the prying eyes and ears of the servants. Only with their eyes could Serine and Rory transmit the turmoil in their hearts.

When finally the servants retired, Serine dared speak.

"How came you here, and why?'' She believed he had come because he loved her, but she needed to hear him say the words.

He took her hand in both of his. "I came because I could not live without you, and I knew you could not come to me.''

Her smile was his reward, but the joy her words brought was even greater. "My need to be with you has been so overpowering that I thought to risk everything and return to Corvus Croft regardless of the danger.''

"There is no danger, dear heart,'' he assured her. "The sickness that plagued the people was confined to the women, and turned out to be the same ailment that swells your belly this moment.''

"You mean...'' Her eyes widened in astonishment.

"'Twas Damask who came forth and told the angry crowd that it was not poison, but pregnancy that sent the women to their beds.''

"But they made it sound as though it was widespread. Half the village was afflicted by some unknown malady,'' Serine told him, still hardly able to believe her ears.

"And so it was,'' he assured her. "Over half the wives will bear children.''

Her laughter rang out through the hall. "I had hoped that one or two of the women would conceive, but never in my wildest dreams did I believe it would be so widespread."

"Damask realized the extent of what had happened."

"Dear Damask, how does she fare?"

"Only Guthrie is happier and more proud. Thanks to you, our land is a place of gladness. I was the one person there who was not bursting with joy."

"Did you come alone, with but the children to accompany you?" She frowned. "How is it that none of the men offered to join you?"

"No one wanted to miss the birthing of the babes. They were not willing to take the chance that we would return in time to see their children born. They cared little that I might never see my own child, nor the woman I love, again. When I realized the extent of their selfishness I decided I owed them nothing and had the right to extract payment for my services."

She came to his arms, unable to restrain herself any longer. "Oh, my Rory." She sighed. "I have missed you."

"And I, you." He allowed his lips to find hers, touching them but gently while the passion sprang up between them as though they had never been apart.

She traced her fingers across his lips. "I would not have known you had I not seen you before without your mustache and beard. Why, even your own brother would hardly recognize you now."

"Do I not make a fine-looking English lord?" he asked.

"You are as fine-looking a man as ever I've seen, and I cannot tell you how wonderful it is just to look at you again." She augmented her statement by kissing the slight cleft in his chin. "I never thought to see you do away with your beloved beard simply to return a few stolen children."

"I come as would any proper English knight, ready to ask for the heart and hand of the woman he loves," he told her self-righteously. "Do I not look the part?" He turned his head this way and that, waiting for her approval.

"You are far more handsome than any man has a right to be, and it may behoove me to make you grow your beard again just to keep the ladies from throwing themselves at your head."

"No woman can tempt me, Serine, save yourself. I would have no other... and no other woman will ever have me."

"And do I truly have you, my Rory?" She could not tear her gaze from the masculine beauty of his face.

"Need you ask?" he returned. "For your love I have betrayed my own people and turned myself into a renegade. Indeed, you, Serine, could return and be warmly welcomed, but I have made myself an outcast by coming to you."

"Do not despair, my love. They will forgive and forget with time. And you and I will find happiness together while we are waiting for them to do so."

She did not tell him that, but a few short days before, she had grieved in that Hendrick might be taken from her. Now she could hardly contain her happiness, and even the thought of Hendrick's prospective absence was tempered by the knowledge of Rory's presence. All would be perfect if she could keep both of them with her. But she would take the bitter with the sweet, and not begrudge Hendrick the right to learn to live the life that was his right and privilege by law, though she would miss him sorely.

The door burst open. A cry of joy escaped Rory's lips as he recognized Drojan. Without releasing his hold on Serine, Rory crossed the space between them. Only then did he let go the woman and embrace his friend.

"I have much to tell you," Rory said as he smiled into Drojan's face.

"The women were in the early throes of pregnancy and that was the cause of their discomfort," Serine told Ethyl, loud enough for Drojan to hear.

"Is this true?" Drojan voiced the question.

"Aye, that it is," Rory admitted. "It was all a cruel mistake. Serine can return anytime she chooses and will be welcomed with open arms."

"Until your people decide I have done something they cannot understand or do not agree with," Serine retorted, ignoring the look of hurt that crossed Rory's face at her words.

"Then she is in far less danger than yourself," Drojan said bluntly.

"What do you mean by such a statement?" Serine challenged. "Rory is in no danger here. I welcome his presence, as does my son, and the people have proclaimed him a hero for returning their children."

"The people have only begun counting the noses of the returned children and have come up short. Several of the parents are asking why their children were not returned." This time it was Ethyl who spoke.

"I brought only the children who wished to return to Sheffield. The others would not desert their new way of life," Rory told them. "Beyond that, I could not carry more children with me, as my boat was small."

"We understand, Rory." Serine beamed at him. "And it was a wonderful thing you did by returning those children. I, too, was told by Tim and some of the older children that they were pleased with their lot and wanted nothing more than to keep to the new life they had found."

"What the children want is of little import," Drojan said. "The fact is that once the serfs have had time to question their childer as to the name of the man who brought them back to the village, they will, most like, be outraged at the truth of Rory's identity."

"By the time they think to question, it will be too late—" Serine set her chin in determination. "—for Rory and I will be married, and he will be, by law, the Lord of Sheffield until Hendrick reaches his majority."

Rory's head snapped about, and Serine caught her breath at her outrageous statement. "That is, if it be your wish, my lord." She curtsied in graceful supplication.

"It is the culmination of all my wishes," Rory told her, "as well you know."

Ethyl assessed the situation quickly. "We must send for a priest and start the preparations for the nuptial celebration. The activity should keep the serfs occupied to the point where they will not have the time or energy to question anything until after Rory has become their legal lord." Without waiting for approval, Ethyl sent one of the servants for Margot and, after apprising Hildegard of the situation, began putting the plans in motion.

By the middle of the week the village of Sheffield was agog with the promise of what was to come. Not only had some of the children been returned, but Lady Serine would wed with their deliverer.

"Who is this man that would wed with our lady?" Hildegard, the alewife, asked her newly returned daughter. "Surely you must have known him while you were away."

"He was one of the men in the Croft," was all the child would say.

Happy to have her daughter again with her, the alewife went about her duties and did not bother to question the child more closely. It was not until Hildegard's husband, Ellis, returned to Sheffield from selling their wool at the market that the woman, as well as the rest of the village, learned the truth.

Having taken the moneys for the wool to Serine, Ellis went to his home and hearth. After greeting the child he had seen but twice in her young life, he turned to his wife.

"I was surprised at the turn of events that awaited me when I came back to Sheffield. I never believed a Celt would chase a woman to her lair as Rory McLir has done." He pulled out a stool and sat beside one of the rough wooden tables on which the guests of the alehouse were served. Several of the other men moved closer, their curiosity piqued. After all, Ellis had gone to the village of the Celt and returned to tell about it. He would know the truth of what he spoke.

Hildegard's mind took an entirely different tack. So the man's name was Rory McLir. The name rang a bell. Ellis had told her that McLir was the name of the headman of the Celts. "Might this be the Celtic headman of whom you spoke on your return from the Isle?" she prodded.

"Nay, 'tis the headman's brother, Rory, who has stolen our lady's heart." Ellis took a long swig of ale and glanced about. He was pleased to once again be the center of attention. After his return from Corvus Croft he had been barraged by questions, but as time passed the serfs had had their fill of his repetitious story of his capture and rescue at the hands of the Celts. Now they again looked on him with interest.

"So it is Rory McLir who brought back our childer." One of the men lifted his cup in salute.

"And why not?" Ellis took a cup from the tray his wife carried. "'Tis the same Rory McLir who led the raid to steal them."

A gasp went up from the gathering crowd. "And our lady would marry him for all that?" one of the men asked.

"He is a fair man, and brave." Ellis gave the devil his due. "He had to go against everything he loved and believed in to return our children to us."

"But he did not return *all* the children," Hildegard told him. "There are but three, and ours one of them."

"Then thank the saints," Ellis told her. "From what I saw, taking even one child from Corvus Croft would be worth a man's life."

"The scoundrel took them," another man declared. "He should have brought them all back with him."

"Yes!" The cry was taken up by many voices. "We will make him take us to his village and force his people to return our children to us."

The men spewed through the door and into the street, hawking their ill-conceived plan as they gathered in numbers and marched toward the castle.

Chapter Nineteen

The sound of angry voices reached Serine and Rory as they dined in the great hall. His hand closed over hers as fear filled her eyes.

"Come," he said, helping her to her feet. "We will resolve this problem together."

Serine went to the door and confronted her serfs. "What is it you want of us?" she demanded, proud that her voice did not waver, though her heart certainly did.

"Give us the man who stole our childer," one of the men shouted. "We will force him to take us to his god-forsaken village and we will take back what is ours."

The men surged forward. Rory drew his sword, and Ethyl appeared from the shadows of the hall, arrow nocked. Her eye fell on Ellis and she turned her aim toward him.

"'Tis your fault, Ellis," she accused. "You could not leave well enough alone and had to tell all you knew. I should have killed you when I had the chance."

Ellis cowered visibly. "I but said what I knew to be true."

"How could you say what is true?" Ethyl demanded. "You, who were so frightened by the thought of being made to face the Celtic test of truth that you fainted dead away and had to have another man stand in your place."

There was a buzz of interest in the crowd. "That is not the story Ellis told when he returned," one of the men ventured.

"All the more reason to take his words with a grain of salt." Ethyl's tone was saccharine.

"We do not care if he boasted about his bravery." Another man stepped forward "We care only if Rory McLir is, indeed, the man who stole our children while we were off on crusade. Be that so, or not?"

"It is true. Just as it is true that I brought back those children who would come with me." Rory spoke before Serine could stop him.

The men grumbled among themselves. They had not expected the Celt to admit to such an offense.

"Why did you not bring all our children if you wanted our goodwill?" the alewife asked.

"I know! I know!" a childish voice piped. The boy who had first asked Rory to take him home squirmed through the crowd and ran up to stand beside Rory. "The others wanted to stay with their new families."

The boy's father made a grab for him, but Serine blocked his way.

"Let the child have his say," she ordered. "He knows whereof he speaks."

The boy looked out over the crowd. Never in his young life had he had the attention of so many people. He swallowed hard. "The big boys did not want to leave, for they are all learning a trade and can keep some of the money for their wares."

The crowd stirred, and the word *freeman* was bandied about. Then a woman's voice arose. "What of the younger children?"

"They are well kept and not made to go to the fields and glean fodder. Their lives are carefree and they remember no other."

"That cannot be so," a young mother wailed. "My baby would never forget me. A child knows his own mother."

"If Corvus Croft is such a paradise, perhaps we should all go there," one of the men suggested despondently.

"You are serfs of Sheffield and bonded to the land," Serine reminded them. "Even if you left Sheffield, you would still be sworn to Baneford and subject to his will."

"Rory McLir." One of the men swaggered forward and stood at the bottom of the stairs looking up at Rory and Serine. "Do you say that our children will be raised free men in your land?"

"Free men with skills to earn their way throughout their lives," Rory assured him.

Again the rumble of voices as the serfs talked among themselves. "In some ways it sounds as though our children may have come into a better way of life than that of their parents," he said. "I would not take freedom from them."

With that he turned and elbowed his way through the crowd, making for his own hut. It took only a few moments before the others followed. The threat was over. The danger circumvented.

Ethyl lowered her bow. Rory sheathed his sword.

"Thank God it is over," Serine breathed as her hand grasped Rory's sleeve. "Think you they are satisfied?"

"Your serfs will do nothing more," Drojan assured them as he strode toward them from across the courtyard.

"I will go to the chapel and give thanks to God," Serine promised.

"Do not be too hasty in your thanks," Drojan warned ominously.

"What do you mean, old man?" Ethyl asked suspiciously. "Do not speak in riddles. It is the truth that we need to hear."

Drojan looked from one to the other. He would have preferred to have told Rory privately, but it was not to be.

"Baneford has been sighted less than a day's journey away. It is obvious Sheffield is his goal. Was he sent an invitation to the wedding?" the seer asked.

"We sent a messenger, who left the invitation with Baneford's steward, since the lord himself was not in residence," Serine explained. "When Baneford did not respond, we thought to apprise him of the situation once the wedding had taken place."

"A wise move," Drojan observed. "At least, it would have seemed wise under other circumstances. We can only hope he has not heard of Rory's presence and guessed his identity."

Serine put her hand to her mouth, but no sound came forth. Her eyes sought Rory's, and she was soothed by the love that shone therein. He placed his arms about her.

"Do not fret, dear one," he told her. "Somehow we will tilt the scales to our benefit. We have come too far to let Baneford or anyone else destroy our happiness."

And Serine could do no more than believe him as he led her into the hall where they joined Hendrick, who had ignored the commotion and continued eating his evening meal. He looked up as his mother took her place.

"When I am grown I shall free the serfs," Hendrick announced, to the amazement of all. "People work harder when they are free." He popped a sweetmeat into his mouth and looked around the table for approval.

"But, Hendrick, how do you plan to accomplish this feat?" Serine questioned.

"Rory will help me." He cast a tentative smile in the direction of his soon-to-be stepfather.

"What do you know of this?" Serine directed her question to Rory.

"No more than yourself," he said. "It is the first I have heard of such a plan, but I concur heartily and am willing to do what I can to see that Hendrick succeeds."

Now it was Serine's turn to smile, for the pact was made between the two people she loved most in the world. Rory and Hendrick had found a common cause that would bond them together.

Trumpets sounded with the dawn. The earth shook from the hooves of many horses.

The people of Sheffield thought it all part of the wedding celebration, but Serine viewed it with trepidation, for she knew it was no part or parcel of the ceremony.

Baneford had come to Sheffield, and with him, his entire entourage.

"We but progress through our fief lands," he said as Serine ushered the tall, dignified nobleman into the great hall of Sheffield. "It seems I could not have come at a better time, since there is to be a wedding." His eyes narrowed in speculation. "Of course, you are aware that as Lady of Sheffield you must by rights ask my permission to wed."

"Only the first marriage," Serine reminded him with quiet dignity. "I am a widow."

"From the tales I've heard, you do not have much need of a man." He chuckled.

"That is not true," Serine objected. "I *do* need a man, and have chosen the one most suited."

Again the dignified chuckle. "And who might this paragon of masculinity be?"

"'Tis Rory McLir of Corvus Croft," she said as Rory stepped before them.

Baneford took measure of the younger man. It was obvious he was of good blood. Young, well dressed and most likely knowledgeable in the care of estates. "Well met, Rory McLir," Baneford said graciously.

"And to you," Rory returned.

The men eyed each other warily.

"So, you would wed Lady Serine," Baneford said.

"I would," Rory replied.

"And if I give my blessing, will you whisk the lady off to your own estates and leave me to manage Sheffield until Hendrick is of age?"

There was no correct answer to the man's question. Regardless of what Rory said, Baneford could turn it to his own purpose. "I am a younger son," Rory told him. "My estate is small. Until Hendrick reaches his majority I will help Lady Serine to hold Sheffield for her son."

"Then you would become my liege man?" Baneford jumped at the chance. This man was young and strong. He carried himself like a leader and would be advantageous to any overlord.

"My services are sworn to my brother, who is overlord of the lands to which I hold title. I can guard your land, my lord, and fight for the rights and protection of those I love, but I will not leave to go on crusade."

Baneford's eyebrows shot upward. "What audacity!" he said aloud. Then he turned to Serine. "Have you told your betrothed that I, too, refused to join the Crusades?"

"Forgive me, my lord, but I fear we have not yet discussed your preferences on war," Serine admitted.

This time the dignified chuckle exploded into laughter. "So be it, then. I will accept Rory McLir's vow of loyalty as husband to Lady Serine and guardian of Sheffield. I will even stay for the wedding. Then I must take Hendrick and go on with—"

"But why?" Serine protested, fighting back tears. "Surely he can be schooled here as well as on your estates."

Baneford motioned the boy forward. Hendrick was small for his age. In truth, it would be some time before the boy would be of a size to perform the services of a page, let alone those of squire. Apparently the mother had gone through a great deal to return the lad to his estate. He considered the matter carefully before asking, "Are you willing to learn your lessons here at Sheffield like a true and diligent student?"

"Oh, yes, my lord," Hendrick agreed promptly. "But I would like to be allowed to come to you when it is time for me to begin training to become a knight."

The boy's candor pleased Baneford and he clapped the child on the shoulder, almost upsetting the lad. "You have my word," he promised. "Now, on with the festivities!"

As if on signal, Serine's knees buckled and she dropped to the rushes.

Rory was immediately at her side, scooping her into his arms and rushing with her from the hall. Baneford glanced around in confusion. "Was it something I said?'' he asked aloud looking for a familiar face so that he might receive an answer to his question.

"My lord, come with me and we shall have some wine and cakes." Drojan indicated the chairs near the hearth, and the man accompanied him there. "It seems the festivities must be postponed until after Serine's child is born."

Baneford settled himself comfortably. "Is this the projection of a seer?" he queried, aware of the other man's reputation.

"No, my lord, it is simply the best guess of an old man." And with his words he caught Ethyl's eye and a smile passed between them.

"It seems a shame to waste all the preparations for such a sumptuous wedding breakfast," Baneford observed, taking in the affection between the seer and the female archer. "You would not know of another couple who might wish to be wed this day?"

The suggestion hit Drojan like a stone. He loved Ethyl, by all the gods, he loved her and never doubted her love for him, but he had never given serious thought to marrying her. Now, somehow, it seemed the right thing to do, and he knew that if he were to read the Runes, they would bear out his belief.

"Give me but a moment, my lord, and I believe I have a solution to the problem." Without further ado, Drojan crossed the hall to where Ethyl stood.

"Have you pacified Lord Baneford?" she asked.

"Nothing will pacify him other than to have a wedding prior to the breakfast," Drojan told her.

"I doubt my lady Serine will be much enthused at the thought right now," Ethyl said cryptically.

"That is why I suggest we come to her aid."

"What do you say, old man?" Ethyl asked suspiciously.

"I say that I love you. Not only in this life, but in the life there is hereafter. I want a bond made between us that can never be broken."

Ethyl caught her breath. "As do I," she managed to say.

"Then I ask you, Ethyl, to marry me and become my wife in this life and throughout eternity." His eyes softened as he beheld her radiance.

"With all my heart," she answered as she bowed her head in what he took to be submission. In fact, she dared not let him see the expression on her face in that moment, for had he seen, Drojan would have realized that had he not asked her to marry him, Ethyl would have asked him to be her husband.

They were wed on the steps of the village church, and as they returned to the hall the wails of a newborn babe reached their ears.

"Aha," Baneford gloated, "it sounds as though the child has been born. Strong and healthy, I vow! A good omen on the day of your wedding. Perhaps you will be next!"

Ethyl shot the man a glance that would have melted iron. She would have welcomed Drojan's child . . . had it been some twenty years earlier. But at this time in Ethyl's life the last thing she needed was a babe, and even if it were possible for her to give birth to Drojan's babe, she could not hope to live to see the child grow to adulthood.

Why wish for the impossible? Why bay at the moon? Ethyl had everything she could possibly want, and resented anyone implying that she should ask for more.

Her expression caused Baneford to recognize the age of the couple to whom he spoke. "Then again, perhaps not," he deferred.

"Amen to that," Drojan and Ethyl said in unison.

The shouts of congratulations were stilled as Rory appeared at the top of the stairs. In his arms he held the smallest of bundles, and on his face was the smile of a man who has been touched by God.

"Rejoice with me!" he called out over the hall. "Rejoice, for my lady has blessed me with the fairest of daughters. A child has been born to Sheffield, and the curse of Corvus Croft has, at last, been broken."

And the people voiced their plaudits, forgiving any misdemeanor that might have taken place prior to this day, lost in the miracle of birth.

Ethyl pressed Drojan's hand and went up the stairs as Rory and his newly born daughter descended. She slipped into Serine's apartment and was pleased to see the younger woman awake, but she was pale against the linens of the bed.

"She is a beauty, Serine, and Rory could not be more proud had you given birth to a score of sons."

"I still hope to do that," Serine said weakly. "Do you think he is pleased?"

"The man could not be happier, and it is the same for us all. Tomorrow Drojan and I will return to Corvus Croft and tell them that a strong, healthy child has been born, and they need have no fear, for, as Rory said, the curse is broken."

Serine took a deep breath. "They told me that while I labored, you and Drojan were married."

"Baneford suggested that it would be a shame to waste a well-prepared marriage breakfast. Drojan and I decided to do everything we could to appease the man."

The women laughed together. "Rory and I will be married this afternoon and you and Drojan can preside on our behalf at the banquet tonight. If it would please you."

"Being Drojan's wife pleases me," Ethyl said bluntly. "All else is of little importance, but I cannot deny that I enjoy it."

She glanced over her shoulder as the door opened and a determined Dame Margot ushered Rory into the room.

"I simply do not recall anyone taking a newborn babe from its mother so soon after it is born," she fussed. "It cannot be good for the child."

The baby looked at them with muddy blue eyes and yawned mightily.

"It looks to me as though the child is none the worse for wear," Ethyl observed. To her surprise, Rory placed the child in her arms and went to Serine's side. His soft voice, rough with emotion, vibrated through the room like music, ages old. The words of a man paying homage to the woman he loves for giving him immortality.

Ethyl watched them, sharing in their love with the knowledge of her own feeling for Drojan... her husband. Her eye misted and she was lost in memories of the past and dreams of the future.

The baby kicked impatiently and Ethyl looked down into the tiny face, the smooth blush cheeks and the intelligent eyes, slightly crossed beneath a puzzled scowl.

The eyes were Serine's and the scowl Rory's, Ethyl decided. A wonderful bundle of pulchritude placed in a small package. The child began to fuss, and Ethyl took the opportunity to place the tiny girl in her mother's waiting arms.

Ah, yes, there was no greater happiness than that experienced at the birth of a babe. A new life, a new beginning, with all of life beckoning. Ethyl backed away from the bed, leaving the little family together, but, as she glanced back one last time to burn the memory of this moment into her mind, she could not help but wonder what a child born of her love for Drojan might have been.

A great warrior? A seer? Perchance a wizard, gifted with the abilities to form the lives of many peoples. Of course, it could not be, but this was a time of miracles, and Ethyl, the woman who had never dared to dream, walked down the stairs toward her new husband with a small, secret smile on her lips.

In the age of miracles there were no limits as to what the future might hold.

Serine looked at Rory with a puzzled frown. "How strange that she neglected even to say goodbye. Think you she is hurt that we have a babe and she is destined to have none?"

"Come, now," Rory chided. "Why would a woman of Ethyl's age desire a child? She could not hope to see him grow to manhood. 'Tis more likely her thoughts were on the journey that she and Drojan will take on the morrow when they return to Corvus Croft."

As he spoke the name of his village, Rory's eyes misted and he looked off through the window of the solar.

Serine put her hand on his. "Does your heart grieve for your homeland? For I know that my soul cried out for Sheffield while I was away, until the day I realized I carried your child, and then the craving ended."

He bent and kissed her hand. "I thank you for allowing me a glimpse into your mind, for, indeed, I believed for a time that your only thoughts were for Sheffield."

"My thoughts and my love are for you alone," she assured him. "And I hope someday it will be that we can again return to Corvus Croft without fear."

"Once Drojan and Ethyl have spoken to Guthrie I have no doubt but that we will be welcomed with open arms," Rory said. "My people decided to steal children because there was no alternative other than annihilation. Thanks to you, that problem no longer exists. Soon the town will again ring with childish voices. The people dare not condemn me for turning their own ploy against them and stealing back the children I had first stolen in their behalf."

"Then perhaps we will return to your home in the future."

"It would seem a shame for our daughter not to know of her heritage."

"Our child is a girl, Rory," Serine reminded him.

"According to Celtic law a woman can inherit," Rory told her. "All I have will be hers when she reaches adulthood."

Serine's eyes glimmered with wonder. "You mean our daughter will inherit McLir Manor?" she asked in wonder.

"I have said it is so," Rory stated. "Hendrick has lands here in England. Estates placed so far apart can be nothing less than a hindrance."

Serine pondered Rory's words. What he said was true, and the sole ownership of McLir Manor made the tiny bit of life that Serine held in her arms a force to be reckoned with. She smiled as she raised her eyes.

"Perhaps now your people will not be so anxious to place the blame of their ailments on the brew." Serine tried to keep the self-righteousness from her voice, but it was a futile effort.

"I have no doubt that my people have already come to the conclusion that the brew does nothing but good for those who would reap the benefits, as we have done." His eyes fell on his little daughter, and went back to his wife. "I have but the deepest respect for the brew of bitter herbs," he said. "Without the brew I would never have lived to know the miracle of our love."

He pressed Serine's fingers against his lips as his daughter's tiny hand closed about his finger and his heart stood still with happiness. "You see, Serine, I love you. And together we will find happiness, for our love burns warm and bright no matter where we abide."

"Warm and good and life-giving—" Serine placed her hand over that of Rory and their daughter "—and burning through our lives, just as the brew burns through our bodies when it heals the hurts of the past and gives us the strength to look ahead to the future."

"To the future." Rory repeated Serine's words as Hendrick's voice floated up to them from the courtyard and their daughter sighed contentedly, secure in the cocoon of their love.

*   *   *   *   *